A BLESSED CHILD

A BLESSED CHILD

Linn Ullmann

Translated from the Norwegian by Sarah Death

Alfred A. Knopf   *New York*   2008

THIS IS A BORZOI BOOK
PUBLISHED BY ALFRED A. KNOPF

3 1257 01777 1485

Translation copyright © 2008 by Sarah Death

www.aaknopf.com

Knopf, Borzoi Books, and the colophon are registered
trademarks of Random House, Inc.

Originally published in Norway as *Et velsignet barn* by Forlaget Oktober,
Oslo, in 2005. Copyright © 2005 by Forlaget Oktober AS, Oslo.

Library of Congress Cataloging-in-Publication Data
Ullmann, Linn, [date]
[Velsignet barn. English]
A blessed child / by Linn Ullmann ; translated from the Norwegian
by Sarah Death. — 1st ed.
p.   cm.
"A Borzoi book."
ISBN 978-0-307-26547-0
I. Death, Sarah.   II. Title.
PT8951.31.L56V4513 2008
839.8'2374—dc22
2007046060

Manufactured in the United States of America
First American Edition

To Halfdan

I

The Road

In the winter of 2005, Erika went to see her father, Isak Lövenstad. The journey was taking longer than expected, and she felt a strong urge to turn around and drive back to Oslo, but she pressed on, keeping her mobile phone on the seat beside her so she could ring him at any time and say that the visit was off. That she wasn't coming after all. That they would have to do it another time. She could say it was because of the weather, the heavy snowfall. The change of plan would have been a great relief to both of them.

Isak was eighty-four years old and lived by himself in a white lime-stone house on Hammarsö, an island off the east coast of Sweden. A specialist in gynecology, he had made his name as one of the pioneers of ultrasound. Now in retirement, he was in good health and his days passed pleasantly. All his basic needs were met by Simona, a lifelong resident of the island. Simona saw to it that he had a hot lunch and dinner every day; she gave the house a thorough weekly cleaning; she shopped, dusted, and did his laundry, of which there was not much. She also helped him with his annual income tax return and payments. Isak still had all his teeth, but in the past year he had developed a cataract in his right eye. He said it was like look-ing at the world through water.

Isak and Simona rarely talked to each other. Both preferred it that way.

After a long, full life in Stockholm and Lund, Isak had moved to Hammarsö for good. The house had stood empty for twelve years, during which time he had more than once considered selling it. Instead he decided to sell his flats in Stockholm and Lund and spend the rest of his life as an islander. Simona, whom Isak had hired back in the early seventies to help Rosa take care of the house (in spite of knowing that Rosa was the kind of woman, quite different from his previous wife and mistresses, who rarely needed help with anything, and especially not with the house, which by Rosa was kept to perfection), insisted that he allow her to take him in hand and cut his hair regularly. He wanted to leave it to grow. There was no one to cut it for, he said. But in order to restore the mutually preferred silence between them, they reached a compromise. In the summer, the crown of Isak's head was blank and glossy and as blue as the globes he had presented to each of his three daughters, Erika, Laura, and Molly, on her fifth birthday; in the winter, he let his hair grow free, giving him an aspect of towering grayish white, which in combination with his handsomely lined, aging face suggested the beginnings of a *rauk*, one of those four-hundred-million-year-old island outcrops in the sea, so characteristic of Hammarsö.

Erika seldom saw her father after he moved to the island, but Simona had sent her two photographs. One of a long-haired Isak and one of the almost bald Isak. Erika liked the long-haired one better. She ran her finger over the picture and kissed it. She imagined him on the stony beach on Hammarsö with arms stretched aloft, hair streaming out, and that long, fake beard he would wear when rehearsing his lines as Wise Old Man for the 1979 Hammarsö Pageant.

Rosa—Isak's second wife and Laura's mother—died of a degenerative muscle-wasting disease in the early 1990s. It was Rosa's death that prompted Isak's return to Hammarsö. In the twelve years the house had stood empty, there had been only occasional visits from Simona. She had swept up the insect life that forced its way in every summer and lay dead on the windowsills all winter; she had the locks changed after a minor break-in and mopped up when the pipes burst and water leaked all over the floor. But she could do nothing about the water damage and rot if Isak was not prepared to pay for workmen to come in and fix them.

"It's going to get run-down whatever I do," she said in one of their brief telephone conversations. "You'll either have to sell it, do it up, or start living in it again."

"Not yet. I'm not making any decisions yet," Isak said.

But then Rosa's body let her down, and though her heart was strong and wouldn't stop beating, Isak and a colleague agreed in the end that Rosa should be spared. After the funeral, Isak made it plain to Erika, Laura, and Molly that he intended to kill himself. The pills had been procured, the deed carefully planned. And yet, he moved back to the house.

Molly was born, against Isak's will, in the summer of 1974. When Molly's mother, who was called Ruth, was giving birth in an Oslo hospital, Rosa threatened to leave Isak. She packed two suitcases, ordered a taxi from the mainland, took their daughter Laura's hand, and said: "As long as you go on sleeping with anything in a skirt and babies are the result of it, there's no place for me in your life. Or in this house."

All this happened just before the premiere of that year's Hammarsö Pageant, the annual amateur theatrical revue written and produced by Palle Quist. The Hammarsö Pageant was a tradition on the island; both tourists and residents contributed in their various ways, and the production had been reviewed in the local paper several times, not always favorably.

When Rosa had her furious outburst, her only one, as far back as Erika could remember, Laura cried, saying she didn't want to go. Erika cried, too, seeing before her the long summer holiday alone with her father, who was too big for Erika to cook for or to comfort all by herself.

Ruth rang twice. The first time, she rang to say the contractions were coming every five minutes. Thirty-two hours later, she rang to say she had given birth to a daughter. She knew at once the child would be called Molly. She thought Isak would, at any rate, want to know. (No? Oh. To hell with him, then.)

Both times she rang from a pay phone in the hospital corridor.

Isak spent those thirty-two hours calming Rosa down and persuading her not to leave. The taxi waiting outside was sent away, then called again a few hours later, only to be dismissed once more.

Isak couldn't live without Rosa, he said. This thing with Ruth was all just a big misunderstanding.

Isak sent Erika and Laura out of the kitchen several times, yet the girls kept inventing new excuses for coming in to disturb them: they were thirsty, they were hungry, they were looking for their soccer ball. In the end, Isak roared and said that if they didn't let him and Rosa talk in peace, he would cut off their noses, so then the sisters hid behind the door and listened. That evening, when Isak and Rosa thought the girls were in bed, they came back to their post outside the door, wrapped in their blankets.

During the night, Isak almost succeeded in persuading Rosa to accept the word *misunderstanding* without, in fact, having to explain exactly who had misunderstood whom—Rosa, Ruth, or Isak himself—or how this sick state of affairs had arisen.

Isak had been away at a conference in Oslo nine months previously, yes. This is true.

He knew Ruth (at the time, just a pretty, fair-haired midwife who admired Isak), yes. Also true.

He had had sporadic contact with her, both before and after the conference, yes. And he is not denying this.

But Isak could not give any proper account of how and why Ruth was at that moment in an Oslo hospital, in labor with her first child and claiming he was the father.

This is where, in Isak's view, some kind of terrible misunderstanding must have arisen.

After many hours of argument, attended by much slamming of doors and muttering of resentment, Rosa made tea for herself and Isak. The two blue suitcases she had packed for herself and Laura were still standing in the middle of the floor. The last thing Erika saw from her hiding place behind the door was her father and Rosa sitting on either side of the kitchen table under the big pendant lamp—also blue—each cradling a cup of tea. Both were staring out the window. It was still dark.

And when Ruth rang, early the next morning, to let Isak know he had a fine, healthy daughter weighing 3,400 grams and measuring 49 centimeters, and that the delivery had generally gone smoothly, he threw the telephone on the floor and shouted DAMN IT. Rosa, who was standing just behind him in a polka-dot nightdress, her long hair hanging loose and tousled, picked the phone up off the floor, put the receiver to her own ear, and listened to what was being said at the other end. She nodded, said something back, nodded again.

Erika and Laura, who had been woken by the ringing of the telephone and their father's DAMN IT, crept out of their beds and back to their hiding place behind the door. They could not hear what Rosa was saying. She was speaking softly. The telephone was red and shaped like a periscope, with the dial in the base and a long cord so you could carry it around the house with you. When Rosa had finished her conversation, she tugged on the flex to gather it up and put the phone back on the hall table where it belonged. She returned to the kitchen and put her arms round Isak, who was standing in the middle of the floor, beside the suitcases. She whispered something in his ear. He laid his head on her shoulder. They stood like that for a long time.

Erika heard him say: "She should never have had that damned baby."

In the days that followed, Erika and Laura talked over what it could mean: that *she should never have had that damned baby.* They realized the fuss was all about some Norwegian woman called Ruth, the mother. Laura said that their father, who knew more than most people about having babies, was cross because the Norwegian woman hadn't waited for him to get there to help.

"Help with what?" Erika asked.

"With getting it out," said Laura.

Erika said she didn't believe that. Their father had said loud and clear that he didn't want it, so why would he help?

Laura said maybe he could have helped shove it back into the mother again.

Erika said you couldn't do that.

Laura said of course she knew that, she was only kidding.

Now, more than thirty years later, Isak would often say on the telephone that he lit candles for his daughters every evening. One candle for Erika, one for Laura, one for Molly, he said. He made it his business to mention this ritual of his to Erika as often as he could. Erika thought it was because he wanted her to pass it on to Molly, who, despite having lost her mother, the fair-haired midwife, Ruth, in a car crash when she was seven and having been sent to live with her grandmother rather than her father, had never stopped loving him.

His lean frame, his slim hands, his narrow feet, and his large head. Erika knew that it wasn't his looks that attracted so many women. It was his brain. That was what it said in the November 10, 1965 edition of *Life* magazine. Under his photograph, it said in so many words that Professor Lövenstad had a *brilliant* brain. The photograph had been taken in glaring sunlight and he was screwing up his eyes as he looked at the camera, which meant you couldn't see them or any of his face particularly well, just a great round head and a shock of fair, curly hair. The article, which was long, said that the Swedish researcher, along with his fellow scientists from Dublin, New York, and Moscow, was on his way to solving one of the mysteries of life.

When Erika went to Hammarsö for her holidays for the first time, in the summer of 1972, Laura took her hand, led her into the living room, and pointed out the article, which had been framed and hung on the wall. Erika could already read English without too much difficulty. The picture of her father with his big head, his fair hair, and his brilliant brain had stayed with her ever since, through her medical studies and then in her professional life as a gynecologist.

But she knew so little about her father, as he told her almost nothing. Now and then he would start a story, then stop in the middle. He would speak quietly under his breath; Erika had to lean in close or press her ear to the telephone receiver to hear. When he was angry, he would sputter monosyllabic roars, carefully chosen poisonous words. But whenever he was trying to tell some sort of narrative or answer questions (and Erika never posed one without considering it carefully), it was as if his voice faded away; the pauses grew longer and she sat waiting in vain for him to continue. And because he spoke so quietly, because Erika had to concentrate each time he said a word, as if what was passing between them was essential, like light or water, and because she could never be sure of having heard the whole story, any conversation with Isak gave her the sense of being let in on a secret.

There had been two husbands. On paper, Erika was still married to Tomas, but he had left her.

Then there was the first husband, Sundt, the father of her two children, who above all was extraordinarily cheap. Isak once pointed out that whenever Erika mentioned him she always referred to him in the past tense. But Sundt was not dead. He also had a first name, but Erika had only ever called him Sundt.

In fact, Erika thought, it would have been better for Sundt if he were dead. Being dead didn't cost anything, and the funeral, gravestone, flowers, as well as prawns, salmon, and roast beef sandwiches, were paid for. After the estate had been divided up, being dead would be free of charge and all cares, something Sundt would doubtless have preferred, if only he hadn't been so scared of it. Sundt lay awake at night, feeling all his bodily irregularities and thinking about everything that could strike him down.

"Cheap people have their own way of counting," Erika told Isak on the telephone. "Let's say, for example, that Sundt was supposed to give me *ten,* let's say Sundt owed me *ten;* well, without a moment's thought *ten* would wind up *four,* and there wouldn't be the slightest explanation; but if Sundt was expecting *ten* from me, then he'd have no problem making *ten* into *sixteen,* which he'd take off me even if I said *it's my last sixteen here and we said ten*—at that moment it would seem as if *I* were the cheap one."

"Yes," said Isak.

"Cheap people always win," said Erika. "Cheap people have all the power. Cheap people have no friends. They start off with lots of friends, then they have fewer friends, and in the end they have none. Who knows whether that bothers them. Do you think it bothers them?"

"I don't know," said Isak.

"Even the skinflint's spouse can never get the better of the skinflint," Erika went on.

"That's true," said Isak.

"Still!" said Erika.

"Still what?" asked Isak.

"Still, one evening I tried to get my own back," said Erika. "One evening I tapped my knife on my glass, rested my head on my husband's bony shoulder, and declared to our party: *This evening is Sundt's treat! Champagne and oysters for everybody! Sundt has been looking forward to this!* And our friends knew exactly what I was up to; they were in on it, a coup d'état against Sundt, an assassination attempt, a temporary seizure of power—our friends gorged themselves on champagne and oysters, reveling in his pain. They saw him sweating and gritting his teeth; they heard his impotent hints about skipping dessert. And it didn't end there. I started spending extravagantly, Father. I twirled around in new dresses, laid down new rugs, unpacked new books and a new stereo, shut out the light with new blinds. We couldn't afford any of it, you see. None of it! Still, I dressed up and laughed and came home late in the evenings."

And as Sundt lay in bed beside Erika at night, feeling all his bodily irregularities (a swelling in his right leg, a sharp pain in his chest, a change in the texture of his gums—possibly a symptom of decay?), she would not put her arms around him and comfort him the way she used to when they were first married. Instead she would tell him he was a wimp, a fool, a pathetic little figure, an affliction, even; then she would roll herself up in her new quilt and sleep through the night without giving his discomfort another thought. And so she was through with Sundt.

The roads were slushy and icy, but for Erika it was still the round-abouts and the road signs indicating the way out of Oslo that were the hardest part. She always ended up in some tunnel leading somewhere she did not want to go.

"It's not that difficult," said Laura on the telephone. "It's sign-posted all the way to Stockholm. All you have to do is follow."

For Laura, this sort of thing was easy. But Erika had, for reasons she failed to understand, always done the exact opposite of what the signs said. If the arrow pointed right, she turned left. In her nine years behind the wheel, she had caused many near accidents and received several fines, just like her mother, who was possibly an even worse driver.

Sometimes people would wrench open Erika's car door in the middle of a road junction just to shout at her. The difference between Erika and her mother was that Erika apologized whereas her mother shouted back.

Laura said once that Erika's nature behind the wheel, so totally contrary to her nature in all other areas of life, grew out of a profound split, an unspoken rage. Erika did not agree. She attributed this lack of confidence to some kind of dyslexia, an inability to read and process simple signs and codes or calculate distances.

Before Erika got into the car and drove off, she rang Laura and said: "Can't you take some time off, too? Can't you come with me?"

"Actually, I've got the day off today," Laura answered.

Erika could hear her gulping coffee and visualized her sitting in front of her computer, surfing the Internet, still in her pajamas though it was nearly eleven. Erika said: "I mean, can't you take the week off and come with me to Hammarsö? You could drive," she added.

"No!" retorted Laura. "It's not that easy to get a substitute teacher. And anyway, none of them want to take my class."

"Can't you come down at the weekend, at least? I'm sure Isak wants to see both of us."

"No!" said Laura.

"It would be an adventure," said Erika.

"No," repeated Laura. "I can't. Jesper's got a cold. We're all exhausted. Everything's falling apart. The last thing I have the energy to think of right now is going down to Hammarsö to see Isak, who, besides everything else, I am sure doesn't want to see us."

Erika would try again. Erika wouldn't give up. It was perfectly feasible to get a substitute teacher. Laura always moaned about her students, but in fact she didn't like entrusting them to other people; she didn't like other people doing her job. Nobody did it well enough, in her view.

Erika said: "What if Isak dies while I'm there?"

Laura laughed out loud and said: "Don't count on it, Erika! The old man will outlive us all."

Every summer from 1972 to 1979, Erika had flown by herself from Oslo to Stockholm, and then taken a smaller plane down to the port on the Baltic coast that was the last stop on her journey. She had a big blue plastic wallet around her neck; inside the wallet were her plane tickets and an official-looking piece of documentation on which her mother had written who was escorting her to the airport in Oslo and who would meet her at the airport in Sweden, as well as her name, age, and other such information.

"In case the stewardess loses you when you're changing flights in Stockholm," Erika's mother told her, putting a large, flowery handkerchief to Erika's nose and telling her to blow. Hard.

"Blow it all out before you get on the plane. Isak doesn't want children with colds coming to visit."

Elisabet had long auburn hair, strong, well-turned legs, and high-heeled, snot-green pumps. Erika was her only child.

"And if the stewardess happens to lose you, then find another stewardess and show her this sheet of paper," she said. "Are you listening, Erika? Can you manage that? All you have to do is show her the paper."

At the airport in the town on the shores of the Baltic, Rosa and Laura would be waiting for her. The drive to Hammarsö took an hour and a half, but sometimes they had to wait in a queue of cars to get onto one of the two ferries that transported residents and tourists between the mainland and the island. Then it would take two and a half hours or even longer. For Erika, it was like a small eternity. Going to Hammarsö was something she did every summer. She sat beside Laura in the backseat and followed their route on the road signs, saying: Now there are only fifty kilometers to go, now only forty, now we've passed the halfway oak and now there are only twenty kilometers to go. Rosa! Rosa! Are we nearly there? Can't you speed up?

"No!" said Rosa. "Do you want us to crash, for the the police to come and pull bits of our bodies from the wreckage?"

Erika looked at Laura, who was to be her sister for a whole month, and laughed.

A kilometer is like a minute.

Ten kilometers are like ten minutes.

Rosa said the girls could watch for the kilometer signs and work out for themselves how far they had left to go without whining.

But it wasn't just waiting in traffic or even the prospect of seeing Isak again that made the ride from the airport seem like a small eternity. It was anticipating the white limestone house and her room with the floral wallpaper. It was her half sister Laura and eventually Molly, too. And it was Ragnar.

It was Hammarsö itself, Erika's place on Earth, with its flat heath, gnarled trees, knobbly fossils, and vivid red poppies. It was the silver-gray sea and the rock where the girls sunbathed and listened to Radio Luxemburg or her friend Marion's special tapes. It was the scent of everything as the ultimate confirmation of now! now it's summer!

The summers in Hammarsö were the real eternity.

The drive was a small eternity on the way to the real one.

Erika drove slowly, talking out loud to herself. Talking out loud to herself was something she had learned from her driving instructor, Leif.

Erika knew she should have failed when she took her driver's test nine and a half years before (the day before her thirtieth birthday), and having somehow failed to fail she should have refused to accept her driver's license, simply giving it back to the authorities.

"You're not relating naturally to others on the road," Leif would say.

"I don't relate naturally to anybody," said Erika.

"Neither do I," admitted Leif. "But if you're going to drive a car, you have to relate naturally to others on the road. That's just the way it is."

Erika had never really intended to take the test. But when she and Sundt got divorced, she decided to learn to drive, and that was how she met Leif. He was a white-haired, quiet, melancholic man who opened his mouth only to pronounce sarcastic statements of the obvious, usually related to vehicular traffic. Erika drove around Oslo in Leif's company for a number of months; she paid for a hundred and thirty-four driving lessons.

"The older you are, the more lessons it takes," Leif said.

The newly divorced can latch on to the strangest people, and Erika latched on to Leif. She viewed him as a wise man, a mentor, if a bit gnomic. Every time he said something, one of those sarcastic statements of the obvious, *a stop sign means stop,* for instance, she would interpret it at a more profound level.

Laura, Isak, and even Molly had thought Erika was spending too much time with Leif. Nevertheless, in that time she did learn to talk out loud to herself when she was behind the steering wheel. This prevented her concentration from lapsing so she could stay focused on the act of driving, if not quite the direction of her trip. It was like this:

Now I'm at the roundabout.
Now I'm stopping at this red light.
Now I'm joining the motorway.
Now I'm keeping my eyes firmly on the middle of the road.

It was winter; she was on her way to Hammarsö; she was driving. She passed a roadside café. She didn't want to stop yet. Although she was hungry, she didn't want to stop yet.

Whenever Erika spoke to Isak on the telephone, and that was often, this was how she visualized him: he is sitting in one of the two armchairs in the living room of the white limestone house, with his feet up on a pouf and his big rectangular spectacles on his nose. He is listening to a piece of Schubert, perhaps the slow movement of the C major string quintet. On the table beside the chair is the black tape recorder that he carries around the house with him. Erika is twelve and Laura is ten. They are lying side by side on the white wooden floor, reading and listening to the music with him. He lets them do that as long as they are quiet. The legs propped on the pouf are grasshopper thin and clad in worn brown velvet trousers. He once bought several pairs of velvet trousers of the same style and make. These trousers were patched over time and otherwise maintained by Rosa.

I bet he's still got those same trousers, thought Erika, but now it would be Simona who patched and stitched them. On his feet, a pair of warm sheepskin slippers. Isak often had cold feet. On the table beside the chair, three newspapers: two national and one local.

It had been a year since Erika had seen her father. The last time had been in Stockholm, one of those dinner dates he liked to make with her and Laura. At first he had invited Molly, too, but she rarely came, so he stopped asking her.

Erika followed the signs, just as Laura had advised. It worked. She was on her way now. She felt sure Isak would not have changed much since she last saw him. He wouldn't have changed, his house wouldn't have changed. She hadn't been there for more than twenty-five years, but was sure he hadn't moved the furniture around or bought any new clothes. He would still eat two thin slices of toast for breakfast, a bowl of kefir with a banana for lunch, and little meatballs with potatoes and gravy for dinner. That would be on Tuesdays. On Mondays and Wednesdays there was fish. And on Saturdays chicken casserole. The same dinners were cooked by Simona that had been cooked by Rosa in years gone by. After serving him his meal, Simona went home. He had told Erika all this on the phone, and sometimes Erika spoke to Simona to ask how her father was. Was he perhaps nearing death without any of his daughters knowing it?

"He'll never die," said Simona.

His face had more pockmarks and furrows and discolored patches, to be sure. But it was the same face. The same eyes, she thought, though she couldn't picture her father's eyes. She didn't even know what color they were. Isak's eyes looked at you and you either existed or didn't exist in that look. He had been old for a long time. He had been old twenty-five years ago.

Once he said on the telephone that he had changed since Rosa died. Isak Lövenstad's formative years, according to him, had been between the ages of seventy-two and eighty-four.

"Really?" asked Erika. "How's that? I mean, how have you changed?"

Erika stared at the windshield wipers moving back and forth without much effect. The snow was coming down heavily. The driving was difficult.

He had said: "I'm maturing."

"You're maturing?"

"Yes."

"What does that mean, you're maturing?"

"I'm reading Swedenborg."

"Oh?"

"And Swedenborg wrote that if you feel you're living too long—and that's certainly true in my case, isn't it—then it's your obligation to mature."

"So that's what you're doing?"

"Yes."

"But what does that actually entail, Isak, you maturing?"

"I understand things better."

"Such as?"

"That I've never cared about other people. I've been indifferent."

"I don't believe you."

"What don't you believe?"

"That you've been indifferent. I don't believe you. It's too easy just to say that."

A little boy with matchstick legs and scabby knees came running toward her, in and out of the light. Just occasionally, he turned to look back. She remembered the boy saying: "We need to find his weakness, where he's vulnerable, but it won't be easy." Erika gripped the steering wheel, but the car went into a skid and grazed the snowy bank before she could regain control. She stopped at the next gas station and bought herself a coffee. She closed her eyes for a few minutes before setting off again.

"That's how people get killed," she said to herself. "They drive in weather like this."

"And yet I told you not to come," Isak would have said.

Elisabet said it wasn't easy to be mother and father at the same time. She said *more* is demanded of a woman than of a man. She said that as a *woman* she had been forced to do *everything* by herself. (Elisabet often spoke in italics.) She said women, simply because they are *women,* are not *heard* the same way men are. That's why I speak *clearly,* she said. To be *heard.* To get your *attention.*

In the spring of 1980, almost a year after that summer when everything happened, everything changed, Erika spoke to Isak on the phone, and he said she would have to forget about coming to Hammarsö for the holidays. It would be the summer Erika turned fifteen. Why? she said. Why must I forget Hammarsö this year? Her father did not like to be questioned, so he snapped his fingers. Erika heard a little snap from far away in Stockholm or Lund or wherever he was, and the frost seeped through the receiver. Yes, the receiver Erika was clutching froze in her hands, and Erika's hands, which her father would sometimes kiss, turned to ice, too. That's the way he is, thought Erika, and so as not to cry, she thought of five reasons why she loved him.

She would have to forget about Hammarsö that year. And maybe next year, too. And the year after that. She wasn't going there; none of them were. Because Isak didn't want them to.

"But why *doesn't* he?" asked Elisabet. "Why, Erika?"

Her mother was standing on her long legs in the living room on Oscarsgate, running a hand through her thick hair. On her feet she had a pair of high-heeled ferry-yellow pumps by Yves Saint Laurent.

Elisabet said: "There is simply no way I can be expected to think up all sorts of exciting activities for the holidays. You'll have to entertain yourself."

She continued: "I shall be *working*. My head's *full* of things that need doing. *Full!* Your father can't just *change* a system that's worked perfectly well since 1972."

Erika knew all about Elisabet's head. It had always been full. Erika was nearly fifteen now, but when she was little, her mother used to declare herself a bundle of nerves. Erika felt sorry for her then, having to drag around that overflowing, tired, and heavy head filled with a bundle of nerves. She hadn't been sure what nerves were, but imagined them to be some kind of maggot. She had thought Elisabet's lovely head might explode at any moment or open up and let out some huge, tangled horror, especially if clumsy little Erika, by her very presence, added to the bundle.

As Erika grew older, her mother ceased claiming to be a bundle of nerves. She just said: I'm just not very *happy* today, Erika.

Erika wasn't going to Hammarsö ("Why? Why? Is the house just going to stand empty, Isak?"), but she had a plan.

"I shall keep out of your way, Mamma. I promise. You won't know I'm here."

"But why, Erika? Why aren't you all going to Hammarsö? I mean, it's so beautiful there. Green sea and everything."

"Gray," said Erika.

"What?" said Elisabet.

"The sea's gray," said Erika. "Not green. It's different sorts of gray."

"But why?" asked Elisabet. "Why aren't you going there? Why isn't anybody going to Hammarsö?"

"I don't know, Mamma."

"What will you do, then? Get a summer job of some kind?"

"Yes, maybe."

Erika had known Isak would come to this decision, of course. All that long winter she had known. How could they stay in that house again as if nothing had happened? How could she possibly go there again? How could he? How could Laura and Molly? How could Rosa, who had sat in complete silence beneath the blue lamp in the kitchen in the white limestone house, go back there? To Hammarsö. To the heaths and beaches and poppies and the bluish-gray sea she had once heard a grown-up man call the Frog Sea. The man intended it in a derogatory way. But Erika liked the idea of her and Ragnar's sea being a frog sea: silent and strange and alive and shallow until it was suddenly deep and ominous. A frog, Ragnar had said, can go slack and play dead for several minutes if he's attacked.

The currents brought things from the Baltic states and Poland that washed up on the stony beach below Isak's house: sodden detergent boxes and cigarette packets, shampoo bottles, driftwood; and bottles that might contain oxygen and be deadly dangerous *(Don't touch anything you find washed up on the beach!),* or even a secret message from the sealed continent on the other side of the horizon, from the communist regimes in the east, from the countries where people were shot or thrown in prison if they tried to cross the border or escape. The cardboard boxes and shampoo bottles had strange words on them, written in strange letters: PRIMA and STOLICH-NAYA, and Ragnar and Erika tried to decipher the words, adding them to their cryptic language. They gathered the things in plastic bags from the shop and took them to the secret hut deep in the woods.

·   ·   ·

So never again. Erika grew up and married Sundt and had a girl and a boy. Both forced their way out of her, took a breath, and found her breast, and now, this winter, her son was the same age that Ragnar had been in the summer of 1979.

Erika and Ragnar. Born on the same day, in the same year. They were exactly the same age and were even born at more or less the same time of night, Erika at five past three in the morning and Ragnar at quarter past three. She remembered how delighted he was at realizing this. We're twins, he said. And a few years later he said: We're best friends. We love each other. Soul mates with the same blood.

So far Erika hadn't made a single mistake. The daylight was fading. It was nearly four and already getting dark. The snow was falling more heavily than ever. She wanted to get as far as Örebro; she had booked a room at the Grand Hotel, where Laura said she should stay, pronouncing it *frightfully nice;* she wanted at least to get farther than Karlstad before she stopped. Otherwise it would be too long a drive the next day. Erika said out loud:

> I'm driving carefully through the snow.
> I'm remembering to look in the rearview
>   mirror every five seconds.
> I'm the one in charge of this car.
> I shall go on to Örebro.

Her children were fine. Magnus was on a school trip to Poland, visiting the concentration camps, Auschwitz and Birkenau of course, but also a couple more whose names Erika could not recall. Now he was in Kraków. He had sent a text and told her he had bought a jacket and a pair of trousers, because it was cheaper there than at home. He said nothing about the camps. Ane was managing by herself, staying with a friend. Ane sent a text saying: *Hi Mum. Have a gd trip :-) Drive safe. OK 4 me 2 stay with N not B? :-) Dad says OK.*

Going to Hammarsö, where she hadn't been for more than twenty-five years.

Going to see Isak, to whom she normally spoke only on the telephone.

His voice had sounded so reedy the last time.

"How are you, Isak?"

He replied: "It feels a bit like an epilogue, Erika."

"I could come and see you, you know."

She regretted it immediately.

"You never want to come here," said Isak.

"Well, I do now," said Erika.

"You haven't been here since you were . . . What were you? Fifteen? Sixteen?"

"Fourteen. I haven't been to Hammarsö since I was fourteen."

"Fourteen years! Goddamn! You haven't been here for . . . ! How old are you now?" asked Isak.

"Thirty-nine," said Erika.

Isak went quiet, then he said:

"You're thirty-nine?"

"Yes."

"So you're not exactly a spring chicken anymore!"

"No, Isak. And neither are you!"

"And how old is Laura?"

"Laura's thirty-seven."

Isak said nothing, but Erika added: "And in case you're wondering, Molly's thirty."

Isak said: "You haven't been here for twenty-five years. I see no reason why you should come now."

"Maybe it's time."

"But now? You're coming now? The weather's awful. They're forecasting snowstorms. Nobody wants to be here in a storm."

"We can think of something to do."

"I don't think anymore. I'm almost ninety."

"You're eighty-four," said Erika. "I'll bring some DVDs. Have you got a DVD player?"

"No."

"All right. I'll bring some videos."

"Don't come, Erika. We'll just tiptoe around being polite to each other, and that's an awful effort at my age."

"I don't care. I'm coming to see you," said Erika.

She didn't want this. She didn't want to see him. She wouldn't be able to cope with the physical proximity. The telephone was perfectly adequate. But she let herself be carried along by her proposal. The little girl let herself be carried along. A reedy, old man's voice on the telephone. The idea of a life without Father. *It feels a bit like an epilogue, Erika.*

There is a photograph: two little sisters with long blond hair, shaking hands—formally, politely, gravely, like the heads of state of two Lilliputian nations.

Every summer from 1972 to 1979, Erika flew by herself from Norway to Sweden to let Elisabet rest her bundle of nerves, which had been gathered up all winter and spring. Erika agreed with her mother that it was *about time Isak Lövenstad took a bit of responsibility for once.*

Elisabet said: "But I want you to know it's a great, *great* joy being your mother, Erika!"

Every time Elisabet mentioned the great joy she felt at being Erika's mother, which she did frequently and in that rather abrupt, random way, she would bend over Erika, gather her in her arms, and kiss her all over. Kiss! Kiss! Kiss! Gorgeous child! It was a mixture of kissing and tickling, and Erika didn't like being tickled; it took her breath away and made her want to pull free and run. And yet she giggled. It was impossible not to when you were being tickled, and it was impossible to be cross with Elisabet.

Erika tried to explain to her mother that she liked the kisses but not the tickling, but it was hard to find the right words. She couldn't do it. Elisabet misunderstood: she thought Erika was fishing for more tickle-kisses and put her arms around her daughter, held her tight, and tickled her even more, and they laughed until they both gasped for air.

Before Erika went to Hammarsö for the very first time—it was the summer she turned seven—Elisabet told her many things. She told Erika to remember to put on clean underwear every day and that she couldn't assume Isak's new wife would lay out clean clothes for her every morning. She told Erika to remember to say thank you for her meals and not to give the impression of being a spoiled brat. She told Erika not to forget to show Isak and Isak's new wife the end-of-year report from her teacher that was full of praise for Erika's achievements at school. Erika was a good reader, a good writer, good in math, good at keeping quiet until it was her turn to speak, good at working with others, and good at working on her own, but not particularly good at sports or making friends. Erika preferred the company of the teachers and seemed lost at recess. Her teacher wrote that Erika could make more of an effort with her drawing: she had—and this was just an example—handed in a drawing of a polar bear that did not look like a polar bear. The picture looked more like a sea monster with huge teeth, slavering jaws, and oozing eyes. The point, wrote the teacher, had been to draw a *lifelike* polar bear. But apart from a few such criticisms, the report was overwhelmingly positive, thought Elisabet after reading it several times, and therefore worth showing to the child's father. Elisabet told Erika to remember to ring her at least every other day to let her know how she was; otherwise Elisabet would worry. Elisabet did not want to ring Hammarsö herself and get Isak's new wife on the line. Elisabet told Erika she must bear in mind her father's nasty, temperamental streak, but also that he didn't mean anything by it, or rather, he meant *something,* but it wasn't as bad as it might seem at the time; Erika shouldn't get upset if he started bellowing. Or at least not terribly upset. Elisabet said Isak had a tongue that could dart out of his mouth like a serpent, spurting poison.

"But you can choose for yourself whether you want to die of it," she said.

Elisabet did not tell her that Isak's new wife had a name, and that the name was Rosa. *(How lovely! Like the flower!)* Neither did she tell her that Isak and Rosa had a daughter who was almost five, and that she was called Laura and that Laura was thus Erika's sister.

Erika and Laura wore shorts and washed-out pink T-shirts that strictly speaking they had grown out of. Both had long blond hair, long tanned Barbie-doll legs, and little handfuls of girlish bottom that wiggled from side to side as they trudged all that way from the shop to Isak's house, each with a dripping ice-cream cone in hand. Men turned their heads and thought unmentionable things, but the sisters took no notice of the men; they were having enough trouble keeping their hands and T-shirts safe from ice-cream drips.

Or they lay in the tall grass in the meadow beyond the white limestone house that Isak had bought when Rosa was expecting Laura.

"We're sisters, aren't we?" asked Laura.

"Half sisters," said Erika. "That's different."

"Yeah," said Laura.

"We've got different mothers, and you have to have the same mother to be real sisters," said Erika.

"And the same father," said Laura.

Erika pondered.

"It's a bit like false croup," said Erika. "It's not the real thing, being half sisters," she added, and sang: "Half. Fake. Lie. Swindle."

"What's false croup?" asked Laura.

"An illness," answered Erika.

"What sort of illness?" asked Laura.

"Children can't breathe," said Erika. "Children go all blue in the face and blue round the mouth and they croak like this . . ."

Erika produced a croaking, coughing, rasping sound in her throat, grabbed her neck with both hands, and shivered all over.

Laura giggled and lay down beside her. Erika felt an urge to take her sister's hand; it was so small and slim and delicate. Instead she said: "I had false croup when I was little. My mummy was all alone in the world. *Alone and abandoned.* And I nearly died. My mummy was all alone, standing outside with me in the winter night, crying."

Laura went quiet; she very much wanted to tell a similar story about her own mother, Rosa, but could not think of one. Rosa was never *alone and abandoned.* Rosa would never *stand outside in the winter night, crying;* she would never contemplate anything so wild. One winter, on her way home from school, Laura had taken her woolly hat off and put it in her schoolbag, and Rosa had been so angry that she couldn't speak for ten minutes, at least. This—being speechless for more than ten minutes—was the craziest thing she could think of with regard to her mother, who was always utterly sensible and calm. Rosa had been convinced that Laura would get pneumonia, and though Rosa was rarely wrong, on that occasion she was. Laura didn't even catch cold.

Erika went on: "But of course, there's something even worse than false croup."

"What's that?" asked Laura.

"REAL CROUP!" said Erika, not entirely sure what real croup might be, but obviously it had to be worse than false croup.

"With croup, you don't stand a chance," Erika said. "You just die. And that's that."

"But—" objected Laura. She wanted more details.

Erika stopped her with a scream. If she screamed, she wouldn't have to give details. She got to her feet and staggered over the meadow, screaming HELP HELP I CAN'T BREATHE, I'VE GOT CROUP, I'VE GOT CROUP, before finally collapsing beside Laura.

Erika lay in the middle of a flower meadow. The backs of her knees and the insides of her wrists and her neck and scalp were itching: it was the insects climbing over her; it was the ticks latching on to her to suck. If you had a tick attached to you, there was a great commotion in Isak's house. In Norwegian it was called a *flått*. In Swedish it was a *fästing*. She liked the Swedish word better. If you had a *fästing*, you would have both Isak and Rosa staring at your armpit, or bent over your bottom or leg, or pushing your hair off your neck so they could study it. It was a bit like going to school in new shoes: everyone said *Aren't you smart*, pointing at your shoes; it was nice and embarrassing at the same time. And then there was the whole business of removing the tick with butter and tweezers, especially when it was big and fat and ready to pop and all bluey-mauve because it was full of blood. If you pressed the tick, blood would squirt out of it. The most important thing was not to leave the head behind. That could lead to blood poisoning, Rosa said. Splinters in your fingers or toes could also lead to blood poisoning if they stayed there too long, or if you didn't manage to get the *whole* splinter out. And blood poisoning could lead to fever and convulsions, which could lead to gangrene, which could lead to amputation, sometimes without anaesthetic because it had to be done in such a rush. So you could end up having your arm or leg cut off, wide awake and conscious while they did it—and all because you hadn't removed the tick or the splinter properly.

Beyond the trees, a hundred meters from the gray, uneven, stony beach and silver-gray sea, lay Isak's white limestone house. Erika said to herself: I am Erika Lövenstad. Isak Lövenstad is my father. We live here on this island and my sister is called Laura and I'm the eldest.

She opened her eyes and stared straight up into the blue sky.

And so, the summer days were indistinguishable, as were the summers themselves. Erika and Laura spent most of their time lying in the long grass in front of that house, reading Donald Duck comics and later *Starlet,* which was really too advanced for them. They ate wild strawberries, staining their hands and mouths red. The sun shone every day, and it was outdoors time, which meant they weren't allowed to go into the house and be a nuisance. Outdoors time was decreed. It was never discussed, had never been explained. Everyone knew what it was. It was unchangeable, like the sun and the moon and the seasons. Outdoors time meant you stayed outside. You didn't go in to get a glass of water or use the toilet, because the pipes would gurgle and Isak would hear. You didn't go to your room to fetch things you'd forgotten to take out with you (like maybe a tennis ball for a game of sevens), because the floorboards would creak. Erika learned all this during her first week on Hammarsö. If Isak was disturbed, it broke his concentration and sabotaged his working day. He would storm out of his room, stand in the middle of the kitchen, and bellow. Laura had stories to tell about Isak bellowing, about how scared she'd been, alone with him in the kitchen, about how his face blanched with all that bellowing. First white, then red, then mauve, like a tick ready to pop. Isak would get so angry that saliva dribbled from his mouth.

There was no reason not to believe this. Her mother had warned Erika before she came to Hammarsö that Isak could be moody; but her mother didn't call it moody, she called it *temperamental.* Elisabet said several times that Erika must not disturb him when he was working, otherwise she risked a flash of his *temperamental* side— and that wasn't good. Erika would sometimes imagine Isak's temperamental side as a ton of plutonium inside his head. You wouldn't even have to disturb him *a lot:* annoying him just a little was enough to make the barrel tip over and the plutonium, pale lilac, run out over the floor.

Day after day Erika and Laura would lie in the high grass in the meadow beyond the house by the sea. It might be two o'clock. They couldn't hear it, but in the living room next to Isak's workroom ticked the grandfather clock that chimed every whole and half hour. They couldn't see him, but they knew Isak would be inside assembling some mysterious invention; it was never really clear what he was up to, but it was his work, and their father's work was of the utmost importance (Laura would tell Erika) and had something to do with women and birth and swelling tummies and dead fetuses.

It was Laura who saw the boy with the matchstick legs first. He was running. Laura nudged Erika in the side and pointed, but neither of the girls said anything. Erika could see what Laura was pointing at, but the figure was running so fast that at first she couldn't see that it was a boy her own age in a T-shirt and shorts; it could as easily have been an animal or some supernatural creature. It was as if he came from nowhere—he just materialized in the landscape around Isak's house—but Erika thought he must have come from the beach, where he probably had slipped and fallen on the rocks. His knees were scraped. The boy didn't notice Erika and Laura lying quite still in the grass, following him with their eyes. He ran across the meadow, so close that they could hear his sneakers pounding on the ground, his breathing louder than their own. He ran right past them and crossed the boundary between the meadow and the private dirt road that swung down to Isak's house, past the gate a little way from the house, past the clump of stunted pines, past the wild strawberry patch, now picked bare, past Isak's green Volvo. Erika looked at Laura and Laura looked at Erika, and both of them looked over at the boy again. He had short brown hair and his T-shirt said I'VE BEEN TO NIAGARA FALLS. And running down the road toward Isak's house, he suddenly fell over on the gravel. Laura got to her feet, but Erika pulled her down into the grass again. The boy lay flat on his stomach. He lay there for a long time, or at any rate it felt like a long time. In the end he sat up and examined his knees. Erika felt a shooting pain in her own knees. The boy had already bashed his knees on the rocks on the beach and now he had fallen on the gravel and would have to pick all the grit out of the open wounds. It would sting. Perhaps she ought to help him. Perhaps she and Laura should get up from the tall grass and go over to him, but they stayed where they were. It was Erika who had to decide. She was the elder of the two. Erika lay there, pressing one hand on Laura's back to keep her there, too. It was the boy who got up. He stood there for a bit, not moving, his body tensed, and he looked about him; then he set off at a run again. He ran all the way down to the house, all the way down to Isak's house, and there he stopped. The boy stopped outside Isak's door and rang the bell. The boy didn't know it was outdoors time. He didn't know outdoors time had been decreed. He didn't even know what *a temperamental streak* was. He rang several times. Erika could see him ringing the bell again and again—even more than thirty years later she could see him at Isak's front door—and when nobody opened he started hammering on it; he clenched his fists and launched himself at the door. Erika turned to Laura, who, though she could hear neither the ringing nor the hammering, had put her hands over her ears and screwed up her eyes. Erika knew that it would not be long before Isak opened the door, but that it was too late to get up and run after the boy to save him.

Erika crossed the border between Norway and Sweden. No one pulled her over and asked her to explain her business in Sweden.

"They never do," Laura told Erika on the phone.

It was five o'clock and Erika had decided to stop somewhere for Swedish meatballs and mashed potato. She said out loud: "Why don't I stop the car and have meatballs and mashed potato. With lingonberry jam."

Erika had a feeling Isak might not have long to live, and that was why she had embarked on this journey, which she was now regretting. The truth was that he lived on and on and on. Isak never died. His grief at the loss of Rosa remained unbearable, and he would occasionally speak of his suicide, planned down to the last detail but never carried out. The pills had been procured and lay ready, interminably, in the drawer of his bedside table.

Elisabet would say, in one of her few moments of insight, that if they were the same pills he had been talking about for the last twelve years, they had no doubt passed their sell-by date, in which case he ought to get some new ones if he was serious. Like Erika, Erika's mother spoke frequently to Isak on the phone.

Elisabet would say: "Your father and I are good friends. We once sat on a rock out on the sea when we were in love, and he said we were *painfully* bound to each other."

Talking to each other on the phone every other Saturday from twelve to half past one was a ritual they had had ever since their divorce in 1968. They had divorced because Rosa's belly had swollen past any point denying she was pregnant or that Isak was the father.

Now Isak had grown old. Elisabet, to be sure, thought eighty-four was no great age. Elisabet's friend Bekky was over ninety and *bright as a button,* Elisabet said, so eighty-four was really nothing to speak of.

And vocal cords do not decay at the same rate as the rest of the body. When Elisabet and Isak spoke on the telephone, they were not two bodies, a source of concern and embarrassment to themselves and each other. Two bodies moving ever more slowly and often hurting. Mamma and Father, thought Erika. Isak with his painful hip and cramps in his legs, and Elisabet the dancer with her aching back and feet.

As a child, Erika would sometimes overhear part of their telephone conversation. Elisabet's voice when she was talking to Isak was bubbly and happy and as light as a length of pink silk ribbon before it has been measured out, cut, and threaded into a shoe.

When Elisabet Lund Lövenstad was a young and promising ballerina, a member of the Swedish Opera Ballet (which was grander than the Norwegian Opera Ballet), one of her boyfriends said that if he had only one day left to live and had to choose between seeing her dance or hearing her laugh, he would choose the day of her laughter. Erika's mother laughed often and loudly. There are women who giggle and women who laugh; Elisabet never giggled. She opened her whole mouth, bared her teeth, tongue, and throat, and uttered sounds that came from someplace deep down inside her. But the exact source was unclear. Her chest, her stomach, her pelvis, her abdomen? Isak must have pondered such matters. He wanted the whole of Elisabet. Not just the beautiful part everyone else saw onstage, the perfect beauty—no, he wanted all the other things as well. Everything that ran out of her. The sounds she made. Her sobs when she cried. The painful cough that kept her awake at night. The rumbling of her stomach, her groans and low snores. It was not enough for him that she stripped naked. She had a fantastically beautiful body. As a ballet dancer she was a vision onstage. Admittedly, she was too big for the international stardom her talent merited. Too tall, too broad, too heavy. There was far too much of her. Too much for the powder-white lace skirts, too much for the male dancers who almost collapsed each time they had to lift her, but not too much for Isak, who always wanted more. Though he was himself a lean man, known for his brilliant brain and his perfect pitch.

With a small team at the University of Lund, Isak helped develop the use of ultrasound. In his old age he was called a pioneer in his field. The female patients were grateful. Tumors were discovered, the unborn checked and assessed. Some might say invaded. Isak's many romantic indiscretions were forgotten as time went by, and those women had grown old, their bodies no longer arousing anything in anyone. Neither desire nor curiosity. Perhaps pity. The female body is predictable that way.

But oh! Isak the lean and Elisabet the voluptuous! As a young man, he would spread her out naked on the bed like a big hand-embroidered quilt. He would not allow a single piece of skin, a single limb, a single orifice to remain unattended. But it wasn't enough. He wanted more. And she let him rub oil on her stomach and move the transducer over her skin so her flesh melted away and they could both see the inside of her body on a screen; he couldn't get enough of it, couldn't get enough of the irresistibly lovely Elisabet: her stomach, bladder, womb, ovaries, birth canal, cysts, tissues, ligaments.

And one day, a fetus inside her! A nine-week-old fetus. A nine-week-old Erika. Or not Erika. Not nine weeks. Something else. Not a human being. Not time. Something that would one day be a human being, be time, be a nine-week-old Erika screaming and screaming for her mother's breast. But now: something dark and mobile, like a jellyfish. A blob or blotch that often merely dissolves and runs out of a woman's body as blood and liquid and grit. But that just as often takes root and eats and grows and bursts out of its skin like a cancer or a tree. Sounds attracted to or repelled by each other: sounds that create an image. A blotch that wasn't there until it appeared on the screen, in the womb, deep within and way up inside Elisabet's divinely beautiful body.

There was a child growing inside your divinely beautiful body, Elisabet. It would not disappear, though you ran up and down all the steps you could find, ran through the streets of Stockholm instead of taking the bus, ran to the shop to buy food for yourself and your husband, the man they declared a genius, ran to rehearsals at the Opera House, where you held your breath and pulled in your stomach though nothing showed yet; ran home, up and down more steps, always more steps, ran to your morning class, ran until you fell over in one practically perfect movement and threw up on yourself and two other girls who came tripping over on tiptoe to help you; threw up on pure white costumes, on diaphanous tights, leg warmers and toe shoes firmly tied, crossed twice around the ankle; threw up so the stench of your vomit overpowered the smell of chalk; everywhere that smell of chalk; you could no longer bear the smell of chalk on the floor, on your shoes. But your child didn't disappear. You went on running, but your child clung on to you and you couldn't stop throwing up. Rehearsals were canceled, classes skipped. You were replaced by another dancer. Get rid of it, Isak! Get rid of it! I don't want it, you must see that! I don't want children! Not this child! Not now! But Isak did not want to get rid of it. That's a life you're carrying, *a life,* Elisabet, he said, and shut the door behind him. Your body lost its shape. It swelled up. What's that smell, Isak? Fried food?

Sweat? Perfume? Soap? Semen? Coffee? Snow? You'll soon be able to see your baby, he said. And if it's a girl she'll be called Karin, because it's the loveliest name I know. Your stomach expanded. Your ankles swelled. You got out the sewing machine and the rolls of pink silk ribbon. You measured and cut four ribbons of equal length and fixed them to your shoes. Like hell she'll be called Karin, you whispered to nobody, and threw the shoes at the wall. That was the last thing you said for a while. Little ballerina! Your ankles were fat and puffy, the hemorrhoids were riveted between your buttocks, your legs were as blue as an old woman's, and now you were certainly too big. Too big to dance, too big to run, too big to sleep, too big to speak. You were a gigantic white whale, Elisabet. A gigantic white whale lying quite still on the ocean floor. And you didn't say a word.

Normally, said Laura, who had made the trip a thousand times before, it takes two days to drive to Hammarsö. Two days, with an overnight stop in Örebro. But Erika had set off in a snowstorm, started late, and only got as far as Arvika. She hadn't stopped for meatballs with mashed potato and lingonberry jam. Isak had been right. It was dark. It was icy. She should never have started out.

Erika said out loud to herself: "This is how people die. Driving when the roads are like this."

She said: "You were quite right, Isak. It was a bad time to come!"

The mobile phone was on the seat beside her. All she had to do was pick it up and ring the number. She was sure he would understand. He would support her decision to abandon the trip. He would be relieved. She continued along the motorway, planning to stop for something to eat in Boda.

"After all, we'd just tiptoe around being polite to each other," Isak had said.

And the boy with matchstick legs knocked and hammered and pounded on Isak's door for what seemed like forever, and the door was at last flung open by Isak himself. Laura, lying on her stomach in the grass, clung tightly to Erika and blurted OH NO OH NO when she saw her father.

"Shush, shush," whispered Erika.

Erika has since wondered whether she really did see Isak tearing out his hair like the mad professor in some comic strip, and whether she really did hear him bellow at the boy DAMN YOU GET OUT OF HERE OR I'LL CUT YOUR EARS OFF AND EAT THEM FOR DINNER YOU FILTHY LITTLE BRAT.

What Erika does know is that the boy with matchstick legs was so astonished to see the door opening and Isak suddenly standing there that he fell over backwards and played dead for several minutes.

She was on her way to Hammarsö, and these were the sounds she could hear: the drone of the engine, the fan, and the snow tires on wet asphalt. Gusts of wind, dark rain, and falling snow, melting in the air and joining the slush on the motorway, and the front windshield wipers swishing to and fro, one-two-one-two-one-two, like black pendulums.

Erika remembered sitting barefoot on the settee, reading a magazine and waiting for the sun to come back, the grandfather clock in the living room ticking, waiting for the overcast sky to clear so she could put on her polka-dot bikini and sunbathe on the rocks with Marion and Frida and Emily and occasionally Eva. And she remembered Ragnar, who smelled of Coca-Cola and of the sea and was ugly and handsome at the same time. It depended how you looked at him, with eyes open or virtually shut.

She remembered Isak stomping out of his workroom and stopping short when he saw her. He'll start bellowing any moment now!

He'll start bellowing because I'm sitting here on the sofa. I haven't disturbed him. I haven't made a single disturbing sound—unless . . . unless . . . unless turning the pages of a magazine made a sound that Isak could hear. Because Isak could hear sounds no one else could hear. She had read that in the article about him in *Life*. That is, it wasn't that he *heard* the sounds; he *saw* them on a screen. A throbbing fetal heart. The outline of a brain, looking like a shriveled date. The shadow of two babies instead of one in the mother's womb. Laura, who knew their father best, used to say Isak could hear *everything*. He could hear what Laura and Erika were saying to each other, even if they were a long way off. He could even hear what they were thinking. Words and thoughts could be picked up and registered as dots and lines on a screen to make a picture. It was better not to say anything or even think anything you didn't want Isak to get wind of. But that was impossible. No talking. No thinking. Two deaf-mute girls in the grass with virgin knots between their legs and in their heads. It was Ragnar, the boy with matchstick legs, who came up with a plan.

Ragnar had five ring binders full of *The Phantom* and *Superman* comics and knew everything about superpowers. Isak had a sort of superhearing and X-ray vision combined, said Ragnar, who also seemed to know things about Isak. But just like Superman, Isak had his limitations, a kind of weakness or vulnerability. "Like Achilles!" Ragnar exclaimed, not bothering to explain to the sisters who Achilles was. The point was to find *Isak's heel* (which wouldn't have to be a heel, exactly; it could be anything), cause pain, and make sure there was a total loss of all superpowers. Only then would the three of them be able to win the war against someone like Isak.

"A superhero without his superpowers is much weaker than ordinary people without ordinary powers," Ragnar said.

Erika and Laura nodded and continued to say nothing. (Erika was not aware of exactly why Ragnar was declaring war on her father, but she and Laura went along and listened and didn't protest.) Ragnar took the sisters to the hut in the woods and said that until they could discover what Isak's weakness might be, they would have to speak and think in a language Isak didn't understand, because then it wouldn't matter that he could hear them. A language that he, Ragnar, had started to develop; it was based on criminals' backslang but was much more complicated: you didn't have the same consonant on each side of the vowel *o*, for example, like you do in the simplest form of backslang. In backslang the word *love* became *lolovove,* which anybody could work out. In Ragnar's language, *love* was *lomovowe* and *I'm in love with you* was *Imon inop lomovowe woxitovhoj yozou;* and what was more, you had to pronounce it as if you were speaking Russian.

In the hut he had a box full of things he had found on the rocky shoreline, flotsam and jetsam from the countries in the east, and that was how he had collected foreign words in foreign alphabets that could be added to his language. The wonderful word STOLICHNAYA from a vodka bottle, for example.

But the first thing Erika and Laura learned to say was *I'm in love with you* or *Imon inop lomovowe woxitovhoj yozou.* Erika remembers repeating the word *lomovowe* to herself when she went to bed at night. *Lomovowe, lomovowe, lomovowe.* It was a lovely word once she had learned to pronounce it. Laura gave up trying to speak Ragnar's language more or less straightaway. She found it too difficult, she told them. But not Erika. She didn't give up. She liked speaking in a language only she and Ragnar could understand.

Ragnar would speak to her, quietly. She lay there in the secret hut with his arm around her; he stroked her hair and said:

Isak, pronounced Isotakol, was the wicked king from the land of Dofeatovhok who had bewitched the island and everyone who lived there—the people, the sheep, the cows, the trees, the fish. He had an ear as big as the tall windows of the community center. He heard everything. Every sound. The slap of the flounder against the stony seabed. Fir cones opening. Your breathing as you run away through the woods.

At a bus stop on the edge of Fagerås, a woman waited for the bus. Beside her was a boy of fourteen or so. The woman and the boy stood motionless in the slush; it was snowing and raining by turns. The bus stop consisted of a pole with timetables mounted on it and a rotting shelter with a disintegrating roof, the bench inside unusable. The woman, dressed in a red checked coat with a tie belt and high-heeled black boots, had her dark hair up and was holding a big black umbrella in her right hand. The boy stood a little apart from her. He was wet and inadequately clad in a cap, a hoodie, and sagging jeans. Between them on the ground were a black suitcase and a yellow nylon bag with the logo of a Swedish soccer team. The woman and the boy were both staring in the same direction, to the left, as if their gaze could impel the bus along the road.

Erika saw the two figures as she drove past them. At first she thought that she was just imagining it, that the boy and the woman were a ghostly vision created by the rain, the dark sky, and the perpetually changing light. But when she looked in the rearview mirror to confirm that it *was* her imagination, they were still there. The woman under the black umbrella. The boy with the hoodie, soaking wet. The suitcase and bag on the ground.

Erika pulled over to the side of the road. She switched on the hazard lights and grabbed her anorak from the backseat and threw it around her shoulders. She opened the car door, got out to face the driving rain, and tried to attract the attention of the woman or the boy. They just stood there, unmoving, staring the other way.

"Hey there! Hello!" she shouted. "Hey there, you two!"

The woman with the umbrella turned toward her. Erika broke into a run. The boy still did not move. He was listening to music; a thin white cord ran from his ears to his jeans pocket. The woman looked inquiringly at Erika, who was wet and freezing cold and out of breath after her run along the road.

"You looked as if you've been waiting awhile," said Erika.

"The bus should have been here ten minutes ago," said the woman.

The boy had now realized that his mother—for the woman with the umbrella must be his mother, thought Erika—was talking to someone. He took out his earbuds so he could hear better.

"Where are you going? I mean, can I give you a lift part of the way?" asked Erika. "You're drenched," she said when neither of them responded. "And the bus definitely isn't coming."

The woman and the boy regarded her as if they didn't really understand what she was saying. Erika switched to Swedish.

"Especially you," she said, nodding to the boy. "You're absolutely soaked."

The boy shrugged his shoulders and looked at his mother.

"We're going to Sunne," the woman said. "Are you going there?"

Erika was heading for Örebro, to stay at a nice hotel, eat good food in the hotel restaurant, and get a decent night's sleep before the long drive to the ferry terminal the next day; everything had been planned in accordance with Laura's instructions.

Sunne would mean a detour of at least eighty kilometers.

"Yes, I'm going to Sunne," Erika said.

And why not, she asked herself as she hurried back through the rain with her anorak over her head to the parked car and its flashing lights, followed by the woman and the boy with their luggage. The boy, who was about the same age as her own son, was wet and cold, and their bus hadn't come, so why shouldn't she drive them to Sunne?

"Do you live there? In Sunne?"

Erika turned up the heat and gave the hoodie boy in the backseat a towel that she had stuffed into her rucksack just before leaving home.

"Yes," said the woman.

The boy had put the earbuds back in his ears. He was listening to music only he could hear and staring out the window. He had big brown eyes and an emphatically etched mouth that stretched from cheek to cheek. Yes, he reminded her a little of her boy, of Magnus. Perhaps because of his tall, slim body (huge hands and feet) well hidden in baggy clothes, or the finely chiseled face that could equally have been a child's or an extremely young man's, depending on the light and the constantly changing expressions.

She looked at him in the rearview mirror and tried to catch his eye. She wanted to give him a smile. She wanted to say: I'll drive you all the way home.

"How old is your son?"

Erika lowered her voice. She could have spoken at normal volume, of course. The boy with his iPod wouldn't hear in any case. From time to time he fished his mobile out of his pocket and his fingers moved swiftly over the keys as he texted someone.

"He's fourteen," said the woman.

"I have a son of fourteen, too," Erika said eagerly.

"He's not my son," said the woman. "He's my sister's son."

"Oh, right," said Erika. "Well, obviously. You're too young to have a son of fourteen. You're much younger than I am."

Erika didn't think the woman looked much younger than she did—in fact there was something old and haggard about her—but Erika was trying to be pleasant; she had a feeling she had already offended or annoyed this woman, and feared she thought her banal and chatty and would never have set foot in Erika's car had it not been for the rain and the dark and the cold and the bus being so late and the boy so wet.

"Well, yes, I suppose I'm really too young to have teenagers," said the woman.

Erika waited for her to say something else, offer some clarification. But she didn't. The woman didn't take off her red checked coat; she didn't loosen the tie belt although the car was nice and warm.

Having thought that she and the woman had sons the same age, Erika had believed there would be something to talk about. The woman was dissatisfied *(With Erika? With Erika's driving? With the weather? With fucking Sweden?)*, and Erika felt an urge to mollify her. Entertain her. Make her laugh or give a nod of recognition or tell something about herself. Their common experiences might bring them to some sense of easy female solidarity. But maybe that worked only when your children were small, mused Erika, visualizing knots of mothers in cafés or parks, rocking; rocking a baby at their breast or a baby in a buggy. Erika didn't dare ask the woman if she had small children.

If a woman in labor lashed out at Erika or begged to be allowed to die, as women in labor sometimes do, she would take the woman's hand in hers and hold it firmly.

Face-to-face with her patients, Erika felt confident. She inspired trust. Unlike Isak, she covered her office walls with photos of newborn babies, photos sent to her by grateful new mothers and fathers. He never put up a single picture. Once the child was out of its mother's body it was no longer his responsibility, he would say.

But beyond the hospital walls, Erika felt clumsy and awkward in the company of other women. Especially other women in flocks. They wouldn't let her in, as if to say: There's altogether too much of you, Erika. You're awkward. You're shallow. You're loud. You're quiet and shy and boring. You're superficial. You're earnest and humorless. You're just wrong. We don't like you. It would be better if you simply dissolved and disappeared. But you can't. You won't.

Ever since Erika and Ragnar were beachcombing and she saw Marion for the first time—Marion, in polka-dot bikini briefs, lolling on the rock farthest out to sea, surrounded by Frida, Emily, and Eva—Erika had felt enthralled. She wanted to be part of that picture. She allowed herself to be enthralled by the formation of four girls on the rock, supreme and inviolable, a secret, shining, unassailable alliance. And she could be part of that alliance or not, depending on Marion's mood, and when she was not a part of it, her exclusion was pitiless and she was left with nothing but her own thin, boring little body, her best friend Ragnar's childish games in the secret hut, and all the gray clouds in the sky.

Many hundreds of years ago, this is what they did when a child was about to be born: when a woman began to have contractions and labor was under way, the other women made haste to let down her hair and unfasten any laces on her dress, her shoes, and everything in the vicinity that was knotted, tied, closed, barred, or locked, such as drawers, chests, windows, and doors. If her husband wanted to help her, he could attack something outside the house. He might take his ax and chop his plow in two.

Erika remembered that she had arrived for her night shift and inquired about the women in labor. The midwife said of one young woman: Tedious. It's going to take time. Nearly twelve hours and only three centimeters' dilation.

And she was no more than a child herself, thought Erika as she stood at the door of the maternity ward and saw the young woman in the light from the hospital corridor. No more than seventeen or eighteen, and alone. No boyfriend or sister or mother. No girlfriend. She was sitting in the middle of the floor in a white hospital gown, small and thin, with her face in her hands and her legs drawn up under her. She neither turned nor looked up as Erika closed the door behind her.

I crossed the floor and squatted down beside you. I took off the elastic band and unplaited your hair so I could run my fingers through it. You looked at me and let me do it, and finally you even rested your head on my shoulder.

After a time, as night became morning, the young woman gave birth to a girl, silently gasping for air and light. One day, thought Erika, she, too, might have her mother's beautiful long hair.

Erika opened her mouth to say something to the woman sitting beside her in the car. After all, she had to say something, didn't she? No. She decided against it. Why say anything? And what about the boy in the back, who had not said a word and was not the woman's son but reminded Erika slightly of Ragnar? She looked at him in the rearview mirror.

"Did I say Ragnar?"

The woman turned to her and replied: "You didn't say anything."

Erika smiled at her: "Sorry. I talk to myself sometimes, especially when I'm driving."

She looked at the boy in the backseat and realized she had been mistaken.

He did not remind her of Ragnar.

Ragnar was spindly, with thin wrists.

This boy reminded her of Magnus.

Erika said: "I need to stop for gas and I must ring my son. I must tell him I shall be spending the night in Sunne instead of Örebro. Magnus likes to know where I am. He pretends not to be bothered but he is."

The woman shrugged her shoulders, her eyes fixed straight ahead. "Well, naturally, it's your car. Do whatever you like."

Erika stared at her. Was that it? Not the slightest veneer of anything polite or friendly? Erika had now even given away that she had been heading for Örebro, not Sunne; that she was actually making a detour of eighty kilometers for the sake of this woman she didn't know. The woman became aware that Erika was looking at her. She looked down, fingering something in her lap.

"We're hugely grateful, of course, that you're giving us a lift."

The woman was looking straight at her now. Her expression was defiant.

"Hugely grateful! You really have gone out of your way!"

What do you want from me?

"No problem," said Erika.

She turned in at the next gas station. She found her mobile phone, opened the car door, and got out into the wintry rain, which would soon turn to dense snowfall. She left the car without saying a word to the woman or the boy. Erika didn't look at her passengers as she shut the car door; she didn't ask if they were hungry or thirsty. The woman could damn well buy her own food and drink. Erika ran into the shop and asked for the toilet. A young man with a scarred face and ginger mustache gave her a key and pointed to the right. Erika took the key and unlocked the door. She went in and locked it behind her. It stank of shit. The toilet was blocked, its seat missing. The bin was full and there was litter all over the floor. Erika imagined the woman in the car, her fellow traveler, who wasn't the mother of the soaking wet boy, wasn't anybody's mother, and somehow this goddamned stinking toilet and everything that stank was all *her* fault. Erika could have been in Örebro by now: in her hotel room, or in the restaurant having dinner. Erika rang Magnus's number. She got his voice mail. She listened to her son's voice, no longer clear and singsong as it had been when he used to lie beside her in bed to have stories read to him. His voice was like the rest of his body: everything was growing, darkening and deepening. Magnus would be asleep in his bed, and when she came into his room to tuck him in she would see a strong, hairy, man-size foot sticking out from under the cover. And now he was on a school trip, in Poland. She said: "Hello, love. It's Mum. I'm taking a detour via Sunne. I'll be staying the night there, not in Örebro. I'll ring you when I get to the hotel."

She hung up. She should have sent a text. Magnus hated it when she left him voice mail messages. It cost money to check messages on your mobile, he said, and it was pointless paying just to hear a message from your mother. He didn't mean anything unkind by it. Or hurtful. It was simply a point of information. Erika sent him a text message. *Hi Magnus. Left you a voice mail, no need to check it. Staying in Sunne, not at hotel in Örebro like I said. Speak soon. Love Mum.*

Erika studied her face in the mirror, which amazingly enough was unbroken and even quite nice and clean. The mirror. Not her face.

"It's not the one in the car who's haggard," Erika said to her reflection. "It's you! It's me! The one in the driver's seat. It's Erika! Here in this hellhole of a gas station, in this stinking shit!"

Tomorrow she would ring Isak and tell him she wasn't coming after all. She didn't want to ring him from her mobile; it just made him nervous, and if he was nervous, it made her nervous. She wanted to sit quietly and calmly on the edge of the bed and use the hotel phone. She wanted to say she couldn't come after all, because something had come up at work and she needed to sort it out. She combed her hair and applied some lipstick, vivid red. She studied herself. Now she looked as if somebody had hit her, as if she had a gash in her face instead of a mouth. Erika rubbed off the red with her hand.

And then it struck her that the woman she had picked up on the road was pregnant. She saw her in her mind's eye, in her coat and boots. The belt pulled tight around her waist. She was pregnant but didn't want to talk about it. Didn't want to think about it. Maybe she was going to have an abortion? Maybe she was about to lose it? Maybe she was bleeding?

When Erika was pregnant with Magnus, she had felt sure it would destroy her. She had felt she would never be able to see the pregnancy through to term. She had felt she would get ill and not have the strength to give birth. She or the child would die. She had survived bringing Ane into the world. A little girl had forced her way out of her, drawn breath, and found the breast.

They had both come through that unscathed.

"God has blessed you," Isak had said on the phone, as if he were not a doctor but a minister like his father.

But this time it was different. With Ane, everything had been so easy. At least, she remembered it as easy. The pregnancy, the birth, the breastfeeding. Erika wasn't ready for this other thing. This blackness. She dragged herself through the nausea, the nausea that never relaxed its grip on her, the nausea that mixed in with everything she ate and drank, everything she wore, the places she went and everything she touched. The nausea in her nostrils, under her nails, in her freshly washed hair. And even all these years later, she sometimes felt a touch of that nausea. It took no more than the scent of lilac to make it well up inside her, because the lilac had been in bloom when she was twelve weeks pregnant. Yet simultaneously, the terror of damaging this child that was not yet a child. She had given it a name. Not a proper name. Not the name that it would one day be given, that would be written in official registers, books, minutes, and lists, but a secret name. Saying it out loud would bring bad luck, just like buying clothes or equipment before the baby was born, or at any rate before the pregnancy was fully visible.

In her eighteenth week, Erika learned she was expecting a boy. She was examined by a male doctor who had been a few years ahead of her in medical school. When he had said that the fetus was lying in a position that prevented his seeing whether it was a boy or a girl, Erika grabbed hold of the transducer and managed to get a picture of the child that showed them both it was a boy.

It was a boy, but was he viable? She checked his head and neck, the length of his legs. Everything looked fine, but Erika left the clinic with a sense of having intruded on her child. It had looked at her from the other side, not wanting to be disturbed, not wanting to be invaded. It was just a glimpse before it dissolved into lines and dots on the screen and a heart beating and beating and beating.

In week thirty-one, she began to think: I won't escape this time. Day after day she was helping women through complicated pregnancies and births, calming them, reassuring them, calling it *the most natural thing in the world,* but she herself was afraid. Afraid lest she bleed to death, lest she not be able to breathe. There he lay like a little suicide bomber, waiting to blow himself and Erika to pieces.

So she asked him if he could manage the journey. Can you handle the choices life is going to thrust at you as soon as the umbilical cord is cut—taking a breath, finding the breast, crying when you need me? Or will you turn inward, into yourself, not have the energy, not cope, not want to? Ane stroked Erika's blue-white full-moon belly and talked about all the games and songs she would teach him. She stood in the middle of the floor and sang:

> *Goosey goosey gander*
> *Where shall I wander?*
> *Upstairs and downstairs*
> *And in my lady's chamber*
> *There I met an old man*
> *Who wouldn't say his prayers*
> *So I took him by the left leg*
> *And threw him down the stairs*

Ane looked at Erika. She asked: "Can he hear us in there?"
"I don't know. I think so."

"What's he going to be called when he comes out?"
"I don't know."

And then you're here. You're mine and I'm yours and I shall never be myself again. First the fear of being ripped apart, and once the baby is born, the knowledge that I have been ripped apart, though not in the way I thought. Night after night after night without sleep and with you held near to me; the blood, the tears, the milk, the fever, and hard lumps in my breast that are only sometimes eased by warm water, warm skin, or your mouth; the loneliness when everyone else is sleeping, except you and me.

She would lie awake in the night, listening to the sounds he made. She would keep bending over the crib, bringing her face close to the baby's to check that he was breathing. She would pick him up and take him into her own bed. His body was so warm and heavy. One night she whispered something in his ear, first into the left ear, then into the right. He can't remember it now, but what she whispered was his name, because she wanted him to be the first to hear it.

For many weeks after the boy was born, he had no name. There were plenty of suggestions—Kristian, Sebastian, Lukas, Bror, Thorleif—all rejected. But one evening, his parents came to a decision. He was lying between them in the bed, not quite two months old. He had a cold, and a fever. His airways were still so narrow, and Erika said several times that if he got any worse, they'd have to take him to the emergency room. She tried breastfeeding him and dissolved into tears when he wouldn't, or couldn't, suckle, his little mouth slack and immobile around her nipple. But as the night wore on, he improved. His breathing grew less labored. He took milk from the breast. He relaxed and let himself slip into a few hours of peaceful sleep. And suddenly, just when his parents could fight their sleepiness no more, he opened his eyes and said, *Let's always remember this moment. Always! No matter what happens, let's not forget that we lay here in this bed, all three of us, utterly alive and utterly still. When I'm older I want you to tell me about this night, how we lay here in bed close to one another and you sang the night away. I know nothing of how my life will turn out, but whatever happens I want you to tell me about our lying here, all three of us, about how much you loved me and how scared you were of losing me.*

The little boy opened his eyes and looked at his parents, and suddenly they knew what they were going to call him. A few years later they split up, parting as enemies and tugging their children in opposite directions, as if the children had very long arms, but on that particular night they lay quietly beside each other in bed with the little boy between them. His mother slept and his daddy stayed awake, or his daddy slept and his mother stayed awake, and the little boy slept and woke, slept and woke, as is the way with very small babies quite new on this earth.

Erika filled up the tank. She bought two bars of chocolate. One for herself and one for the boy in the backseat. She considered buying a bar of chocolate for her pregnant passenger but decided not to. She came out of the shop and ran to the car, then turned and ran back in again. She bought oranges. She had had a taste for them both times she was pregnant herself. It wasn't far to Sunne. She got into the driver's seat, turned the key in the ignition. The woman beside her was staring straight ahead. She hadn't taken off her coat or loosened the belt.

A few months before Erika's thirtieth birthday, she went out to a restaurant with Laura and Molly. It was something they did from time to time. First they had dinner and then they went to a bar and drank vodka and talked about their husbands, their jobs, and a little bit about the old man on Hammarsö. It was a mild summer's evening and Erika drank too much. Erika couldn't take much alcohol. And it was then that she met Tomas. Nine years later, on her way to Sunne in the car, she had the feeling she had never really sobered up since that day; as if that last sip of spirits, the one that illuminated the room and set the orchestra playing, had still not evaporated but had left vague little traces in her body.

Tomas was sitting at a table on the other side of the bar, drinking beer. It was Molly who saw him first. Then Laura saw him. And finally Erika saw him, too. Later that evening, she threw up over him in the taxi.

"I'm not used to drinking this much," she kept saying, as she tried to wipe the sick off his shirt. Tomas helped her upstairs, maneuvered her into the bathroom, sat her on the floor of the shower, and let the warm water flow. He washed her hair and dried the back of her long, slender neck with a towel. He said she had the palest neck he had ever seen. Like a ballet dancer, he said.

"My mother's a ballet dancer," she said, and began to cry.

He gave her clean clothes, a cotton shirt and a pair of sweatpants, and put her in a chair in the living room. He went out to the kitchen to make coffee. She did not want to lose him. She was tired and she ached all over, as if she had given birth without a moment to rest afterward. Everything just carried on. She sat in the chair in his living room and knew she must not lose him.

"Can you hear me, out there in the kitchen?" she called.

"I can hear you," he called back.

Erika sang:

> *I wish, I wish, but it's all in vain,*
> *I wish I were a maid again;*
> *But a maid again I never shall be*
> *Till apples grow on an orange tree.*

The idea had been for them to make love, and then for her to go home to Sundt and the children, slip under the covers beside Sundt, and wonder whether Sundt could smell Tomas on her body even though she had showered, sense the stinging red all over her skin, her lips swollen from the kisses of a man who was not her husband; but then she had been sick in the taxi and none of what was planned had happened, and now she was sitting in the chair knowing only that she must not lose him.

"You've got a nice voice," he said.

He spoke quietly. There was no need to shout from the kitchen.

"I've had too much to drink," she said.

"You've got a nice voice even when you've had too much to drink," he said.

No, she must not lose him. She got up, crossed the living room—
her legs would carry her now—and went into the kitchen. She
didn't really know what it meant, this knowledge that she must not
lose him. She fell to her knees and wrapped her arms around him,
resting her head at the back of his knee.

"Don't go."

He stood motionless.

"Erika, I can't make coffee with you hanging on to me like that,"
he said.

"I don't want coffee."

"What do you want, then?"

"I don't know. I want to live here with you."

"You can live here for a while," he said.

Ragnar ran through the long grass, past Erika and Laura as they lay dozing in the sun. He turned left and ran into the woods. If you turned right, you came to the sea; if you went straight on, as Ragnar had done the first time they saw him, you came to Isak's door. Ragnar ran and ran and ran.

It was windy. The wind gave you goose pimples and you needed an anorak even though the sun was shining. Erika and Laura had found a sheltered patch in the grass. At breakfast that morning, Isak had told Erika and Laura they weren't to go down to the beach; they would have to stay near the house. He said the way it was looking, a storm was likely to blow up and then both of them, small and thin as they were, could be carried right out to sea. Rosa agreed. Erika and Laura ate nothing; they ate like two little mice, and such nibblers couldn't stand up to the sea the day it decided to come and get them. Nibblers would have to ride the waves all the way to the Soviet Union, or even farther, and there they would have to stand in a queue for the rest of their lives to buy a few wretched potatoes, and they would never be able to go back home, because everybody who tried was shot at the border. So Erika and Laura ate two more slices of bread with cheese, although they were too big to believe stories like that, and they each drank a glass of O'boy, which tasted best if you took it with a dessert spoon, as if the chocolate milk were an elegant soup, although Rosa never let them; nor were they allowed to put more than two teaspoons of O'boy powder in each glass, and that wasn't enough: three teaspoons was the absolute minimum, and five tasted really nice, especially if the powder formed lumps in the milk—like syrupy chocolate bubbles that would melt on your tongue.

Isak was strict about a lot of things. Outdoors time, for example. And bedtime. And dinnertime.

Every so often, Erika and Laura would be ordered out to find Molly, who used to hide in the woods. For on the stroke of six, *dinnertime,* Isak would come clumping through the living room into the kitchen and yell, *I'm as hungry as a bear,* and Molly, who nearly always had a blue dress on, would shout back, *Not bear! Not bear!* Then they could all sit up at the table and be served by Rosa.

But he was not strict about the O'boy. He saw no reason why the girls shouldn't be allowed to gulp down as much chocolate milk as they wanted, and he didn't care if they drank it from a glass or laboriously with a spoon. When Rosa went to the mainland to shop, he said they were welcome to tip the whole packet of O'boy down their throats if they liked, provided they didn't expect any sympathy when they were sick afterward.

When Ragnar ran past them through the grass on his way into the woods, Erika and Laura decided to run after him. He had the wind at his back and was running faster than usual; his feet barely touched the ground, and from a distance he looked like some woodland creature, an elf or an ogre. Laura could run faster than anybody Erika knew, but not as fast as Ragnar, and it was Laura who whispered to Erika that Ragnar looked a bit like an ogre. Erika didn't like that.

He wasn't good-looking, with his matchstick legs and thin wrists, it was true. And the worst thing was the little lump or growth between his eyebrows that made him look like a boy with three eyes or two noses. But as time went by and Erika got to know him, she and Laura didn't talk so much about his looking like an ogre. Erika told herself that if she squeezed her eyes almost shut and squinted at him, he was actually okay, even good-looking; but she didn't say that to Laura, who was too young to know if a boy was good-looking or not, anyway.

Erika and Laura got up from their sheltered spot in the grass and ran after him. They knew his name was Ragnar. They knew he lived alone with his mother in a summer cottage of brown-stained wood, ten minutes' walk from Isak's house. They knew he was in year five of a school in Stockholm. They knew his favorite shirt was the one that said MY DAD WENT TO NEW YORK CITY AND ALL HE GOT ME WAS THIS LOUSY T-SHIRT. Or at any rate, that was the one he nearly always had on as he raced past them through the long grass behind Isak's house, along the stony beach, along the gravel track and past the shop. That one or NIAGARA FALLS. They even knew he had a hut somewhere in the woods, a hut he had built himself. But they didn't know where it was. It was secret.

Many summers later, when Erika and Ragnar were thirteen and were lying in the long grass eating wild strawberries and drinking Coca-Cola they'd stolen from the shop, she told him about when she was little, about the first years on Hammarsö, before she knew him, when she had only one new sister, Laura, before suddenly, one summer, there was a carriage outside Isak's house with a baby in it who screamed and screamed and screamed; she told him how Isak and Rosa had teased her, saying she was so small and thin that she could get blown out to sea any minute and die a horrible death on the other side of the horizon. Ragnar listened, stroked her hair, and said: "It's the big trees that fall over in the storm, not the little ones."

He bent over her and kissed her on the mouth. His mouth felt rough, not like a girl's—she had kissed a number of girls in her class, so she would know how to do it properly when it really mattered— and he tasted of salt and Coca-Cola.

"What do you mean?" asked Erika.

"It's a well-known saying that your father, Isak, obviously never heard—I mean, when he said that about you being blown away in the storm."

Erika looked up at the sky: not a cloud anywhere, not the slightest mackerel streak. *Your father, Isak,* Ragnar had said, and he meant something by it, but she didn't know what. At any rate, it was a strange way of putting it. Erika wouldn't have said *Your mother, Ann-Kristin.*

On Hammarsö, the trees were small and crooked, so perhaps it was true that the big ones fell first.

"But we're not trees," said Erika out loud, nudging him in the side.

He looked at her and smiled.

"We're not trees," she repeated.

And she really didn't know if she wanted to kiss him some more, or tip the rest of the Coca-Cola over him and run.

One evening, Tomas took her hands and loosened her embrace, finger by finger, and left her. They had lived together in the flat by Sofienberg Park for nine years.

For nine years, Erika and the children ate food that Tomas had cooked. Hearty, fragrant meat stews, extravagantly spiced, with big chunks of beef or pork. And long after Erika and Ane had gone to bed, Tomas played computer games with Magnus. Erika said: He's a child; he's got to go to school. The pair of you can't stay up all night playing computer games. You can't do that, Tomas. Magnus has got to get some sleep. He's a child.

She remembers that he said: I stayed with you longer than I really wanted, because of Magnus and Ane. But they're not my children.

In the days after he left her, she went through all the things he had bought with money they didn't have and that he had then left behind, like relics; among them an idiotic cordless doorbell you could carry around the flat with you, if you happened to be in the toilet or in bed and were afraid of not hearing a ring at the door. What was more, you could adjust the volume and choose how you wanted it to sound. Tomas chose church bells. They had spent some time contemplating that. They had discussed the pros and cons. Shall we have this ring tone or that one? They didn't talk about what was happening in the world, the fact that one war was succeeding another. They didn't talk about the icon Tomas had bought in Paris for almost a hundred thousand kroner. It was supposedly from the sixteenth century and reminded him of a *Ukrainian actress, beautiful as an icon,* whom he had met at Nice airport. He hung the icon over the bed. She took it down. He put it back up. Don't you realize they're going to kick us out, Tomas? We can't afford to borrow a hundred thousand kroner from the bank. We can't afford to borrow ten thousand kroner. We can't afford to borrow one thousand.

Erika talked like Sundt.

She objected like Sundt.

She *was* Sundt.

The icon turned out (and it came as no surprise) to be a forgery, worth a couple of hundred at the most. Tomas stared at Erika wide-eyed when she told him. He wanted to sell the icon, he said. It's worth two hundred kroner, she said. Don't you understand? Then we'll throw it out, said Tomas. After that, he forgot all about it. Erika left it hanging there over the bed.

Now and then she missed Sundt. He was cheap, but he wasn't crazy. Sundt watched over the children in the night. Tomas didn't watch over anybody but himself, and scarcely that. Tomas didn't sleep in the double bed with her. He slept on a red sofa in a basement storage area he rented from the housing association. He'd actually been planning to use it as an office; it had a window, and he wanted somewhere to do his translation work without being disturbed by Erika and her children. But he'd gradually moved down there, where, in the end, he spent virtually all his time.

.   .   .

They laughed a lot toward the end. Told stories and laughed. Tomas bought wine, music, books, and that weird doorbell, and they laughed! Erika stopped mentioning the money slipping through his fingers.

Erika was *not* Sundt.

But she threw the bags of music and books into the car and drove to the different stores. Can I have the money back? I don't want a credit note. I want cash back. And please don't let my husband buy any more books. Or any more CDs.

But they talked about the new bell.

All those ring tones.

And you can carry it around the house with you.

He left her a note before he disappeared.

"For good," the note said. "This time I'm going for good."

"We're nearly there now," the woman beside her said. She was happy. She almost sang the words.

Erika turned to her and smiled.

Oh, so you're talking now, she thought. Having sat beside me in the car, eating oranges without a word, without even loosening the belt of your coat.

Throughout their ride together, the woman had made Erika feel that she'd done something wrong, put her foot in it, rushed in where angels fear to tread, or worse: that she had soiled something pure and delicate simply by taking up space.

Now you listen here! I've met people like you before! My father, for example, when he was younger and I was still afraid of him. Or Tomas, my husband. He could read something out to me, something elegantly phrased he'd translated or written himself, and I'd make some comment, and it was always wrong, see? It was totally wrong, and Tomas would look away and say, Forget I ever asked you. Forget it!

When Erika found Tomas's note (he had put it on the kitchen table under a hand-painted blue teapot, as if afraid it might blow away), she went down to the storage area in the cellar to check that he hadn't hidden away there or hung himself. How long ago now? Four months? Four months, three weeks, and two days. The cellar window was open; it was just getting light outside. Afterward she had found herself thinking he must have escaped through the window, like the Indian in *One Flew over the Cuckoo's Nest*. Outside the cellar window it was snowing or raining and she stood there, staring. Not a wet, snowy mass but gray, virtually transparent flakes, light enough to be indifferent to gravity, like particles of dust, though wetter and colder. There was a scattering of dry brown leaves on the window ledge and the linoleum floor; they must have blown in and he hadn't bothered to collect them or vacuum. Erika lay down on the red sofa that had been moved down to the cellar when she refused to have it in the living room; she hadn't expected Tomas to move down with it. The sofa smelled of him and of other things, too. But mostly of him.

The first time Erika saw her was in the summer of 1977. She was lying draped on the rock farthest out to sea, with long brown legs extending from her polka-dot bikini briefs.

Erika knew at once that she was the one called Marion.

She stopped and looked. She dropped the Russian tobacco packet she had found on the beach and stood quite still.

Ragnar grabbed her arm and said, "Come on, come on, Erika! Don't gawk at her. She's a moron. Come on!"

He picked up the Russian packet, which was still pretty much intact and bore the name PRIMA.

"Come on," said Ragnar. "Come on, Erika."

It was Marion who said that the perfect boob was the shape of a champagne glass. Her father, Niclas Bodström, had said so. But Niclas Bodström hadn't used the word *boob;* he'd said *breast.* Niclas Bodström had a summer place on the west side of Hammarsö and wasn't just anybody. Erika didn't really know what he did or even what he looked like, but she knew he wasn't just anybody.

To illustrate what Niclas Bodström meant by this statement, Marion produced a crystal champagne glass from her shocking-pink beach bag. Not a champagne flute that you might confuse with a white wine glass, but a wide, rounded champagne saucer.

Erika would be lying on the rock along with Emily and Frida. She had been invited. It was Marion's rock. None of the girls would lie down on the rock without having been invited by Marion. Laura was too young; she wasn't allowed to lie on the rock. The first summer Erika got to know Marion, she wasn't allowed to lie on the rock, either.

"What was your name again?"

Marion stood face-to-face with Erika outside the shop. As usual, she had Emily and Frida with her; Eva was there as well.

"She's that Norwegian girl," said Emily.

"The one whose little sister always tags along," said Frida.

"And much worse than that! She's the one who hangs out with Psycho Boy," said Marion.

The champagne glass wasn't clean; there was a huge lipstick mark clinging to the glass like a leech.

"My mum's lips," said Marion, pointing to the lipstick mark.

She got up and stood on the rock, letting the wind catch her long black hair. Erika could see she was posing; Erika could see that in fact she seemed a little bit ridiculous, standing there on the rock, pretending she was being photographed for *Vogue* or something. But so what? Just because Ragnar kept filling her head with shit about Marion. How vain she was. How stupid she was. What a slut she was. She was pretty fabulous, too. The most gorgeous girl Erika had ever seen. No wonder Ragnar talked shit.

Erika looked out across the sky and the sea.

"Absolutely perfect!" said Marion, lowering her breast into the glass.

Now, more than twenty-five years later, she was on her way to Hammarsö again. But first she would spend the night in Sunne. Ragnar was gone. Only his breath in Erika's lungs. His blood in Erika's veins. A flood of pain and waves and breathing. Ragnar's breathing in her lungs, in her mouth, Ragnar's blood in her veins.

She spoke of him to no one. Ever.

Ragnar was gone.

It wasn't so hard to say.

Erika said it inside herself: Ragnar's gone, she said. Then she said: I am this car. I am this road. I am this snow, falling outside. I am these windshield wipers. I am the pregnant woman beside me and the boy in the backseat.

They were almost at Sunne. The woman asked if they could stop at the next gas station to use the toilet. It was something of an effort for her to have to ask. Erika took the opportunity to ring Laura. It was snowing heavily now.

"Sunne, oh yes! They've got a spa in Sunne! I think it's dreadful there. But you can eat pesto and greens and take steam baths until trees grow out of your ears," Laura said over the phone.

Laura tried to laugh, but Erika could hear something was wrong. Laura seemed uneasy, breathless. Erika asked what was the matter.

"It's the neighbors," said Laura.

"You're always worrying about the neighbors," Erika said. "You've got to stop."

"Yes," said Laura.

"I might ring Isak and tell him I'm not coming," said Erika. "I want to come home."

"You needn't decide now," said Laura. "Sleep on it."

"I've got passengers in the car," said Erika.

"I know," said Laura. "You told me."

"I don't quite know what to do with them. The woman's pregnant."

"But don't they want to be dropped off in Sunne?"

Erika opened her mouth, stuck out her tongue, and tasted the snow.

"I hope so," she said. "I have to get some sleep."

I'm awake, said Ragnar. I'm wide awake; I've never been so wide awake in all my life. If this isn't being awake, if this is sleeping, I want to sleep like this always. Erika, don't leave me. Soon we'll be fourteen and we have to stay together. I love you. Day after day, month after month, year after year I will love you and lie beside you in the grass on Hammarsö and listen to the music on the waters.

II

The Colony

Everybody said they were so lucky to live just at that location. Laura stretched her arms up to the sky and took a deep breath. An idyllic oasis in the heart of the capital, wrote the real estate agent when he was drafting the property description.

"Explain to me what that means," Laura said.

"What what means?" asked the real estate agent.

"An *idyllic oasis.* I want to know what it means."

Jonas Guave, top real estate agent, senior partner in Prospero Properties, was known for talking people into offers that were more than they could afford. Laura had called him one morning when she was bored and said she wanted to sell her house.

"Old-fashioned charm and modern comfort combined," he said. "It's incredible what you've done with the house, Laura. It's exactly what everybody wants."

Laura, skinny as a strip of film negative, sat on the stone wall outside the kitchen door, dangling her legs. Gangly, bony little-girl legs. Her dress was white, her skin tanned. Next year, Laura would get just as brown, maybe browner, and anyway she wouldn't be sitting here swinging her legs and waiting for Isak to come out of his study and play Yahtzee. Next summer she'd be glorying topless on the beach in polka-dot bikini briefs, just like Erika and Marion and the rest. *Fabulous Erika!* Laura once heard an almost grown-up boy say exactly that. The boy, who might have been seventeen, stared at Erika for a long time and said to his friend, There goes that fabulous girl. Laura's hair was matted and sticky and pale blond, virtually white. She hadn't washed it for several weeks. Summer holiday dirty, said Rosa. Summer holiday beautiful, said Isak. He'd be here soon. Laura shut her eyes and visualized him in there, in his study. Now he was putting his papers away in the drawer. Now he was switching off the lamp. Now he was going over to the shelf to get the Yahtzee or maybe Chutes and Ladders. She hoped it would be Yahtzee. Chutes and Ladders was for little kids; even Molly could play Chutes and Ladders, though she generally messed it all up. Now she could hear his footsteps coming through the living room. He would open the door any minute and yell: "I'll be damned if it's not time for a game of Yahtzee, Laura! What do you say? I'm going to beat you sense- less! You don't stand a chance!"

She had left her socks and shoes on the kitchen floor. She sat on the wall, eating a pear lollipop, swinging her legs, looking out at the beach and the stones and the sea beyond the pine trees.

She had called the real estate agent Jonas Guave on impulse. She hadn't said anything to Lars-Eivind. It was a perfectly ordinary January morning, cold and dark, with heavy snow falling. Laura was looking forward to being alone. The kids, particularly Jesper, had been sulking and wouldn't eat their breakfast; and Julia wouldn't say a word. Lars-Eivind broke a glass and got milk on his jacket, which had just been dry-cleaned. It wasn't the kids' fault. It wasn't Laura's fault. It was nobody's fault. All of a sudden, Lars-Eivind dropped the glass on the floor and milk splashed everywhere.

"Fuck!"

Julia and Jesper looked at their father. Jesper started to cry.

"Calm down, Lars-Eivind," Laura said.

The jacket, bought in New York two years before, was to be worn for an important meeting. Lars-Eivind had an important meeting. First Lars-Eivind had to go to the doctor's, just a routine thing, and then he had the important meeting. There's an awful lot hanging on how this meeting goes, he had told Laura the previous night, at three o'clock. They were lying in bed, cold, and Lars-Eivind couldn't sleep. She had squeezed his hand and told him it would be absolutely fine. Now he'd have to find another jacket. The one he had had dry-cleaned for the occasion smelled of milk. Laura scrubbed it with warm water and green soap, but it didn't help. Julia had been dressed and ready for ages and was sitting on a chair in the living room, waiting to go. She sat in silence, watching her mother, father, and brother. Jesper had a runny nose. He had had a runny nose the previous evening before he went to bed, and it was worse now. Not terrible, but worse than the evening before. Laura felt his forehead, put her hand to his cheek, stroked his hair. Quick, efficient maternal hand movements. Jesper stood stock-still.

"He doesn't feel feverish," said Laura.

She didn't take his temperature, couldn't face getting him out of his wool underwear and his padded snowpants and everything; couldn't face the idea of Jesper staying at home on her day off. A whole day to herself. She felt his forehead one more time.

"He's a bit hot," she called out to Lars-Eivind. And added, mainly to herself: "But then, it is rather hot in here."

"I've got an important meeting," called Lars-Eivind irritably.

He was in the bathroom, brooding about his jacket.

"You'll have to sort it out. I haven't got time," he added.

Laura squatted down by Jesper in the hall and wiped his runny nose. She looked him in the eye.

"If you feel poorly or your cold gets worse, I'll come and fetch you right away. Is that okay, Jesper?"

Jesper nodded.

"But only if you really feel bad, understand? Not if you feel okay but just want to come home. Not then. If you're okay, you have to stay at nursery all day."

Julia, who was two years older than Jesper, looked at her mother. Laura got up and ruffled her daughter's hair. *For goodness' sake, stop looking at me like that!*

"And please look after yourself especially well today, Julia? Don't take off your mittens—you always do that, so don't."

Julia neither nodded nor shook her head, just went on staring at her mother.

Laura went on: "It's so important to keep wrapped up and warm and not take off your hat and mittens and scarf out of doors, even if you get hot playing."

Julia shrugged.

What am I doing wrong? thought Laura. *Stop looking at me! I haven't done anything wrong.* She abruptly embraced her two children, the six-year-old and the four-year-old in their snowsuits and wool hats, with big blue eyes and red-tipped noses.

"This evening we'll treat ourselves to hot chocolate and whipped cream," said Laura. She pointed to each child in turn and said: "You and you and Daddy and me. Hot chocolate and cream and waffles."

When Lars-Eivind left with Julia and Jesper, to drive them to school and nursery and then go on to the doctor's and to work, Laura didn't yet know she was going to ring the real estate agent Jonas Guave. She didn't even know of his existence. She cleared the breakfast table, made herself a coffee, sat down at the computer, and started surfing the Internet. She found his name there. She studied houses up for sale, looked at the pictures, saw how people had arranged their homes, their living rooms, bedrooms, bathrooms, and kitchens, imagined herself living there, or there, or there. Jonas Guave was the agent name attached to the most exclusive properties. When Erika rang from her mobile, insisting that she should come to Hammarsö, Laura didn't want to talk. Drive to Hammarsö, now? No way. Laura just wanted to sit here surfing the Internet, maybe hoping to find out a bit more about this Jonas Guave. She ended her conversation with Erika and dialed the number of Prospero Properties.

"We haven't definitely decided to sell yet," she said on the phone. "We're considering it, but we're not sure."

All she really wanted to know was how much she could get for the house. To see what it was worth. Jonas Guave said he could come right away. Laura barely had time to shower, put on her makeup, and slip into a pair of tight jeans. She twisted to and fro in front of the mirror. Lars-Eivind always said she had the nicest ass in Oslo, and she wanted the top real estate agent to see it.

She gave Jonas Guave a glass of ice water. He didn't want coffee, just water with ice. Laura let him go around the house making notes. Everywhere it was clean and tidy, but she apologized for the mess. She always apologized for the mess, no matter how pristine her home was looking. She left Jonas Guave in the living room and went into the kitchen, opened the freezer, and tapped one of the ice cube trays on the counter to make the ice cubes jump out; she never had the patience to press them out. That annoyed Lars-Eivind, who said it was the wrong way to do it. There was a special knack to getting ice cubes out properly, he claimed. Lars-Eivind had had a strange smell about him lately. It wasn't sweat or bad breath, but an unpleasant body odor that developed when he was tired—and he had been very tired during the reorganization at work, and because he wasn't sleeping well—or when he was afraid of something. Laura didn't know why she thought he was afraid of something. Lars-Eivind had nothing to be afraid of. The reorganization meant he was having to work harder just at the moment, but it would be to his advantage in the long run. His salary would go up. They would be able to afford to do things they'd dreamt of for years. Have a new bathroom, do up Julia's and Jesper's rooms, strip and polish the floors. Maybe even rent that dream cottage in Provence for a whole summer. Take things much easier.

When Erika rang for the second time, it was to ask how to get out of Oslo. There was something so helpless about Erika, Laura thought. Erika was the eldest, the clever one, the one Isak was proudest of, a doctor like him, but there was still something distinctly helpless about her.

Jonas Guave and Laura were sitting next to each other on the cream-colored sofa under the big southwest-facing window with the view over parts of the garden and the Oslofjord in the distance, having a discussion of sorts: *Attractive view of garden with lilacs, apple trees, and berry bushes. Fjord vista.*

Laura wondered whether you could call being able to see out into the garden a *view*. Jonas Guave said he had his terms down pat.

"The fact that the house has a fjord vista is the same thing as having a view," he said. "It's important that your line of vision isn't interrupted, and here it's not."

Laura nodded.

"Have you ever thought that if your line of vision is interrupted, your thoughts will be, too?" said Jonas Guave.

To be strictly accurate, the house hasn't got a fjord vista, thought Laura. But if the new owners can be bothered to stick their heads out the window and crick their necks, peering sideways . . . She put down the draft property description and looked at Jonas Guave, who was sitting beside her on the sofa, drinking his ice water, oblivious. It lasted only a few seconds. But Jonas Guave was engrossed in his water glass, like a child with his first Coca-Cola. Laura could stare straight at him without his noticing. He wasn't on guard. He was sitting on her sofa with a glass of ice water in his hand, and for a few seconds he was utterly oblivious. He had lots of tiny, almost invisible acne scars on his face. A tough time in his youth, thought Laura; lonely, confusing. Not the sort the girls liked. They taunted him. Pretended they wanted to kiss him and when he finally believed them, when he finally believed the prettiest girl wanted to kiss him, they all laughed and shouted Eww and God no and Get lost. They're even leaking. Your pimples are leaking! Disgusting! All that had changed now that he was grown up and lived in Oslo and had been a regular at the gym and got rid of his acne, maybe with some kind of antibiotic. He set the empty glass on the table in front of him. She asked if he wanted any more water. Jonas Guave shook his head.

"Okay then," said Laura, indicating the draft description. "This is looking incredibly good, but I think we ought to change the expression *idyllic oasis*. I think it sounds stupid."

Jonas Guave smiled at her.

"Stupid?"

He was waiting for an explanation. Laura groped for the right words. What can you say to a man who doesn't realize the phrase *idyllic oasis* is stupid? Cloying. Is *cloying* the word? Can you call a phrase cloying? Jonas Guave looked at her. Laura leafed through the sheets of paper on the table. She could feel his eyes on her body, her breasts, her face. Laura was not oblivious. Laura was never oblivious. Was he thinking: Is Laura Lövenstad in distress? Laura looked up and smiled. Top real estate agents don't use words like *in distress*. Actually, no one uses words like *in distress*.

"I mean, such a stupid expression in the property description?"

Jonas Guave leaned back on the sofa.

"A breathing space, a haven from the daily grind, Laura. Life is hell for most of us, isn't it: stress all day, longing for something but not knowing what, because we've got everything we need. And then we come home. Here! To this garden. To this house, to this idyllic oasis, Laura—everything falls into place!"

"Come here, Laura. I want to show you something," called Isak.

She jumped down from the wall and went to her father. She noticed him looking at her. Her white dress. Could Isak see that she had grown pretty, that she had long brown legs and a firm butt? She was eleven now. Isak was over by the birchwood writing desk nobody was allowed to touch because of all the important papers kept there.

"Stand here and I'll show you something special," said Isak.

First he opened the pull-down front of the desk to reveal two big rows of drawers, and between them two more rows of little drawers. All the drawers had white ivory knobs. If you inserted your hand between the two rows of little drawers and pulled aside a small protruding trim, presumably (if you didn't know better) just decorative, there turned out to be another drawer in the desk. A secret drawer. An invisible drawer.

"Guess what I've got here," said Isak.

"Important papers," said Laura.

"Not at all," said Isak. "Guess again."

"Pictures of dead fetuses," she said dubiously.

Isak smiled, put his hand into the drawer, and pulled out a dainty green box with gold lettering.

"Fancy chocolates!" he said. "Do you want one?"

Laura nodded. Each chocolate came in its own individual envelope, thin as tissue paper; the chocolate was dark brown and rough textured, with mint cream inside. Laura ate her chocolate. It was delicious, all the more so because it was gone so quickly. You immediately longed for more.

"Can I have another one?"

Isak shook his head and put the green box away in the drawer.

"We're not allowed two. We're only allowed to take one. Very occasionally we might be allowed two. But never three."

"Yummy," she said, and smiled. Then added: *"Yozumonmonyoz!"*

Isak gave her an inquiring look. Laura was speaking in the secret language that not even Isak understood. He shrugged his shoulders and went into his workroom. Laura was left standing by the writing desk.

Erika and Ragnar thought that she'd given up, that she'd never mastered the secret language. They were wrong, but she let them go on thinking it.

ABANDON HOPE ALL YE WHO ENTER HERE

The huge hand-painted banner, made communally (each household responsible for its painstakingly measured letter), was fixed over the entrance to the Colony residential area.

ABANDON HOPE ALL YE WHO ENTER HERE

Tuva Gran had told Laura that somebody had finally bought the dilapidated old property next door to her house, that it was a family with no children (pity!), and that a single man called Paahp had moved in.

Of course the message didn't read ABANDON HOPE ALL YE WHO ENTER HERE.

It read: WELCOME TO THE COLONY. PLEASE DRIVE WITH CARE! LIVELY CHILDREN AT PLAY! THANK YOU FROM ALL OF US IN THE RESIDENTS' ASSOCIATION.

Laura pulled her shopping trolley after her and said in an affected voice: "Thank you from all of us in the Residents' Association. Thank you from all of us in the Residents' Association."

Laura and Lars-Eivind and the children had been allocated the *V* when they had made the banner; Tuva and Leif Gran and their twin girls got the second *Y*.

"We can all give free rein to our creativity and imagination here," said Ole-Petter Kramer at the June meeting of the Residents' Association. The only item on the agenda was the design and production of the banner, for which Ole-Petter Kramer and Alf Krag had responsibility. The team was to start work within the week. Laura was confused. It might in fact be Geir Kvikkstad who was in charge of the project. Or Lars Krogh. She knew Lars Krogh was on the banner committee. Geir Kvikkstad, too. But Ole-Petter Kramer had overall responsibility being on the design committee as well, which was different from the working committee she sat on along with Tuva Gran.

"Is it meant to be 'lively children' or 'love children'?" asked Laura.

"Lively," said Ole-Petter Kramer.

Then Mikkel Skar said: "I think it's important . . . I think it's important not to let the lettering on the banner *sprawl* too much. We could end up with rather an overdose of variety and creativity and imagination and all that. We have to draw the line somewhere. Creating something is as much about working within limitations as it is about letting rip."

Mikkel Skar was a designer and the creator of the logo for the new breakfast cereal Krazykrunch. Mikkel Skar was often described as an asset. Lars-Eivind, Laura's husband, was also described as an asset on the strength of his job. But where the banner was concerned, Mikkel was undoubtedly the greater asset of the two.

Mikkel Skar thought there was a risk of the banner looking too . . . *homemade*. Laura sat on a chair, squeezed between Tuva and Leif Gran, and looked at Lars-Eivind sitting in his chair, flanked by the Åsmundsens' three children. He was rubbing his eyes with his fists. Like a sleepy baby, thought Laura. She wanted to reach out and stroke his cheek.

Lars-Eivind wasn't really following the discussion. He was on one of the committees but didn't know which and didn't dare ask. Everybody in the Colony Residents' Association was on some committee or other. Lars-Eivind was looking at an old man in a suit too big for him, who was sitting alone at a table at the end of the dining room, eating a plateful of brown scouse stew. He was a small, thin man; his suit, which must once have been royal blue, was stained. He ate slowly. There was a hearing aid lying beside his plate. His hands were shaking; from time to time he had to put one hand over the other on the table, as if the first hand's job was to pacify the second hand. It was the shaking that made the meal take such a long time. The man lifted the glass from beside his plate and slurped a little water.

Full meetings of the Colony Residents' Association took place six times a year and were held in the dining room of the Fryden Nursing Home, but they rarely saw any of the old folk. The patients' normal dinnertime was two p.m., and the meetings usually started at seven. By that time the old people had been put to bed for the night. Their lights had been turned out.

Lars-Eivind looked at the man. He looked at Laura and then at Mikkel Skar. He said: "Good grief, Mikkel, how the banner looks isn't that crucial, you know. This is for the sake of the children, isn't it? We're doing this for the kids."

"We're going to see it every day," said Mikkel. "And I'm thinking of the children, too. It's important for children to see beautiful things. There is such a thing as aesthetic education."

"Is there?" interrupted Laura.

"Is there what?" queried Mikkel Skar.

"Is there such a thing as aesthetic education?"

"I'm just saying we don't have to make it all sparkly and over the top," replied Mikkel Skar.

Laura looked over at Lars-Eivind again. His eyes were fixed on the old man, who had been sitting alone until a moment before. Now another man was sitting at the table. The other man was neither eating stew nor drinking water. He was wearing a gray coat. Neither man spoke. Laura wondered whether the man in the coat was a brother or a son. Must be a brother, she thought. Tuva Gran leaned over and whispered: "You see him?"

"Which one?"

"The younger one."

"Yes."

"Well, he's the one who's moved in next door to us. It's Paahp. He's . . . I don't know . . . He gave each of my girls a bracelet today."

"Bracelet?" Laura whispered back.

"Yes, he made them himself, I think. Just some beads threaded on string. He stopped the girls on their way home from school and asked them if they'd like a bracelet each, and they said yes and accepted them. I've told them we'll have to give them back."

"Are you going to?" asked Laura.

"I wish someone else had moved in instead," Tuva Gran said.

Laura lay in the overwide bed she shared with Lars-Eivind.

She said: "Are you in pain?"

"No, not exactly."

"Well, what is it, then?"

"I don't know."

"Then go to sleep!"

Laura turned on her side.

"Must you wake me up, too, when you can't sleep?" she said.

"Yes."

"Why?"

"Because I can't bear lying here on my own with all this."

"All what?"

"I don't know. Backache. Clammy sheets. Afraid."

Laura dreamt she was walking barefoot through the snow along the snow-covered road, over the steep, snow-covered ground, and she was dragging the banner behind her in the snow, but it was the size of a coat or a flying carpet or a circus tent. It was white and heavy and sometimes she dragged it along after her and sometimes she carried it with outstretched arms, as if it were a standard. Laura cut her bare feet on the stones sticking up through the snow. Her feet were bloody, but it didn't matter. She felt no pain. She laid the standard over the spindly boy's body in the overwide bed.

"I thought you must be cold," she whispered in his ear.

"I *kolnopowox yozou arose woxetov.*"

"We've definitely decided to sell," said Laura.

"And are the neighbors nice?" asked Jonas Guave.

"Oh yes. Very!" said Laura.

"Families with children, mainly?"

"Mainly. Except for Paahp. He lives alone in a run-down house a bit farther up the road."

"Paahp?"

"Yes. He makes bracelets of beads and gives them to the little girls in the neighborhood. Julia, my daughter, has had several of his bracelets."

"Is everybody okay with that?"

"No, maybe not entirely," said Laura. "There have been a few petitions to try to get him out."

"It might be a smart move to wait and sell in the spring," said Jonas Guave. "When the lilacs are in bloom."

Laura smiled.

"My sister can't stand it when the lilacs come into bloom each

year. She can't stand the smell. It reminds her of when she was pregnant and was sick all the time. Did you know that morning sickness
is very similar to the effect of chemotherapy?"

Jonas Guave looked at her. He said: "But lilacs have such a wonderful smell."

"All I'm trying to say," said Laura, "is that we want to sell the
house now. By the end of January, preferably. As soon as possible,
really."

Laura took Jonas Guave out into the garden. First they stood side
by side in the tiny hall and put on their outdoor things. Anorak,
scarf, gloves, warm shoes. It was a lengthy procedure. Laura didn't
want to look at Jonas Guave while they were doing it. When they
finally got out into the fresh air and took a gulp, their frosted breath
swirling from their mouths, Jonas Guave stopped in front of the old
birch in the back garden, put his arm around Laura, and asked her if
she'd ever climbed to the top.

"No," said Laura.

"You haven't?"

"No."

"You should always climb trees if you've got any," said Jonas
Guave. He put his hand more firmly around Laura's waist.

"But you know how it is," said Laura. "Children . . . work . . .
sometimes it's as though you don't get time for any of the things you
really want to do."

Laura felt vaguely light-headed. Perhaps it was his arm around
her waist? It was just a thought. A light-headed thought. She turned
and looked toward the snow-covered gate at the end of the garden,
thinking that it would be perfectly possible to go back into the
warmth with Jonas Guave. Laura smiled at him and leaned against
him. It was so simple. Like plucking a ripe berry. She could take him
indoors, up the stairs, up into the overwide bed that she shared with
Lars-Eivind, and let him part her legs and take her from behind so
she didn't have to look at him. Jonas Guave said he was a bit of a gar-
dener in his spare time.

"You know, Laura, a beautiful garden makes you live longer!"

He added various suggestions for how to make your lawn look its best after the winter.

"Our garden looks dreadful after winter," said Laura.

"I won't put that in the property description," he said, and laughed as if he'd said something very funny. But there was no trick to it, really. All you had to do was sow some extra seed and feed it well and not cut the grass too often to begin with.

Not looking, thought Laura. Not knowing. Not thinking. Not speaking. Naked on all fours, strange hands around my waist, around my neck, through my hair.

"That's a mistake everybody makes," said Jonas Guave.

"What?" asked Laura.

"Cutting the grass too often in the spring," said Jonas Guave.

He was warming to his theme, she could tell, because he started expanding on the topic.

"It wouldn't take much work to make this garden look fabulous, you know. As I said: Plant an apple tree. Build a playhouse. Keep the gate ajar to suggest openness. Closed gates indicate closed minds."

Laura nodded. Jonas Guave had cookie crumbs in the corner of his mouth though she hadn't given him any cookies. How strange that she had noticed it only now and not when they were sitting next to each other on the sofa. He was tall, his physical presence slightly oppressive.

"You stand on your veranda and your eye stops at the gate," said Jonas Guave, "and when your eye stops, so do your thoughts."

Laura wondered how often he would say that.

She was overwhelmed by the urge to open her mouth and laugh, but instead she tried to concentrate on a red spot on Jonas Guave's chin, an old cut, she thought, the result of careless shaving, perhaps. She smiled at him. What else should she do? After all, it wouldn't do to laugh. Or to hit him. *When your eye stops, so do your thoughts.* Blah blah blah. *Idofiotov! Poqrosicodkol!*

Laura wanted Jonas Guave to go. He was welcome to sell the house, now or in the spring, but she wanted him to go. She didn't want to explain . . . She didn't want to have to explain the closed gate. Laura smiled. It hurt, but she smiled all the same. It was a sort of exercise in self-control: Don't hit him!

"We keep the gate closed so Yap doesn't escape and get run over," she said.

"And Yap is . . . ?" asked Jonas Guave.

"My daughter," said Laura.

Jonas Guave looked disconcerted again.

"I'm joking," said Laura. "My daughter's name is Julia. But I said that already, didn't I? Yap would be a good name for her, though. But Yap is our dog. Well, it's Julia's dog, really. You know how it is. The kids nag you to have a dog, then they get one, and after a week they can't be bothered to take it for walks and so it sort of became ours, mine and Lars-Eivind's. Yap is with some friends this week, in the country."

Jonas Guave nodded. Laura talked. Don't hit him. Be nice to Jonas Guave. It wasn't Jonas Guave's fault that Laura had wanted to go upstairs with him or climb trees with him five minutes before, and now just wanted him to go. Get lost. Laura talked softly. It had started to snow. It was snowing on them. They would be completely covered in snow if they continued to stand here motionless in Laura and Lars-Eivind's garden. She looked straight at Jonas Guave. The red spot on his chin. Maybe not a cut. Maybe just a little birthmark he had scratched.

"We got him from a shelter. And they warned us . . . I mean, this is why we keep the gate closed. They warned us. Yap has no traffic sense. He runs out in front of cars. Just like my sister. No traffic sense. She keeps ringing up and asking how to get to places. She's distinctly helpless. Right now she's on her way to Sweden to visit our father. He's dying."

Laura paused for breath and could see that Jonas Guave would soon have had enough.

"I'm going soon, as well," she added.

"To Sweden?"

"Yes. I'm going to drive down and visit our father. He's terribly old now. I may never see him again if I don't go now. We're all going at the same time, traveling separately and meeting there. My sisters and I."

Laura looked at Jonas Guave and laughed. Every morning she plaited her hair and the plait reached almost to her bottom.

"And when I get back home we can sell the house, all right?"

Laura decided to buy flowers. She would go into town to do some shopping, and she would buy flowers and make everything look nice at home.

Jonas Guave had gone, and now she would spend the rest of the day cooking dinner and surprise Lars-Eivind when he got home late that evening. First she would serve a soup. Her mobile rang; it was Erika.

"Have you changed your mind?" Erika asked.

Erika was sitting in the car. She had crossed the border and stopped at a service station to have a coffee and perhaps take a nap in the car. Remembering that Magnus was in Poland on a school trip to some concentration camps, Laura knew Erika would be thinking about the boy all the time.

"No," said Laura. "Or rather, I don't know. I've got so much to do here at home, things I have to sort out."

"So you might come after all?"

"No. It's difficult, I think. Maybe."

"I hope you will."

"In that case," said Laura, "we all ought to come. I'll ring Molly and ask her what she's up to these days."

"It would give him a shock."

"A shock?"

"It would give him a shock if all three of us showed up at once."

Laura suppressed a laugh.

"Then a shock is what he'll get."

And she added: "It wouldn't be a bad idea for him to see who we are and to know our names, for him to see us face-to-face before he dies."

"He'll never die," said Erika, "but he claims this is his epilogue."

Laura could hear that Erika was preoccupied with something. Perhaps a paper cup of hot coffee. She hoped her sister wasn't spilling hot coffee all over herself while driving.

Erika said: "What is it you've got to sort out before you leave?"

"Sort out?"

"You said," Erika reminded her, "that you had something to do at home. Is everything okay?"

"Everything's okay, but I think we're going to sell the house and move."

Laura heard Erika sigh. And then: "Why move, then, all of a sudden?"

"I don't know," said Laura. "Because we're not happy here. All the neighbors are so uptight. They're virtually forcing an old man to move out because he gives bracelets to little girls around here."

"Why does he give bracelets to little girls?"

"I don't know," said Laura.

She wished the conversation would end.

"I can understand people feeling uneasy," said Erika.

Laura sighed and said: "Yes, but they can't force a man to move just because they don't like him."

"People do such strange things," said Erika. "I wouldn't let Julia accept any more bracelets from that man."

"Yes, yes," said Laura, and changed the subject. "If you're talking to Lars-Eivind . . . if you ring here, say, and he happens to answer, don't mention what I just said about selling the house. It's not as much of a priority for him at the moment as it is for me, if you see what I mean."

"I've got to go now," said Erika.

"Okay then," said Laura. "Call me again in a little while and let me know how you're doing."

She raised her head and looked out the window, at the snow covering everything, the grass, the flower beds, the birch tree, the green gate. Later today she was going to spend some time out in the garden with Julia and Jesper. She wouldn't be in a rush or answer them irritably. She would take her time. As long as Jesper wasn't feeling too poorly. He was always so sick once he'd gotten a fever; he woke up in the night, crying and saying it hurt, and it was impossible to comfort him. He wasn't happy at that nursery, either; on the playground, he wandered about on his own with an old man's frown and didn't want to play with the other children. Maybe she should have kept him at home today? No, no, it was all right. His cold wasn't that bad. His face was slightly hot and flushed from traipsing around the living room in his outdoor clothes while she was looking for Julia's mittens. He'd be fine. Later today she would build a snowman with a carrot nose and a big checked scarf around his neck; she would make waffles and hot chocolate with cream for their supper; she would let them fall asleep in her and Lars-Eivind's bed, both Julia and Jesper. She would let them sleep there all night and it wouldn't matter if they kicked in their sleep or lay crossways. Laura and Lars-Eivind weren't usually able to get much sleep when the children were sharing the bed, so the rule was no children in the bed at night, but tonight it didn't matter if they got no sleep and it didn't matter if the children slept in their bed. It would be nice. Everything would turn out fine.

"Drive carefully," she added to Erika, but Erika had already hung up.

The cramped little hall had a black tiled floor and the walls were of untreated pine, studded with hooks and pegs for all sorts of winter garments—garments that generally ended up lying on the floor in little pools of melted snow. For the third time that day, Laura stood in this detestable, dark little room that she dreamt of redecorating in the style of the spacious, spotless white halls pictured in the interior design magazines. *(If the kitchen is the heart of the house, then the hall is the open hands of the house. It is the hall that welcomes you, your family, and your guests every day!)* She put on an extra woolen sweater, her anorak, thick boots, a long scarf, and a hat. Her gloves were lying in one of the puddles on the floor; they were wet through, and she had to rummage in the cupboards to find some others. She found a yellow woolen mitten and a brown lined leather glove that some visitor must have left behind. They would have to do. Eventually, when she was nearly at the shops, she would take off the mitten and the glove and put them in her trolley. Laura was going into town to buy the dinner. First to the Turkish shop, where they had the freshest fruit, the fresh vegetables; then to the fishmonger; then to the wineshop; and finally to the supermarket. She left the car where it was and took her blue shopping trolley. This evening, once she'd put the children to bed and read and sung to them (without rushing it), Lars-Eivind would finally be served a well-composed meal. It was a long time since she'd last done that. Soup first: possibly a clear meat broth, made from scratch, with horseradish. Laura felt in her anorak pocket to check that she had her money; then she opened the front door and went out, pulling the shopping trolley after her. Sometime today, in a little while, maybe even on the way to the Turkish greengrocer's, she would ring Molly. *Hello, it's Laura. Erika's on her way to Hammarsö. Shall we go, too?* Neither Laura nor Erika had spoken to Molly for several months, and there was no other way of asking her. *There's always the risk he could die soon,* she might add, though it would sound melodramatic. Molly would say no. She would say no in her ringing voice, and then she would laugh. Molly would say she didn't care if Father died. She had once cooked a dinner for him, when she was just seventeen, and he hadn't turned up. When Molly was little, Isak used to lift her high in the air and spin her around the living room, and then Molly would stretch her arms wide and pretend she was a big bird.

Laura was seven. She had walked a long way. She had walked to the shop and back for her mother, Rosa, and for that she got an ice cream. It was a summer's day on Hammarsö in 1975, and Laura had a shopping trolley even back then. The shopping trolley was full of groceries and she pulled it after her along the dirt road.

"There's nothing more practical for shopping than a decent-size trolley," Rosa would say.

As soon as Laura had put the groceries away in the kitchen cupboards and drawers, she would lie down in the tall grass below the white limestone house and read Erika's Norwegian magazines.

If a Norwegian opened his or her mouth and said something, Laura didn't understand a word; Norwegian was almost as incomprehensible as Danish.

Erika had told her that everybody who lived in Norway could understand Swedish. That was because the Norwegians had Swedish TV. They had Norwegian TV *and* Swedish TV. In Sweden, nobody understood Norwegian, and nobody had the Norwegian TV channel, either. But as far as Laura knew, nobody minded. Swedes didn't care about not understanding Norwegian and not having the Norwegian TV channel, so Erika didn't have to be so snooty about it. Erika spoke both Norwegian and Swedish. Erika was half all manner of things. Half Swedish. Half Norwegian. Half sister.

When Laura was younger, she had no idea that she had any siblings, half or whole, big or small, sisters or brothers, but then Erika appeared on Hammarsö and called Laura's father Daddy, and then Rosa had to explain that Isak had been married before to a woman called Elisabet and they had had a baby. Frida, Laura's friend, said it wasn't impossible that Isak Lövenstad, *the well-known womanizer,* had a whole gaggle of kids spread about the island. Frida had heard her dad say exactly that to her mum. And that must mean, Frida reckoned, that Laura had a whole heap of brothers and sisters.

That made Laura say: "It would be great to have a big brother."

Frida had a big brother who occasionally bought her licorice sticks, and licorice was the best thing Laura could think of.

First Erika arrived, then Molly. All it took was for Laura to squeeze her eyes shut and open them again, or walk to the shop and back and be gone less than an hour—and these things happened. She opened the gate, shut it behind her, and walked the little way remaining down to the house, the shopping trolley behind her, and just outside the house stood a red carriage, and in it was a child with a red hat on its head, screaming. It wasn't a newborn. Laura approached the carriage; it wasn't a newborn because it was quite big and could sit up by itself, and in fact had to be strapped in so as not to fall out. Laura wasn't entirely sure, but it looked like a girl. At any rate, it was too little to be able to talk properly and say who it was. Laura looked around her. HELLO, she called. HELLO THERE, DOES THIS BABY BELONG TO ANYBODY? She had allowed the shopping trolley to topple over, and two lettuces and a jar of jam had rolled out. Laura retrieved them, picked up the trolley, wheeled it to the door, and shouted HELLO. She looked at her watch. It was outdoors time, which meant she couldn't go on shouting like that. Erika was with Ragnar somewhere and Rosa could have gone to the mainland on errands. Isak was in his workroom and was not to be disturbed for any reason. Laura didn't think mislaid babies would count as an exception. Laura looked at the child. It was clearly a girl—nobody would put a hat like that on a boy's head—and now it had screamed so much and for so long that it was too tired to do more than sob. Snivel. Isak would start bellowing if she gave the child to him. This was Laura's problem. When Rosa got home, it would be Rosa's problem, but until then it was Laura's. She looked at the child. She made a plan. First, she thought, she would slip into the kitchen and put all the shopping away in the fridge and larder, and then she would take the child for a walk and hope Rosa would be home soon.

Laura started pushing. She had to shove hard to get the carriage moving; it was much bigger and heavier than the shopping trolley. They made slow progress. One wheel caught on a stone and the carriage almost tipped over. She managed to right it, but the child began to scream again.

"Hello, you," said Laura, pushing the carriage. The wheels squeaked. "My name's Laura."

The child looked at her and screamed; its eyes were red-rimmed and puffy, and now and then it raised its hand and pointed into the air and shouted semirecognizable words: *mummy, nanna, mummy, see! see!*

Laura said: "We're going for a ride, and you're going to sit in your carriage and be completely and totally quiet."

The child looked at her and sobbed. Laura walked faster. She marched along the dirt road, pushing the big red carriage in front of her. No more close calls now. Laura gripped the handle more firmly, went through the gate, and turned onto the path through the woods. The silent green forest light seemed to soothe the child; it looked around, pointed at everything, and kept saying See! See! There were the stunted, windblown trees and outstretched branches scraping the carriage; there were the stumps and roots and rotten trunks and one or two dead birds (sometimes something even bigger, like a dead fox); and there were other paths that led right down to the sea, to open green heathland, to the secret patches of wild strawberries that Ragnar had shown Laura and Erika the summer they first met him. Now Erika and Ragnar didn't want to be with Laura anymore. They said she was too little. They said Laura didn't know where the secret hut was, but she did. She had been there many times; she had even helped Ragnar to make a curtain and hang it up over the big split in the timber, which served as a window.

Once, a long time ago, Laura, Erika, and Ragnar had been sitting in the hut, in the dark, and Ragnar had taken a penknife out of his trouser pocket so they could all cut their thumbs and mix their blood. Laura had taken the knife and cut herself and made her thumb bleed as easy as anything. But when they passed Erika the knife, she sat fiddling with her thumb and didn't dare cut deep enough. There wasn't a drop of blood.

"Come on, come on," said Ragnar.

Ragnar and Laura's Tom Thumbs were both bleeding and they were ready to rub them together, and if Erika didn't hurry up the blood would dry and they would have to do it all over again.

"Come on then," repeated Ragnar angrily.

"I don't want to," said Erika.

"You've got to," said Ragnar.

"You've got to," said Laura.

"I don't want to," screamed Erika, and then Ragnar got tired of waiting.

He took the knife from her, grabbed her hand, held it tight, and jabbed her thumb. Immediately the blood began pouring from the wound. Erika screamed and pulled her hand away. She screamed and screamed, and then she cried. Laura almost cried herself, afraid that Ragnar had cut too deep and her sister would bleed to death, but both collected themselves and held out their hands when Ragnar said it was time to rub their thumbs together.

"Now we're blood brothers and sisters, in life and in death and for all eternity, on Hammarsö, in Sweden, on Earth, and all over the universe," Ragnar said.

Erika and Ragnar were nine now (they had the same birthday, like twins!) and Laura was only seven, too little, they had said. And they thought Laura didn't know where the hut was, simply because Ragnar had told her so many times: *You don't know where the hut is, you don't know where the hut is, you don't know where the hut is.* Ragnar believed he could hypnotize people. He believed it because he had once stared at Frida and said: *Frida loves Ragnar, loves Ragnar, loves Ragnar,* and then Frida had giggled, stretched her hands out in front of her, walked unsteadily over to Ragnar as if she were a sleepwalker, and kissed him on the mouth, long and hard. Afterward, Frida whispered to Laura that she'd only been pretending. Frida had kissed Ragnar because he was so disgusting and you sometimes had to do disgusting things, she said, like gulping down the skin on your milk, or drinking warm Coca-Cola. Laura and Frida had been summer holiday best friends for years, but now Frida didn't want to be with her anymore. Frida would rather be with Marion, the girl with the long black hair.

Laura looked at the child in the red carriage. It had been quiet for a long time now. Every so often its eyelids would droop and it would look as if it were about to nod off. The carriage joggled over branches and fir cones and twigs.

"I don't know what I'm going to do with you," said Laura.

She was tired and out of breath, and it had gotten cold and cloudy. She had walked farther than she'd meant to. Laura found the brake, parked the carriage under a tree, and looked about her.

She wasn't sure now which way she had come, or which was the way back. When the child began to scream again (maybe because the carriage had stopped joggling), Laura shouted at it to stop.

"Stop that! Stop that!"

Laura wanted to find her way out of the woods to fetch Rosa, and she'd be able to do it quicker if she left the carriage under the tree. The carriage was much heavier than she had thought when she set out on this walk.

"Wait here. I'll be back soon," Laura said.

She turned around and started walking. She was doing everything wrong now, it was all falling apart, people would be cross with her and shout at her or ignore her at the dinner table; she shouldn't have taken the child into the woods in the first place, and then she shouldn't have left it under the tree. But she had to find Rosa. Only Rosa knew the right thing to do in situations like this. Laura didn't know the right thing to do. Laura had never even touched a baby before. The child's screams turned to crying. Laura walked briskly on without turning around. After all, nothing could happen to it there, half sitting, half lying, and strapped into the carriage. It wouldn't be on its own for very long. Laura would find Rosa as quickly as she could, and Rosa would know what to do. The child no doubt wanted food and milk and was bound to need a clean diaper.

"Won't be long!" she called, still without turning around. "I'll be back soon!"

There was no danger. Nothing could happen. There were no bears in this forest. When Laura was little, four or five, she had been afraid of bears. It was Isak's fault. Rosa had tried to hush him, not wanting her daughter scared, but Isak thought it did children no harm to be scared, so he told the story of the Hammarsö bear, which had the run of the island. The Hammarsö bear had white fur and could travel by land or sea, half mammal and half sea creature as it was. It had sharp teeth, gleaming eyes, sharp claws, and slavering jaws that gave heavy sighs when it was hungry, which it always was.

And if it got the chance, it would tear a little girl apart and eat her body, bit by bit.

Laura could hear a rustling among the trees and a branch creaking a little way off. One path looked much like another. She could no longer see the child, but she could hear it crying. Laura stopped and listened. The crying was different now, as if the child was on the verge of giving up.

Laura went on walking, but stopped again. It was no good. The child couldn't be left alone. She would have to go back and push the carriage out of the woods as best she could. It wasn't *that* heavy. If she had managed to push it into the woods, she would surely be able to push it out again? She would find the way home. She would find Rosa. Laura ran. First she saw the tree, then the carriage, and then the child, which had tried to get out of its harness but had gotten tangled up instead, so it could no longer move its right arm. Laura ran to the carriage, unclipped the harness and picked up the child.

"Hush, hush," she whispered, rocking the little girl in her arms. "Hush, hush. I won't leave you again. I promise."

Laura took the white wool blanket from the carriage, wrapped the body of the sobbing baby in it, and sat down on the ground, under the tree. Soon she would set about finding the way home. But first, she and the child would sit here under the tree and rest. The little girl was so tired from all her crying that she immediately fell asleep in Laura's arms, her heavy head resting on Laura's shoulder. With one finger, Laura stroked the girl's forehead and nose, the back of her soft neck, her thin wrists and little hands.

As long as the girl slept, she would sit here under the tree and not move.

Isak, Rosa, Erika. She heard their voices calling.

She had put the baby back in the carriage and was trying to find her way out of the woods.

"Laura! Laura!" That was her father's voice.

"Hello, Laura! Are you there?!" Her mother's.

And then a strange woman crying: "Molly! Come to Mommy, Molly!"

"LAURA!" That was her father once again, angry.

Isak came running toward her along the path. It was an unusual sight: Isak running along the path, more frantic and petrified than angry, his curly golden hair sticking out in all directions. When he saw his daughter with the carriage, he ran even faster, and it was hard to tell whether he was going to throw his arms around her or smack her on the ear. He did neither, perhaps because he was so out of breath. He looked down into the carriage and saw that the child was alive and unharmed. Laura opened her mouth to say something, but Isak raised his hand and that meant she had better be quiet. He was still breathless, too breathless to say anything himself, and he had to squat down to recover. And then, in a low voice: "Where have you been, Laura? What the hell have you done? What's going on in your lizard brain when you take a carriage with a child in it and run off?"

Isak stood up, having caught his breath. He stood up, growing big and mighty before her, and he opened his mouth and roared: "We had to call the police! They're on their way now! Have you any idea what you've done?"

Laura folded her arms and squinted at her father. She wasn't scared of him. No, she wasn't scared of him. She repeated that to herself. I'm not scared of you. But the little child in the red carriage had never heard Isak's roar before; she would be hearing it many times in her life, but that time on the path through the woods she was only a year old and had never heard anyone roar in such a way, and she was so taken aback that she, too, started screaming. Laura picked her up, fixed Isak with a look, and said: "Roaring like that you'll frighten the little baby."

Isak shut his mouth and looked at Laura, then at the baby.

Just then, Rosa, Erika, and a woman Laura had never seen before came running toward them along the path. When the unknown woman caught sight of Laura and the baby, she accelerated, ran up to them, grabbed the child, and pressed it to her. Laura saw that the woman was crying, and had been crying for a long time. Her face was blotchy red and swollen. Rosa had stopped running and was now walking calmly along the path toward them with Erika sauntering along behind, chewing gum. Laura could see at once that Erika approved of the situation. It was a little like watching a show, and nobody was shouting at her. It wasn't Erika who had run off into the woods with somebody's baby and scared the wits out of its mother and forced Isak to ring the police, who were on their way from the mainland: a long column of black-and-white cars. Rosa laid a hand on Laura's shoulder and asked her quietly why she had gone off with Molly.

"I didn't know she was called Molly," Laura said angrily.

She stared at the child, now in its mother's arms; she stared at the unknown woman, tried to work out whether she was being dismissed as a delinquent.

Rosa's hand lay heavy on her shoulder.

"The point isn't whether you knew her name or not," Rosa said in that quiet voice. "The point is that you took the carriage and went off without saying anything to us."

"You weren't there!" said Laura. "You weren't there. I called you, and you weren't there."

Rosa's big broad hand maintained its grip on Laura's shoulder. Laura peered furtively up at Isak, who was standing beside his wife, merely nodding. Whatever her mother said, he nodded. As if everything she said was obvious.

"We were on the veranda having coffee, with Ruth," Rosa said. "Daddy and I were on the veranda. We were on the veranda the whole time. Molly was in her carriage, asleep just outside the house, and we were on the veranda."

"I called out," said Laura. "You weren't there. You didn't hear me."

Rosa said: "If you had called, we would have heard you. We had the veranda door ajar so we'd hear Molly if she woke up."

And she went on, sounding more conciliatory: "Ruth's come to Hammarsö with her daughter, Molly. Now she's going back home, and Molly's staying with us for a while. Things haven't exactly got off to a good start for Molly and Ruth, or for any of us, have they? We've all been terribly scared and awfully worried."

It was as if her mother's hand on her shoulder was burning its way deeper and deeper into Laura until it reached the place from which all the tears and snot and sick welled up, and Laura, who had begun to shake all over, opened her mouth and screamed, I called you, Mummy, but you weren't there! Laura flailed her arms about her before bending over to be sick. She couldn't stop. It just kept coming out of her mouth in waves. Rosa's hand let go of her shoulder and moved to her forehead. Laura took a breath and shut her eyes. She was seven years old. She wiped her mouth with the back of her hand, repeating: I called you and you weren't there.

Paahp moved into one of the properties in the Colony sometime in the spring of 2004, to be near his brother, a resident at the Fryden Nursing Home. When his brother died at the end of October the same year, Alfred Paahp was left alone in his dilapidated house with no big brother to care for. None of the Colony residents knew where he was from originally. Someone suggested Eastern Europe, but someone else said Paahp wasn't an Eastern European name. Maybe he was simply a Dane? Was Paahp a Danish name? Mikkel Skar said expressions like *Eastern Europe* were no longer valid, not since the fall of the Wall and the breakup of the Soviet Union. But *Central Europe* was okay, he said, without expressing any view as to whether Paahp was Danish or not. The Residents' Association was holding one of its meetings—seven o'clock in Fryden's dining room as usual. Paahp appeared as a separate item on the agenda, after the item "Autumn working party at Marie and Nils Åsmundsens'." The reason for this special item on the agenda was the following: Paahp had not mowed his lawn, not even once. He had not raked up the leaves. Paahp was letting his house fall into a terrible state of neglect. When some children threw a stone through his window, Paahp made no move to repair it. He did not phone the glazier. He got a sheet of cardboard and taped it in place as best he could.

"It looks terrible," said Mikkel Skar. "It looks like a goddamned war zone there."

Lars-Eivind said maybe Mikkel Skar hadn't watched the television news lately, since he saw fit to use the phrase *war zone*.

"I don't weigh my every word," said Mikkel Skar sourly.

"Well, maybe you should," said Laura.

"I think you're all overreacting," said Tuva Gran, supporting Mikkel Skar.

Everybody listened to Tuva Gran. After all, she and her family were Paahp's closest neighbors. Tuva had been hoping for a family with children.

It was a day in October, and Laura's little girl pointed at Paahp, who was sitting on a park bench, in the light, opposite the school. She said: "His brother's dead."

Laura looked down at her daughter.

"He's dead? How do you know?" And then she added: "Don't point your finger."

Julia shrugged her shoulders.

Laura said: "I think we should go over and express our condolences."

Julia shrugged again.

"Expressing your condolences means you say you're sad to hear somebody's died," Laura explained.

"But I'm not sad," said Julia.

"No, but Paahp is, so you and I can be sad with him for a bit."

Julia folded her arms and looked at her mother. She had just learned to roll her eyes.

"Come on, we'll go over to him, Julia!"

Laura regretted not having simply walked on, letting the matter lie. She dragged her daughter across to Paahp's bench and sat down beside him. She said quietly: "I hear you've lost your brother."

Paahp turned slowly to Laura. His eyes were big and blue, like a child's. Big and blue, with long black lashes. He took her hand and squeezed it.

"It all goes quiet when the crows die," he said.

Laura nodded; she smiled at him.

"It all goes quiet," said Paahp.

"Yes," said Laura.

"It all goes quiet when the crows die," he repeated.

"I don't quite understand what you mean," said Laura.

"I moved here because of him," said Paahp.

"Because of your brother?"

"Yes, because of him. I moved here because of him." Paahp buried his face in his hands and sobbed.

Laura patted his shoulder.

"Please accept my condolences," she said, getting to her feet.

The words *accept my condolences* hurtled out of her like a locomotive. She took Julia's hand and started walking. Paahp went on weeping. Laura squeezed her daughter's hand and kept walking.

When they had gone a little way, Julia said: "Paahp's disgusting."

"Disgusting? Why is he disgusting?" asked Laura.

"Because he is," said Julia.

"Yes, but why?"

Laura studied her daughter's face.

"Has he ever done anything or said anything that you thought was disgusting?"

"No," Julia said. "He gives me bracelets. They're made of stones and beads and sometimes bits of fir cone. He threads them on a string. They're nice. But Paahp's disgusting—everybody knows that."

It wasn't just a question of raking up leaves and cutting the grass. That was part of it, certainly. But everybody knew it was really about the bracelets. Mikkel Skar and Ole-Petter Kramer had both informed Paahp that the Residents' Association didn't want him stopping little girls on their way home from school and giving them bracelets, but Paahp went on doing it. And the little girls went on accepting them. All the children in the Colony residential area, particularly the girls, were ordered by their parents not to talk to Paahp under any circumstances, and not to accept bracelets, or anything else for that matter, from him or from any other stranger; they were just to say no thank you and keep walking. It didn't help. There were bracelets everywhere. Around wrists. In schoolbags. In bedside tables. In jewel boxes. In dolls' houses. Under pillows. In Lego sets. Around dolls' necks. On windowsills. In trouser pockets. Down the backs of radiators. Deep inside beds.

The matter for discussion now was whether there was any way of obliging Paahp to move. Getting rid of him, to be blunt. There turned out not to be. Andreas Knudsen and Line Disen were both lawyers; they lived in the Colony; they were married and had children. They had looked into it and reached the conclusion that there were no legal grounds for doing anything at all. Paahp's sitting pretty, they said. We've got nothing to go on. He hasn't done anything wrong. So the Residents' Association decided that Ole-Petter Kramer, who had three daughters himself, would try talking to Paahp one more time.

It happened sometimes. After Laura had gone to bed and turned off the light, Isak knocked on her door, opened it a crack, and whispered: "Are you asleep, Laura?"

"No, I'm not asleep."

"Shall I read to you?"

"Yes, please."

Isak sat on the edge of the bed and leafed through that book of poetry he always brought with him.

"Here!" he said, and carried on turning the pages. "No, here!" He turned more pages. "No, here: look, this is a beautiful one! Are you ready?"

"Yes, but don't ask me afterward what I think."

Isak looked at his daughter in the gleam of the bedside light. Before she went to bed, she had undone her plait and brushed her hair. It was long. As long as Rosa's hair. His other daughters didn't have such long hair. Laura lay in bed under the covers with her head and her beautiful long hair on a big white pillow.

"You're lying there shining at me," said Isak, and stroked her cheek.

"Come on, Daddy," said Laura.

"Are you ready?" asked Isak.

"Yes."

"What do you mean, I'm not to ask you what you think?" asked Isak.

"I don't always understand the stuff you read," said Laura. "But it doesn't matter. It's nice anyway."

And Isak read:

> *And no one hears those songs*
> *hears the whisper*
> *calm and light*
> *and oblivion the memory*
> *this day—absorption*

"That was the first verse," Isak said. "Now I shall read the second verse."

> *In a hymn the day goes*
> *light and still*
> *and as song sounds everything*
> *and against the misty island of a cliff*
> *and as in agony to touch the beach*

Isak looked up from the book. He said: "Do you want me to read the poem again?"

"No," said Laura. "I'm going to sleep now."

Isak leaned over her and kissed her forehead.

"Good night, Laura. Sleep well."

He stood up and moved toward the door. Laura sat up in bed.

"Daddy!"

Isak opened the door. He paused in the doorway in the light from the hall.

"What does *absorption* mean?" she asked.

"I think," Isak said, "it must be a sort of swirl of darkness."

"A swirl of darkness?"

"Yes . . . it tugs at you and you fall into it, slowly. But it isn't unpleasant. One day you'll long to be there."

It was Marion with the black hair who decided who was to be punished, and how. Before that it had always been Emily. Once it was Frida, but Frida always started giggling, so everybody turned against her and punished her instead.

"Don't you ever get to decide?" asked Laura.

"Decide what?" said Erika.

"Who's going to be punished," said Laura.

Laura was eleven in the summer of 1979; her plait swung from side to side as she walked along the road to the shop. Erika was always with Marion and Frida and Emily now. Or else with Ragnar. Anyway, Erika never had time to walk to the shop with Laura.

If they were to be together, it had to be at night. Sometimes Molly would sleep with Laura in Laura's bed and then Erika couldn't be bothered with Laura. But there were times when Laura slept with Erika in Erika's bed, and then they would talk until four or five or six in the morning. Rosa said everybody was to sleep in her own bed in her own room, but nobody did. Sometimes, after Rosa and Isak had gone to bed, Erika crept out and went to sleep with Ragnar in the secret hut in the woods. Erika didn't think anybody knew, but Laura knew; Laura knew much more than Erika could ever imagine.

Erika said: "I was there when we punished Marion, once."

"I didn't think anyone ever punished Marion."

"Oh yes, even her. Nobody gets let off. We all punished her together. Frida, Emily, Pär, Olle, Fabian, and Ragnar, too."

"Was Ragnar with you?"

"He is sometimes, only not so much these days. He always acts so weird when there are many of us. Jumps up and down and makes faces or sings out of tune just to get attention. And he's so clingy with me. It's annoying. It makes me want to hit him."

"Why do you hang out with him, then?"

"He's different when we're alone together, when it's just him and me. Actually, it was Ragnar who came up with the idea."

"What idea?"

"Punishing Marion."

"How did you do it?"

"We made her cry."

"But how?"

Erika giggled, and squirmed closer to Laura. She whispered: "We forced her to eat the tick off Fabian's butt."

Laura stared at Erika in the darkness. They were lying so close together that Laura could feel Erika's breath on her cheek.

"Disgusting," said Laura. "Did she do it?"

"She had no choice," said Erika. "We made her. We were hanging out in Emily's garden and Marion tossed back her black hair and said, Can't we go to the beach instead of sitting here. I'm bored. And then Pär told her to shut up."

"Isn't Pär Marion's boyfriend?"

"Uh-huh. They've been together for ages. And he told her to shut up and then Fabian started laughing. Then Ragnar started laughing and then Olle. Everyone was bored and I think they thought it was good that Pär told Marion off. Nobody ever tells her off. It's good that he was a little tough on her. Anyway, she got all red in the face and nobody stood up for her. Not even Emily, who's, like, her best friend. Then Pär asked Fabian if he still had the tick stuck to his butt. It had been there forever. Fabian wanted to see how fat it would get before it dropped off. Luckily, he said, it was far enough up for him not to squish it when he planted his big bum on a chair. Fabian just laughed and took off his trousers and underpants and showed his butt to everybody. The tick must have been there over a week. It was the size of a grape, brown and disgusting and shiny and ready to pop. Then Ragnar said to Fabian, I think Marion should take it off for you. Interesting idea, Fabian said, and wiggled his ass. Yes, very interesting, went Pär. How do you think she might do that? Frida, Emily, and me just giggled, and then Ragnar went, I think Marion, since she's such a bitch, should bite it off and chew it and swallow it. Marion screamed that Ragnar could go to hell and that he was a bastard—You're a complete fucking psycho, she told him—and then Ragnar warned her to take that back. She was to stop it. And that was when Pär put his arm around her and said, Maybe you shouldn't call people psychos, Marion, and then he kept hold of her and said if she didn't eat the tick off Fabian's butt he was going to cut off all her hair. You know Pär always has a knife. And he had it that day, too, and he held it up for Marion to see, so she'd know he was serious. Then everybody started laughing again. Even Marion laughed a bit and said, Lay off, Pär, let's go to the beach now, or to the shop for some Coca-Cola, but then Fabian bent over and stuck his butt in the air and Pär grabbed Marion's hair and said, Go on, do it, you fucking cunt. He didn't mean anything by it. He was only joking, probably. But that was when Marion started crying. Tears started running from her eyes. She didn't say anything. She just cried. Then Emily and me told Pär to lay off, but Frida couldn't stop giggling."

Erika paused. It was the middle of the night. Laura thought it was great, lying there talking about stuff like that.

"I was totally hoping," Erika said, "she wasn't going to do it."

"Do what?" asked Laura. "You mean she ate it?"

"Yes," said Erika. "She kind of braced herself. She couldn't stand us seeing her crying, so she really braced herself. She shook off Pär and stood there, sort of swaying. Okay, she said, and tossed back her hair. It's okay. She squatted down behind Fabian, who naturally hadn't put his underpants back on, and bit his big butt so he screamed. Then she straightened up to let us all see the tick between her teeth, I'm sure it was still alive, and then she closed her mouth and started crunching."

Laura sat up in bed and stared at her sister.

"Did she swallow it?"

"Yes."

"I bet it was full of blood."

"Yes."

"Did she start crying again?"

"No. She didn't cry."

"Poor Marion," said Laura.

"But everybody was laughing," said Erika. "Even Marion laughed. I think everybody thought it was disgusting and wanted to go home and forget the whole thing, but everybody laughed. Then Pär suddenly stopped laughing and said Ragnar was a total psycho. It was Ragnar's idea, eating the tick. And Pär said, You really are a psycho! Get the hell out of here, Ragnar! Then everything went back to normal. Ragnar got up and went. Marion threw an empty Coca-Cola bottle after him and the bottle clipped his head, and then he started running. He ran out of the garden and up the road and into the woods."

"Poor Marion," repeated Laura.

"Don't feel sorry for Marion," said Erika.

"Poor Ragnar, then."

"You don't have to feel sorry for Ragnar, either."

Erika pulled Laura toward her. They lay still beside each other for a while.

"The point is, there's no need to feel sorry for anybody," said Erika. "Nobody."

Laura giggled and turned to her sister.

"Yes, there is," she said. "The tick!" She paused. "I feel sorry for the tick."

Her mobile phone rang. Laura had a large brown leather bag over her shoulder. In that bag, it was chaos. In her shopping trolley she kept things in order. But in her shoulder bag there was chaos. Keys, money, cards, tram tickets, receipts, Jesper's pacifier, packets of chewing gum, chocolate wrappers, a small bag of pork rinds, which were the tastiest thing she knew, class schedule, pens and notebooks, a leaflet from the church about christening and funeral services that she'd been meaning to copy and hand out to her pupils so they could discuss what a ritual was. She'd had so many plans when she began teaching the thirteen-to-sixteens, but she never got through half of what she wanted. If she put her hand into her bag to find something, like twenty kroner for the underground, she would often stab herself on some object and make the tip of her finger bleed. A safety pin. A pen nib. She had to empty out her bag. Her phone flashed. It was Lars-Eivind. The doctor had wanted to do more tests than he had expected, and he almost hadn't made it to his important meeting.

"And the meeting was awful," he said. "I didn't manage to say a single thing I'd planned. I was stupid and clumsy."

Laura was standing at the counter in the Turkish greengrocer's, considering one tomato against another. She said: "Why did the doctor need to do so many tests?"

"Just routine."

Laura pressed the phone to her ear.

"Are you sure?"

"They always do lots of tests, Laura. I'm sure."

Laura stared at the tomatoes. Another customer elbowed her from behind.

"I'm sure you were fine at the meeting."

"No, I wasn't. I fucked it up."

"I'm cooking something nice for you tonight."

She could hear Lars-Eivind's breathing at the other end. He was breathing. He was alive. He was nearby. He had a face and a body and two hands and a voice that was talking to her at this moment. Laura put both tomatoes into her basket. She needed many more things; she had planned a big meal and would need more vegetables; then she would go to the fishmonger's and the wineshop and the supermarket, but right now she couldn't focus on anything but the two tomatoes.

"What have you been doing today?" asked Lars-Eivind. "On your day off?"

"I don't know," Laura whispered. She had to get away from the greengrocer's counter. "I haven't done much. Talked to Erika. She's on her way to Hammarsö. She's going to visit Father."

Lars-Eivind faded out for a moment. Someone wherever he was called out to him or demanded his attention. Then he was back.

"Speak to you later, Laura. I'll ring later this afternoon. Everything's all right."

Laura was lying alone in her own bed, in her own room. That was the way Rosa wanted it to be. Each sister in her own room, in her own bed. In summer, it never got completely dark. Maybe in August, but in June and July it never got completely dark. Not on Hammarsö, at any rate. The Hammarsö Pageant marked the transition from July to August, summer to autumn, light to darkness. After the Hammarsö Pageant ended, there would still be three weeks of the summer holidays left, and yet in a way the summer holidays were over. In August it got dark quickly in the evenings and everybody asked if you were looking forward to the start of term. And even if you weren't looking forward to it, even if you hated going to school, you had to say you were. It was expected, said Rosa, who always knew what you should say or do in any situation. You were meant to look forward to seeing your teacher and your classmates and to learning new things. But now, at this moment, August was a long way off. It was only the beginning of July, and as always at the beginning of July it was impossible to shut out the light, even though Rosa had been to the mainland and bought curtain material that promised to do just that. The light always found a chink or crack or hole to creep through, or a threadbare patch to dance on. The window was usually left slightly open, and although it was hot, with hardly a breath of wind (yes, they said it was the hottest summer since 1874), the curtains were moving vaguely to and fro, and that made it easy for the light. If Laura opened her eyes she could see the radio on the bedside table; on the walls the pictures of dogs, horses, and pop and film stars; the Donald Duck comics on the floor; the clothes she had been wearing and had taken off and would put on again the next day, in a little pile on the chair.

Laura closed the veranda door behind her. She was going to take the shortcut down to the beach to go swimming. She had packed everything she needed in a big blue bag that was hanging from her shoulder. Bikini, towel, tape recorder, magazines, potato chips, soda, chocolate, sweets: everything she had bought with her own money, hoarded and kept hidden from Rosa's eyes. Rosa said you were allowed to eat only half a packet of chips and one bar of chocolate a week, and that had to be on a Friday or a Saturday and on no account on a Wednesday, for example.

Right outside the house, under a tree, a bird lay on the ground, quivering. It flapped its wings but couldn't take off and fly; it just lay there struggling. It wasn't cheeping or twittering or singing or crying; Laura didn't know what sounds birds were supposed to make when they were lying on the ground and couldn't fly. This bird was silent, at any rate, not a sound from its beak. The only thing she could hear was the noise of its wings beating against the ground. The bird didn't give up. It tensed, and braced itself, and flapped its wings as hard as it could, and when nothing happened it folded in on itself and waited awhile before trying once more. This happened over and over again. Laura wished she hadn't seen the bird. She was on her way down to the beach to go swimming and the day stretched before her, long and bright, and then the bird was lying there struggling; it was in a terrible way and would die soon and it was her responsibility to help it. She could just walk on, of course, leave it lying there, flapping its wings, convince herself that she'd be able to forget it as the day wore on. And maybe she would forget for a little while, but something was bound to remind her. It could be absolutely anything: the swans on the sea, a stone at the water's edge, a song on her tape recorder.

Laura looked at the bird that had become her responsibility now. Stupid bird! Stupid bird! Everything had been so nice, and now this stupid bird was demanding that she do something, anything to put an end to the pain. She'd have to kill it; that was what you did with birds who couldn't fly and lay on the ground flapping their wings and got tangled up in themselves and flapped their wings again. Laura prodded the bird with her foot and the bird gave a start and that startled Laura, too. She sat down on the ground beside it and felt the tears coming and stroked the little bird body with her finger. It was like stroking a patch of moss. I've got to kill you, stupid bird, I've got to, because you can't fly. She went on stroking it. She thought she could stamp on it, but then she'd feel it in her foot for the rest of the day, maybe the rest of her life. She could stand up, shut her eyes, and drop her beach bag on it, which was heavy; but then she would get dead bird on it, blood and goo and feathers and bird guts, and she wouldn't be able to use it anymore.

As she sat there puzzling, Isak came along. He often took a walk around the house at about that time. Round and round. He had a part in the Hammarsö Pageant, and when he walked around the house like that in the mornings, Laura knew he was practicing his lines. He could never remember them, of course. He had the script in his hand and had to keep checking. Isak could do everything, remember everything, even difficult poems nobody understood, about sinking into absorption, but he couldn't get a handle on his lines for that year's Hammarsö Pageant. Isak stopped when he saw Laura and the bird on the ground.

"Oh, dear," he said, and prodded the bird with his foot just as his daughter had done. "Well, we'll have to kill it," he said. "Put it out of its misery."

The bird flapped its wings. Isak sat down on the ground and sighed; he rested the whole weight of his big body on the ground, and Laura thought that if only he had sat on the bird it would all be over by now; but Isak didn't sit on the bird, he sat so he and Laura had the trembling bird between them. Laura went on stroking its body with her finger. Isak frowned.

"Maybe I could give it an injection," he said. "Or I could pick it up and hurl it at the ground, that would do the trick. Poor bird," he said. He looked at Laura. "I feel sorry for it, don't you?"

Laura nodded.

Neither of them did anything. Laura was glad her father had come, for now it was no longer her responsibility to kill the bird, but why didn't he get on with it? Why was he just sitting there on the ground, doing nothing? Sometimes it seemed her father wanted the two of them to talk about important things together, now that Laura was bigger. It seemed as though he wanted to hear what she had to say; it was as if he was expecting something from her in the form of words, for her to open her mouth and share her insights, ideas, thoughts, and visions with him. Once he had even asked her what her vision of the future was, but Laura didn't know what a vision was so she just shook her head and shrugged her shoulders, and then her father had looked disappointed. Laura knew it was because he loved her most. He loved her more than Erika and Molly. Not because of anything she had done herself or because she was so special, but because he loved her mother so much, because Rosa had saved him from the abyss, he would say, and Laura had no idea what he meant by that.

You are a love child, he would tell her, you are special, and as time went by it came to sound like a sort of reproach. She wasn't small and pretty and funny like Molly, or tall and striking with good marks like Erika. She couldn't come up with any interesting things to say as they sat there with the dying bird between them, and she had no vision, she was more or less sure of that, at least not the kind Isak would nod appreciatively at and say, Yes, Laura! Yes! That's right! What a wise girl you are! Laura had asked Rosa if she had visions, but Rosa said that all she had was clothes on her body and food in her belly and sleep at night and that was all she needed, too, and that Laura should stop putting on airs with fancy pleas nobody had any use for.

Laura looked at her father. He smiled at her.

"So here we are, you and I," he said.

"Yes, but aren't you going to kill it soon?" said Laura impatiently. "I was on my way to the beach to sunbathe."

Isak sighed and looked away.

Laura took her father's hand and squeezed it.

"But now we're here, you and me," she repeated, and then he smiled again.

Laura and Isak sat there on the ground for a long time, holding hands, and the bird flapped its wings occasionally and quivered, and Laura was aware that her father thought this was an important moment—he even said so: he said, You'll remember this moment all your life—but Laura wanted to get up and stretch her legs, she needed to pee, she wanted to go down to the beach for a swim before it clouded over and turned chilly. And at last Rosa emerged through the veranda door with a thermos flask in one hand and a newspaper in the other. Rosa liked to spend time on her own in the morning, drinking coffee and reading. When she saw Laura and Isak sitting on the ground, she stopped short, put the flask and paper down on the garden table, and said: "What in the world are you doing?"

"We're sitting here watching over a bird dying," replied Isak.

Rosa came a few steps closer, frowned, and put her hands on her hips. She nodded in Laura's direction.

"Get up, girl," she said. "You'll get a chill and end up with a bladder infection, sitting on the ground like that."

She nodded in Isak's direction.

"Do you want Laura to get a bladder infection? You call yourself a doctor? Get up, the two of you!"

She stretched out her arms, gave them each a hand, and pulled them up.

Then she bent down to look at the bird.

"We'll have to finish it off," she said, and turned on her heel and disappeared behind the house.

Laura and Isak stood there, saying nothing. Laura looked at the bird. When it wasn't flapping its wings but was just lying there to rest between its exertions, she could see the little body rising and falling. It was breathing. Its heart was beating. This wasn't *absorption*. Laura looked defiantly at Isak. She said nothing. But the bird wasn't longing for absorption.

It was a swirl of breath and warmth and light.

Rosa came back with a shovel that Isak had bought the previous summer to dig ditches round the house. She went straight over to the bird.

"Out of the way, both of you," she said, gesturing impatiently. Laura and Isak took a few steps back.

Rosa raised the shovel, took a breath and brought it down sharply.

"There!" she said.

She turned to Laura and Isak.

Rosa always had such flushed red cheeks.

She tugged on Laura's plait and said: "Don't forget to change into a dry bikini after you've been in the water! A bladder infection is no laughing matter."

But that's how it always is, thought Laura. It was snowing again and in less than an hour it would be entirely dark. What a waste of a day! Before long she would have to fetch Jesper from his nursery and Julia from her after-school club and nothing she had planned had got done. She had bought two tomatoes and a bunch of white tulips and was now standing on the pavement somewhere between the supermarket and the church, letting the snow fall on her, on her shopping trolley. But now I'll get a grip. I'll go to the wineshop, the fishmonger's, and the supermarket, and then I'm going back to the Turkish shop to buy everything else I need. Then I'm going to fetch Jesper from nursery and Julia from after-school club. We will play in the garden. We will make a snowman. I will not rush it. I will cook a delicious dinner. She stood there. She thought: If I say right foot up and take one step forward, then it will automatically rise and take one step forward. And if I say left foot up and take one step forward, then it will automatically rise and take one step forward, and then I'll be walking, right foot, left foot, right foot, left foot, through the snow. I will get my mobile phone out of my bag and ring Jonas Guave and tell him we're not selling the house after all. Lars-Eivind sometimes talked about wanting to die in that house. Not now, but after many years. He wanted to see the children grow up; he wanted to surround himself with grandchildren; he wanted to grow old with Laura and then he wanted to die. All in the same house. So what I said this morning was just a whim. The whole lot. Jonas Guave could forget he had ever met her. I will do all those things. All those things. She stood there. It was snowing on her hat, on the plait sticking out from under her hat, her anorak, trousers, shoes, and the shopping trolley that wasn't properly closed, so it was snowing on the two tomatoes and the white tulips inside. Laura shut her eyes and opened them again. Here we go. Right foot first and then the left. Still nothing. She stood there. Laura stood there until a young man came along on the pavement, talking on his phone and carrying a bag from the supermarket. The man bumped into Laura and walked on. It didn't hurt, but the contact was still hard, disturbing, intrusive, invasive. The man had walked straight into her, into her and through her and on along the pavement as if she weren't there, as if she didn't exist or occupy space.

"Excuse me!" she called after him.

The man turned around. He still had his mobile clasped to his ear.

"Excuse you," he called back.

"You walked straight into me!" said Laura. "You can't just walk straight into people!"

"If people stand in the middle of the pavement and can't be bothered to move aside, then I can," he said.

He walked off. Laura took hold of her shopping trolley and followed him. He couldn't just run into her and then walk off like that. She wanted to call after him. She wanted to fight, but she didn't know how. She wanted to kick him in the back and then, when he turned around, punch him on the jaw. The man walked faster. Laura walked faster. He should leave people in peace. Laura simply wanted to be left in peace. The man stopped; he turned and looked at her.

"Hey, lay off!" he said. "Just drop it!"

"But couldn't you have just let me stand there?" asked Laura. "Couldn't you have just let me stand there on the pavement in peace?"

The man shook his head, fed up with her, and walked on. He crossed the road and vanished around a corner.

And it was then that Laura found herself standing outside the church. She and Lars-Eivind had lived in the Colony for six years, and this was the church they belonged to; in this church they had been married and their children had been christened. The door was locked, of course.

When Laura was twenty-four and her mother fell ill and could neither move nor speak (Rosa was in a wheelchair and communicated with her eyes or by typing the words *yes, no, tired, enough* into a small computer), she asked her daughter to take her to church occasionally. So Laura did.

And long before that, long before Laura was grown up and Rosa fell ill, long before Erika and Molly came into her life, Laura would go with Rosa to the shop on Hammarsö. On the way home they went past the stone church; they always went past the stone church on the way home from the shop, and Rosa would tell her that it was many hundreds of years old, that it held many secrets and its bells struck every hour and half hour, all day and all night, all year round. On Hammarsö the church door was never locked (the islanders maintained that they remembered God even though God had forgotten them), and Laura had tugged at Rosa and asked if they could go inside and look. So they did. Then Laura tugged at Rosa again and asked if she could have fifty öre to light a candle.

"Who are you going to light a candle for, then?" Rosa asked.

"I don't know," said Laura, and laughed. "Maybe I'll light a candle for you, if you give me fifty öre."

Rosa gave her fifty öre.

A thin woman with beautiful long dark hair, wearing a short orange-striped dress, came gliding silently over the floor of the church and stopped beside them.

The woman said quietly: "So here you are, Rosa Lövenstad, lighting candles with your daughter."

Rosa jumped and quickly turned to the woman.

"Ann-Kristin! You scared me."

The woman laughed, almost to herself.

"I expect I often do that."

"Do what?" said Rosa.

"Scare you."

Rosa took Laura's hand and said: "No, Ann-Kristin, you don't scare me."

"Ragnar's been ill. He's had a temperature. I'm tired."

"But he's better now?" Rosa asked.

"Yes, he's better now," the woman said.

"That's good," said Rosa.

"Say hello to Isak for me," said the woman.

"I will or I won't," said Rosa, pulling Laura away from the lit candles and out of the church with her.

"Who was that?" Laura asked.

"Someone Daddy knew a long time ago," Rosa said. "She lives here on the island in the summer and in Stockholm in the winter, like us."

"But who's Ragnar?" Laura asked.

"He's a boy."

"How old is he?"

"I don't know. Older than you. Six, perhaps."

Years later when her mother lay dying, Laura had asked her if she believed in God.

Her mother no longer had enough muscles in her body to be able to nod or to shake her head, and neither could she smile. She had a little movement left in her index finger and used it to type words into her computer. *Don't know,* she wrote. She looked at Laura. *Ask Isak. He talks. I'm tired.* Her look was more penetrating now that she had only a few words at her disposal. Laura thought at the time that her mother had a secret, an answer to a thousand questions, but then she decided everybody who was dying no doubt gave the impression of having a secret. It was the desire of those who lived on for meaning, coherence, insight, consolation.

When she finally died, it was Laura who washed her and laid her out and dressed her in the soft floral-patterned dress she had had for years and the blue canvas shoes she liked wearing in the summer. Her mother had smart, high-heeled shoes, too, but neither Laura nor Isak thought she should lie in her grave in high-heeled shoes. Laura had brushed and braided her mother's hair the way she brushed and braided her own. Laura then studied her mother's face. She found a lipstick in her bag and rubbed a little red into the pallid skin. There! Laura took a step back so she could survey all she had done. Floral dress, blue canvas shoes, a long plait, glowing cheeks. Now Isak could come. Rosa was ready.

Laura turned and went home. She would put the shopping trolley away and get the stroller. Jesper could never walk all the way home from nursery, at least not when it was snowing and cold. It wasn't even four yet but it would soon be completely dark. The special dinner didn't really matter. They could order pizza. She would decorate the pizza with her two tomatoes, and her hair and her daughter's with white tulips. Afterward they could all snuggle up in bed together and watch television. Laura would put her arms around Lars-Eivind and Julia and Jesper; her arms were long enough. They would eat pizza and snuggle up in bed and the children could sleep there all night if they wanted, lying crossways.

"Molly, is that you?"

Laura walked along the road, past the banner. LIVELY CHIL-
DREN! She turned right; she was almost home now. LIVE CHILDREN!
She held the mobile phone to her ear. Molly sounded happy. When
Laura married Lars-Eivind and moved from Stockholm to Oslo, she
thought she would be seeing a lot more of Molly. But it hadn't
turned out that way. Now and then they met up, all three of them,
Erika, Laura, and Molly, and talked about one thing or another and
promised they really would meet more often in the future. They
were sisters, after all.

"Molly, it *is* you!"

Molly laughed.

"I know we haven't spoken for about six months, so let me just
say what I rang to say, then you can think it over and ring me back."

"So, what did you ring to say?" asked Molly.

"Erika's on her way to Hammarsö to visit Father," said Laura.

"Father?" said Molly.

"Yes, Isak," said Laura. "He's old now."

"Yes, he is," said Molly. "But I haven't spoken to him for years."

"Exactly," said Laura. "So Erika and I thought it might be a good idea to spend a few days with him."

"On Hammarsö?" said Molly.

"Yes, on Hammarsö," said Laura. "So he can look at us and we can look at him, if you know what I mean."

"I haven't been to Hammarsö since I was—what was I—five, I think."

"You were five," said Laura.

"Do you mean go right away?" asked Molly.

"Yes, now! Right away!" said Laura. "That is, I'm leaving early tomorrow morning. Erika's already on her way, but she's taken a detour via Sunne. And I'm going tomorrow morning. I can give you a lift."

"Yes, but I can't do that. I start rehearsals in under a week. I can't just ... out of the blue like that ... My life isn't about Isak anymore."

"I'd decided not to go down there, either," Laura interrupted. "But now I've decided to go after all."

"Do you and Erika think he's going to die? Is Father ill?"

"No, we don't think he's going to die, Molly. He's old, not ill. He says he's going to die soon, but he's been saying that for the last twelve years."

"I often think it would be a relief if he died," said Molly.

"Why?"

"I don't know. That's just how it seems to me."

Molly's mother, Ruth, had died when Molly was only seven. Laura, who was fourteen at the time, passed the half-open kitchen door in the Stockholm flat and heard Rosa and Isak talking about whether Molly should come and live with them now that her mother was dead. Isak was her father, after all. Whispering voices: "But you're always at the flat in Lund," said Rosa. "You're never here with me. I have to look after Laura on my own, and now you want me to bring up this cuckoo in the nest as well?"

"No," said Isak. "No. I don't want that. She can live with her grandmother in Oslo. That will be best."

And for many years, Laura and Molly did not speak to each other. They grew up quite separately. Laura trained as a teacher and Molly went to the theater academy in Oslo and became a director.

"And why couldn't she have trained for a proper profession and gotten a proper job?" was Isak's reaction.

Laura and Erika leapt to their little sister's defense. They said Isak should be proud of her. They said she was very good at what she did. They said everybody agrees she's very good.

But as the years passed, Laura and Molly had lost touch.

Molly! I had my arm around you in the narrow bed, in the dark room on the island we believed would be our island for all eternity. We lay close together in bed, listening to Isak's voice in the next room. He was in Erika's room. He was sitting on the edge of Erika's bed, trying to comfort Erika. It was the middle of the night, but everyone in the house was wide awake. It was that night nobody slept. It was that dreadful night when nobody could sleep, you know why, and I told you to forget everything you'd seen. And then—do you remember, Molly?—Isak started singing! He had a deep, rumbling voice. And you looked at me and smiled your lovely smile and said: Bom, bom, bom!

For many years there had been this silence between them, but when Rosa died, Laura got a letter from Molly.

Dear Laura, the letter said. *Now we are both motherless. Perhaps that makes us more like sisters? I'm eighteen now. I still live with Grandmother, but I shall be moving out soon. If you come to Oslo or I come to Stockholm, maybe we can meet up. Yours, Molly.*

P.S. Give Father my best wishes. Erika says he wants to kill himself after what happened with Rosa. I don't think he'll do it. I think he'll live to be a very old man.

In her schoolbag, Julia had a note addressed to all the parents in the Colony, signed by Mikkel Skar, Geir Kvikkstad, Tuva Gran, and Gunilla and Ole-Petter Kramer. The letter referred to the Colony Residents' Association meeting in December, when Paahp's behavior had been under discussion once again.

Back at the start of November, Ole-Petter Kramer had tried to talk to Paahp. It had gone well, or so Kramer thought at the time. They had sat on hard wooden chairs in Paahp's seedy kitchen. They had drunk insipid instant coffee together. Paahp had nodded and said it wouldn't happen again; he realized the little girls of the neighborhood should not get the idea that accepting bracelets from strangers was all right; he realized it worried their parents. He also realized, now that they were having this frank exchange, neighbor to neighbor, man to man, that it was important not to let his house fall into such disrepair that it impeded on the well-being of the community, of his neighbors. Paahp promised to ring a glazier and rake up the leaves in his garden the next day, and to clear the snow from his driveway when the time came. Paahp concluded by taking Kramer's hand and saying something about crows, which Kramer didn't quite catch, but Kramer interpreted the conversation as having been entirely successful. Thus it was Ole-Petter Kramer who showed annoyance at the December meeting. Anger, even. He clenched his fist and said, To hell with this idiot! The December meeting was traditionally devoted mainly to pleasant social interaction and mulled wine; the only item on the agenda was the Christmas workshop under the direction of the Krag family. But the pleasant social interaction evaporated as one family after another spoke of yet more bracelets. The little girls knew now, after innumerable lectures from their parents, that they weren't to talk to Paahp or to accept his bracelets. Yet they still did. They accepted the bracelets, slipped them onto one another's wrists and compared the beads, shells, stones, and bits of fir cone; and when they got home they hid them in their dolls and teddy bears, in empty CD cases, inside the books of fairy tales they no longer read, and behind the windows of their advent calendars. Then the parents found one and then another, and then one more. Things could not continue this way. Paahp would have to go.

"I don't understand it," said Ole-Petter Kramer. "I don't understand it. We talked to each other. We sat in his filthy kitchen and drank that dishwater he calls coffee and he understood everything I said. I didn't use a single word he wouldn't understand. He grasped how serious it was. Yet it just goes on. Is he laughing at us? Does he think we can't see him? Does he think we are fools?"

He stretches out his long, thin old man's arms to our girls, stops them on the way home from school, talks to them, gives them presents; he takes their soft hands in his hands.

A committee was set up, a sort of semiofficial committee, a shady committee, somebody thought, since it had no name and operated outside the usual structures; a think tank to come up with various proposals for a definitive solution to the problem that had arisen in the Colony residential area.

"So this is the solution?" said Laura into her mobile phone.

She was pacing up and down the garden, talking to Tuva Gran. She had the letter in her hand. It was dark outside now, and Julia and Jesper had reluctantly started making a snowman. Julia wanted to watch television instead, and Jesper wanted to sit on Laura's lap, but Laura said it would be fun to build a snowman: they would give it a carrot nose and tie a scarf around its neck, and it would stand in the garden ready to say hello to Daddy when he got home later in the evening.

Then she read the letter she found in Julia's schoolbag.

"It's a symbolic act," said Tuva Gran. "Putting down a silent marker, telling him in a civil way to stop tormenting our children."

"He's not tormenting our children," said Laura, looking across to where Julia was helping her little brother roll a snowball.

"We don't know what he's capable of," said Tuva Gran quietly. "I've heard stories. My girls say he's disgusting. Why is he disgusting, Laura? Why do they say he's disgusting?"

"I don't know," Laura replied.

"My girls say he asked them if they wanted to go home with him. Why does he want them to go home with him? They say that Jenny Åsmundsen, who's four—four, Laura—told them he gave her a bracelet and pointed to his genitals."

"Children say so many things," said Laura.

"Why should they lie?" said Tuva Gran. Her voice was shrill. "The children told me this of their own accord; I didn't ask them a single question. They said Jenny Åsmundsen got a bracelet and then he pointed at his private parts. What they said was 'and then he pointed at his willy,' if you want to know the exact words. And we're supposed to sit back and let it happen? Is that what you want?"

"No, of course not," said Laura. "But I just don't think he . . . I don't think Paahp is . . . I think he's just a lonely old man."

"In any case, it's not normal behavior," Tuva Gran interrupted, "for a grown man to seek out little girls and tempt them with presents. You know that! You know that, Laura! And he continues doing it even when we've begged him to stop."

In the letter, the committee requested that all parents go through their daughters' rooms and find as many of the bracelets as they could. A list of possible hiding places was appended. Next, the parents were requested to hand over all the bracelets to Mikkel Skar, Geir Kvikkstad, Tuva Gran, Gunilla Kramer, or Ole-Petter Kramer. The committee would collect all the bracelets (in a bucket? in a bag? in a cardboard box?) and return them directly to Paahp.

"You're welcome to come along when we go to hand them back," said Tuva Gran. "We're meeting at Fryden's at nine this evening and going in a group to Paahp's house."

"How many of you?" said Laura. "How many of you are going in a group to Paahp's house at nine?"

"I don't know," said Tuva Gran. "Lots, I think. He's got to grasp, once and for all, that he needs to keep away."

Laura looked at Julia and Jesper. "I need to hang up now," she said to Tuva Gran.

Her kids needed help. They couldn't make the snowman without her, and here she was, pacing up and down the garden talking into her mobile. It had been her idea. She had said it would be fun to build a snowman, and now the three of them were wading around in the dark, in slushy, wet snow, getting cold. The snowman still had no head, and the children wanted to go inside. She took a deep breath, grabbed their hands and said: "Right, it's time. Time to make a gigantic snowball. We'll roll and roll and roll, all together, and when we've finished rolling we'll have a head."

"With a carrot nose!" shouted Jesper.

"Of course with a carrot nose," said Julia.

Laura looked at the children. She had forgotten to buy carrots.

"Tomato nose!" said Laura. "This snowman is going to have a big red tomato nose, and that's much better."

She looked at her daughter. *I won't let anyone touch you.*

"Isn't it, Julia?"

Julia opened her mouth and closed it again. Jesper wiped his face with his mitten and jumped up and down to keep warm, and every time he jumped he whispered, Roll, roll, roll, roll, roll, roll.

"A tomato nose is cool, too," said Julia quietly.

Laura ran. She could run faster than anybody. Only Ragnar was faster. Laura had always been quick. She ran through the gate, out into the road, round the bend, past Tuva Gran's house, as far as the snow-covered drive nobody had cleared since it started snowing, and along it to the run-down house with several smashed windows. She knocked on the door. The old man opened the door and looked at her.

"Do you want to come in?" he said.

"Yes," said Laura.

"Shall we sit down?" asked Paahp.

"Yes," said Laura.

He went first, stumbling across the floor through a dark hall and a dark living room. Laura followed. They sat down in his kitchen. The furniture comprised two hard wooden chairs and a big yellow table. From the ceiling hung a naked lightbulb. On the window ledge stood four potted green plants. They were not wilting. On the yellow table there were various boxes containing beads, fir cones, bits of glass and shells. Laura was given an instant coffee. It was insipid. Paahp did not ask why she had come. And she didn't really know, either. She had told Lars-Eivind there was something she had to do, and he should order pizza only for himself and the children.

"But weren't you going to cook dinner?" he asked, surveying the all-too-pristine kitchen.

"Yes. And so I will, another day," said Laura. "But now there's something I've got to do—and anyway, it's too late to start cooking now."

So here she was, sitting at Paahp's and not knowing what to say. It was a few minutes past nine.

Paahp said: "As you know, I've lost my brother."

Laura nodded.

"He was the last one. Now I have nobody."

Laura nodded again. She said: "I've always wished I had a brother."

"I can be your brother," said Paahp. "Then it won't be so quiet."

"I don't think so," said Laura. "I'm not much of a sister."

Paahp bent over his boxes and selected a big red bead. He placed it in her hand.

"To my sister," he said.

And then there was a knock. Laura could hear voices outside the house. There was another knock. A voice called: "OPEN UP, PAAHP!"

Paahp looked at Laura.

"More visitors," he said.

"Yes, but I don't think you should open the door to them," she said.

"Why not?"

Laura moved her chair to the other side of the table and sat down beside him.

Someone out there had clenched his fist and started hammering on the door. She could hear more voices now. "OPEN UP! OPEN UP!"

Paahp sat hunched over the table. He quickly pushed the

boxes away. His back was a thin pillar. His hands were slender. "OPEN UP!"

"Why shouldn't I open the door?" he repeated.

Laura hadn't eaten all day. Paahp's coffee stung her stomach. There was more hammering at the door. "OPEN UP! OPEN UP! OPEN UP!" She put her hand over her mouth. She shook her head. She couldn't hold back the tears. She couldn't hold back any of what was coming out of her. Everything just steamrolled on. She couldn't hold it back. She put her arms around Paahp and her head on his shoulder.

"Don't be afraid," she said.

Paahp didn't move. She couldn't hear his heart beating, but she imagined she could. She visualized Paahp as a big, red, beating heart, one that he had given to her, carefully placed in her hands. The people standing outside the house went on hammering at the door. Sometimes they knocked, sometimes they hammered, now and then they shouted, now and then they jerked the handle up and down although they knew the door was locked. They would give up eventually; they would turn around and go home, their mission unaccomplished. But for now they were pounding and hammering at the door, and it seemed as if it would never end. It was as if they would stand there pounding and hammering forever and she would sit here with her arms around this man forever and it would never end.

She pulled him close to her and whispered again: "Please don't be afraid."

Lars-Eivind and the children knew Laura was going. They had all slept in the same bed, some lying straight, others crossways.

It was early morning and still dark when Laura got into the car and drove the short distance from the Colony to Majorstua. Molly lived in a three-room flat on Schønningsgate. Laura didn't need to ring the bell to tell her to come down. Molly was standing outside, ready and waiting. She had a big red suitcase on the pavement beside her.

Laura had to get out to help her load the suitcase into the car.

"Are you thinking of moving in with the old man?" Laura asked, short of breath, indicating the big suitcase. "Are you going to move to Hammarsö and put some life back into the Hammarsö Pageant?"

Molly laughed.

"As director?"

"Naturally."

Laura started the car.

"I can still remember some of my lines from that summer," Molly said.

She looked out at the road.

"Let's hear them, then," said Laura. "I can't remember any of mine."

"And though the night is falling," said Molly slowly, *"the full moon is bright as day."*

"And what comes next?"

"That's all. That's all I remember."

Laura got on the E6 motorway and drove toward Stockholm.

"We can stop in Örebro," she said. "We can get a good dinner there and spend the night at a very nice hotel, then drive on in the morning."

"Fine," said Molly. "Good idea."

Laura located her mobile phone without taking her eyes off the road. She was a good driver. She rang Erika's number.

"Hello," she said. "We're on our way now. Can you ring Father and tell him we're all coming to Hammarsö?"

She looked at Molly and smiled.

"Tell him all three of us are coming."

III

The Hammarsö Pageant

Molly hop-skips her way along a path through the woods that she's never seen before; it's not really a path, just a thin rut on the ground, and at the end of it the woods open out and there's a little green meadow, and in it stands a crooked wooden hut. Molly knows that if she lies down on the ground a little way from it, behind some scrub or a bush, lies down in the long grass, then no one will be able to see her. She'll be invisible. She can lie here by herself under the sun and eat wild strawberries until she's red all over. That's what she's going to do.

If God happened to open His big black eye and look down on the little island of Hammarsö, He might be surprised that He had ever created such a striking, weather-beaten place and then gone and forgotten it. Admittedly there are places on Earth more striking and weathered than Hammarsö, and Hammarsö is not the only island in the world that God has forgotten. The truth is, every time God went through His creation and called every thing and every place by its proper name and decided whether it was good or bad, Hammarsö was no more than a tiny speck among all the things God had neglected to name. To be forgotten by people is painful enough, but to be forgotten by God is, many say, to live without grace, like staring down into the abyss; but as far as the residents of Hammarsö could tell, God's memory lapse where they were concerned had not resulted in any major catastrophes there. Year after year they had cleared soil and broken stone—tilled, dug, and plowed—and it proved possible to subsist, if only just, as they coped in spite of everything, the men and women going out to sea and hunting seals, some-times returning and sometimes not—and so the history of Ham-marsö could be that of virtually any stubborn little island in the world. Starvation and toil and storms and children crying and death and drowning, yes, all that, but no more of it than could be expected of any spit of barren land in the sea. The residents—who grew ever fewer as subsequent generations gradually moved to the mainland—lived on, reconciling themselves to the long winters, the inhospitable heath reminiscent of the African savannah, the pale lakes, and the silent white cows with their wide, bleak gazes; to the music upon the waters, beautiful yet unbearable; to stories of the dead who could find no rest and haunted old kitchens, the pigsty, the lilac hedge, or the space under the spiral staircase, frightening the wits out of little children and dogs; they lived on and reconciled themselves (at least in part) to a God who had forgotten them. *Dear God,* their evening prayers ran, *who reigns over Sweden, Norway, Denmark, and large parts of Hammarsö, bless our children and let many great ships loaded with gold run aground here that we might live happily all the days of our lives.* The residents of Hammarsö had their friends and their ene-mies and it had always been that way. They could boast a murderer or two, and the murders were described in graphic detail by those who could still remember them; and there'd always been madmen, there was always somebody who would set fire to a barn, or engage in bestial acts with sheep or spread lies about other people, and there was always somebody who didn't get enough at home and chased things in skirts; there was Big Dick himself, and Big Dick's son and grandson, these things ran in families, they said on Hammarsö. But apart from a few minor things like that, the people of Hammarsö had lived peaceably with one another whether as friends or as ene-mies. It was only the tourists to whom they couldn't reconcile them-selves. Not that they complained. The tourists, who started coming in the late fifties and spread like weeds or poisonous algae, proved profitable; they bought food in the shop, hot dogs and newspapers at the kiosk, and sheepskin slippers and landscape paintings at the community center's summer craft fair; but as for their being friends or even considered worthy of enmity—never!

If God ever did catch a glimpse of Hammarsö, He would most definitely be astonished by the scenery, the people, and everything He had created and forgotten. Perhaps He would catch sight of the little girl squatting down to pick wild strawberries, threading the berries on a stalk of straw to make herself a necklace of red pearls. She puts the chain of berries down between some stones in the tall grass in the meadow above her daddy's house and forgets it. She's going to do something else now. Perhaps someone's calling her or perhaps she's going to take a dip in the sea while nobody is looking. One can only imagine the girl's pleasant surprise when she awakes the next morning and remembers her treasure lying hidden in the grass, waiting for her to come and adorn herself with it, or to eat it up and turn herself red all over. God would raise His huge, heavy fist and rub His great black eye so He could view all this very clearly, and then He would see not only the little girl with the wild strawberries; He would see children playing on the beach, building peculiar things out of stones and objects washed up by the sea; He would see an old widower sitting alone at his kitchen table, and two girls, each with a dripping ice-cream cone, on their way home from the shop; He would see a gaudy cockerel in the middle of the main road—the road that winds its way from the ferry terminal in the north to the sandy beach and summer cottages in the south—and a perspiring family of mainlanders cranking down the window of their Volvo to shout at the cockerel to get out of the way; He would see a dying lamb under a tree, rejected by the flock because its mother wants nothing to do with her offspring and the farmwife has decided the little wretch is not to be raised on the bottle—that's the way it is, she says, and nature must take its course; He would see vivid red poppies on a heath and a spindly boy running and running through the pine forest with a procession of clamoring children after him; He would see a crooked, hidden hut on a patch of heath, and He would see a man donning a long white fake beard and doing his best to declaim something to his wife, but the words he utters are mere nonsense and not even God can understand what he is saying. All this God would see if He looked down for a moment at this little splinter of forgotten things. He would look at it all and tell Himself, That's the way it is, I created this and everything has a name, this island is a place on Earth and these people exist now.

Palle Quist (known among the children of Hammarsö as Emily and Jan's dad) was the brains behind the locally renowned Hammarsö Pageant. Every year from 1971 to 1979 he wrote a brand-new full-length revue, which after a hectic period of rehearsals with amateur actors and extras was performed at the community center at the end of July, before the summer visitors packed their cars and left. Palle Quist was not a writer by profession, but he had published two novellas in the 1960s. One was ninety pages long, the other eighty, and then his "creative vein ran dry," as he put it in an interview for the local paper in 1979. In the sixties he divorced his first wife, Magdalena, the mother of his then two-year-old daughter, Emily. In the seventies he remarried and had another child, a son, Jan, and was also appointed to a minor position in Olof Palme's first government. "Once a writer of incomprehensible novellas and active member of the Communist Party—now a loyal Social Democrat with a Volvo, a family, and a dog—he has rediscovered his creative gifts on Hammarsö," the newspaper squib ran. What the journalist failed to mention was that Palle Quist had twice—in 1976 and 1977—attempted to write plays with political overtones. The indirect but nonetheless malicious portrayal of Prime Minister Thorbjörn Fälldin in the play *Sweden, My Homeland* upset a few members of the audience, but to be perfectly honest it was the spiteful royal palace parody that made many get up and walk out. Palle Quist swore he had not had Carl Gustaf and his bride Silvia in mind when he wrote the scene. On the contrary: he worshipped Silvia!

The year before, he tried his hand at a play about nuclear power and its dangers. It was entitled *P!P!P! Plutonium,* and the review in the local paper was lukewarm. Much was made of the fact that nobody knew what *P!P!P!* stood for. Was it a secret message? Or did *P!P!P!* simply stand for the word *plutonium?* In that case it was utterly superfluous and merely proved the playwright was trying too hard to impress, thought the reviewer, a twenty-two-year-old on summer holiday from Örebro who did not bother making any reference whatsoever to the plot, the overall message, the acting, direction, or stage design. This hurt Palle Quist, who had hoped by *P!P!P! Plutonium* to mobilize the younger generation in particular. In the late seventies, Palle Quist took the decision to avoid all controversial political subjects and, as appropriate for Hammarsö, concentrate on writing spectacles inspired by old ballads, classic drama, music halls, and folk tales.

Palle Quist shared the director's chair with Isak. The newly written pieces were produced jointly by these two gentlemen, with general meetings twice a week at which everybody who was involved in any way could make suggestions, whether about the script, the direction, or the scenery. Palle Quist thought on principle that a non-hierarchical organizational system was the only way to live and work together, but the truth was, he hated nonhierarchical organizations. He hated the general meetings because the proposed changes to the script and direction always led to the trivialization and intellectual dilution of his vision.

All residents and summer visitors who wanted to try their hand

at acting and were on hand those three weeks of July were welcome
to join in. This applied in 1979 as in all other years. The only condition was, as ever, that they register their interest by the start of May,
the tenth at the latest—either by letter or by telephone to Palle Quist.

The demanding work of writing began as early as June. The
players were expected at every rehearsal in Linda and Karl-Owe
Blum's garage and at every general meeting. Absence resulting
from, say, nice beach weather could lead to your being written out of
the play without notice.

In the summer of 1979, Isak asked to be excused from the rigors
of co-direction; he wanted to try his hand as a performer, he said.
Palle Quist immediately agreed, and sat down at his typewriter to
write the tailor-made part of Wise Old Man, an omniscient narrator
or prophet, a part with which Isak was content, though he admitted
privately to Rosa that he had misgivings about the long, rhyming
poem that concluded the play, about the longing of the dead to come
back to life. That year's Hammarsö Pageant—a tribute to the natural world and the people, history, and rich storytelling tradition of
the island—was Palle Quist's most ambitious piece of theater to date.

The reason Palle was so keen to accommodate Isak's wish to act
rather than direct was that Isak had as director displayed certain
tyrannical tendencies toward the ensemble. The year before, he had
criticized one crucial scene in Palle Quist's script, a scene with which
Palle Quist himself was particularly pleased. Isak thought the scene
sentimental and lacking originality and he, as one of those artisti-
cally responsible, could not defend it. Later the same day, he told off
the Hammarsö Pageant's faithful leading lady, Ann-Marie Krok
(Marion's grandmother), for not remembering her lines; he even
managed to cast doubt on Ann-Marie Krok's suitability as Queen of
the Elves.

It was basically the same cast that took to the stage each year, and
by degrees the Hammarsö Pageant became as much of a fixture as
the Hammarsö Open Tennis Championship and the annual community sing-along in the living room of Caroline and Bosse Althof

(Pär's aunt and uncle). In 1978, the pageant had finally received good reviews in the local paper, and Palle Quist was therefore feeling himself under such pressure to win favor again that the whole project almost came to nothing.

In the summer of 1979 the rehearsals once again lasted twenty-one days, and as usual they planned three public performances: the dress rehearsal, the premiere, and the closing night.

Ragnar is running through the forest. Ragnar is faster than all the others. They don't know where he hides. They know nothing about this island. They come here every summer with their parents; they come here to hate him and they know nothing. NOTHING! Marion is the worst. Marion is a whore. Psycho boy, she shouts whenever she sees him, but she's the psycho. It's Marion and her whole gang who are psycho. He can hear them, a long way behind him. He can hear them shouting at him. He can hear his own breathing and his own pounding feet, then suddenly he can't even hear the pounding. Only the breathing. He goes swiftly, almost as if he isn't touching the ground. He's out of breath, but he's still got something in reserve. He hasn't got a stitch. He's faster than them. Marion has roped in more of the gang this summer; she's got some of the boys as well. Before, Ragnar used to hang out with the boys who are running after him now. Ragnar showed them the island and everything you could do there (except the hut!), and he stole a few dregs of whiskey and vodka and gin from his mother's liquor cabinet and mixed them all up in a Pommac bottle and like a brother shared it with them all. Now the boys all preferred the idea of fucking Marion, and if they didn't manage to fuck Marion they would have Frida or Emily instead. He had always run faster than them. He knows Fabian, Olle, and Pär are running after him, running and running, along with Marion, Frida, and Emily. Erika hates Marion. When Ragnar and Erika were younger, they planned to creep into her room one night and cut off all her long black hair while she was asleep. Pär has grown gigantic and hairy since last summer, big and hairy and muscular. I'M FASTER THAN ANY OF YOU! Ragnar turns round. He stops for a moment and catches his breath; he shouts: FUCK OFF! FUCK OFF! LEAVE ME ALONE! His voice carries. They don't dare touch him. Marion, who now has Pär as her boyfriend, says she's going to rip off all his clothes and force Jocke Junior to give him one up the ass, or she's going to stick her grandma's knitting needle up his dick, or maybe one of the girls will sit on the lump between his eyebrows and rub her pussy on it. YOU'RE SO FUCKING UGLY, RAGNAR!

In the crooked hut in the woods, which he built himself and repairs and extends every year, hangs a mirror. He has a birthmark between his eyebrows, but Erika leans over him and kisses him, first on the mouth, then on the eyes. He isn't always ugly. It depends on the light; it depends on the faces he makes and what he's wearing. In the checked sun hat from London and a size XXL T-shirt, he looks kind of handsome. The birthmark doesn't show then. If he sees himself through Marion's eyes, he's deformed, a mongol, a fucking monster; but if he sees himself through Erika's eyes, he's none of those things.

The face in the mirror, if he concentrates all his energy into his eyes, looks okay in a rugged sort of way. In a city like London people would leave him alone. Or New York. He doesn't belong here. He hates Sweden. He hates all the damned Social Democrats and damned social workers. He stares at himself. *You talking to me? You talking to me? You talking to me?* They can't find him in the hut, and the summer holidays on Hammarsö are not so very long, and after the holidays he and his mother go back to Stockholm, where there are more places to hide. In parks and cinemas and on a bench under a streetlight, where nobody else sits and which he calls his own. He wants to sit on that bench with Erika one day. Erika lives in Oslo. One day he'll go to Oslo. But life is no better in Norway; it's the same shit there. Maybe they could run away to Los Angeles or even farther, to Sydney or Hong Kong. In Stockholm the bastards aren't called Marion and Emily and Frida and Pär and Fabian and Olle; they have other names there. But they're out to get him, whatever they're called. Ragnar makes another face. *You talking to me?*

Once, many years ago, before he got to know Erika, he and Marion had been best friends. Going out together, even. Eight years old and they were a couple. He's almost forgotten it; it was so long ago.

"I don't believe you," says Erika. "You and Marion?"

Erika is often with him in the hut. She brings cinnamon buns and milk and O'boy and sometimes a drop of wine she's managed to get her hands on without Rosa and Isak's noticing.

"It's true. We walked along the beach, hand in hand, and said we were going out together."

Erika turns to him.

"Why does she hate you now?"

Ragnar doesn't answer. Most of all he wants to lie still on the mattress with Erika and not say anything, or at least not talk about Marion and the others. It means nothing.

"It means nothing," he says.

It's awful, this: counting the days until he and his mother will have to leave Hammarsö and go back home to Stockholm, away from those bastards. It's true, he prefers the bastards in Stockholm to the bastards on Hammarsö. Marion isn't in Stockholm. That's to say, she is in Stockholm, but not in his Stockholm. They live in two different cities. Just as they live on two different islands here. Nobody knows Ragnar's Hammarsö, except perhaps Erika, a little. And nobody knows Ragnar's Stockholm.

Once, last winter, he ran into Marion in town, outside Rigoletto on Kungsgatan. They nodded to each other as if they were perfectly normal acquaintances. She had a cold and looked washed-out, and wore a stupid hat pulled down over her ears and a quilted jacket buttoned right up to her chin. He couldn't see her long black hair. He would never admit, even under torture, that he thinks Marion is beautiful, and that day on Kungsgatan she wasn't beautiful or even cute, just a very ordinary girl in a stupid hat. In his Stockholm there is Puggen, and Puggen is grown up. Puggen and Ragnar are friends. It's awful! The problem with counting the days until he leaves Hammarsö is that he'll also be counting the days until he leaves Erika. When he was little, he counted the days to Christmas and his birthday and even his name day (as if there were anything to celebrate if your name was Ragnar!) because his mother would always give him a present. But not even a lunatic counts the days until he's going to be plunged into acid or leave the person he loves. Ragnar can't be bothered counting the days to his birthday anymore.

Ragnar and Erika have the same birthday.

This year they're going to be fourteen. And when that day comes, there will only be three days to go until the opening night of the Hammarsö Pageant and six days to go until he and his mother return to Stockholm. Six days. That's not even a week. Six days, however you look at it, is an unbearably short time.

Ragnar studies his face in the mirror. *Then who the hell else are you talking to?* One day he's going to have an operation to remove the birthmark between his eyes, and then he'll come to Hammarsö and everyone will gasp. SHIT, IS THAT RAGNAR? they'll say. Because not only has he got rid of that goddamned mark, not only has he got a smooth, tanned forehead, but he's also grown; he's taller and stronger than Pär and all those total losers. And he'll grab Marion's black hair and drag her along the road after him. He winks at himself and shoots with his index fingers from his hips, a pistol in each hand.

The dress is blue. Molly has got other dresses, too, but she likes wearing the blue one best. Molly's mother has washed the dress in the washing machine many times, wearing the fabric very thin. Whenever Molly wakes up in the night, she heads for her mother, who is asleep in bed in the next room. She curls up in her mother's big bed, beside her mother's warm body, and folds herself deeper and deeper into her mother's long arms.

The reason Molly doesn't want to sleep in her own bed at night is that there is a bear in her room, in the wall.

In summer it's Rosa who washes the blue dress in the washing machine. Sleeping in Rosa's bed at night isn't allowed, because Isak sleeps there. If Molly tries—creeps quietly into Rosa's room and climbs into Rosa's bed—Isak wakes up and starts bellowing.

Laura's the only one who doesn't mind hearing about the bear in the wall.

Laura says: "You can sleep with me, in my bed."

Molly nods and looks down at the floor. She has two sisters

called Erika and Laura. They are sisters for the summer and only then.

Laura says: "I've got nails as sharp as claws and I can gouge his eyes out, and I've got teeth as sharp as spears and I can bite his neck and make the blood spurt out."

Laura isn't big and round and soft like Molly's mother, but spindly and sharp-edged, just like her bed. Laura's bed isn't meant for two girls. The girls are meant to stay in their own beds and sleep all night. That's what Rosa says. When Molly wakes up in the night and is afraid of the bear, Laura whispers in her ear that she will slaughter the bear with one of her knives and then skin it. She'll sell the pelt in the shop and make lots of money that she won't share with anybody, not even Molly. Laura wants to keep all the money for herself.

"It's my bear," says Molly.

"But I'm the one killing it," says Laura.

Lastly she'll boil up the bear to make soup, and serve it to Isak, who eats that sort of thing.

"He never does!" says Molly, unsure.

It is dark; the night is long. The grandfather clock in the living room strikes three. Laura says Molly must sleep, but not rest her head on Laura's arm, because that hurts. Laura sings Molly's song:

> *Dance to your daddy*
> *My little lassie*
> *Dance to your daddy*
> *My little one*
> *You shall have a fishie*
> *In a little dishie*
> *You shall have a fishie*
> *When the boat comes in*

When Rosa has washed the blue dress, she hangs it, still dripping, on white rails in a hot cupboard in the laundry room. Molly's mother hasn't got a laundry room. Only Rosa has a laundry room. In the laundry room Rosa washes Isak's socks, shirts, and trousers, and then she hangs them up on white rails in the hot cupboard. Every day there are socks, shirts, and trousers in the hot cupboard, and sometimes the blue dress is hanging there, too, among Isak's clothes, on white rails.

You're not allowed into the laundry room and you're not allowed to open the door to the hot cupboard and you're not allowed to sit in the hot cupboard to get warm after you've been swimming in the cold sea. You could die if you do that. If the door slams shut, say, and you can't get it open again. But it's nice and cozy, crawling in under Isak's damp trouser legs, sitting there to get warm, with Laura. When Erika comes into the laundry room, it's nearly always to rinse out her bikini in cold water, not because she wants to sit in the cupboard. Erika's too big to sit in the cupboard.

On the drying cupboard in the laundry room, Isak has put up a notice, and the notice says: THIS DRYING CUPBOARD IS NOT TO BE USED BY CHILDREN AFTER SWIMMING! ANYONE WHO BREAKS THIS RULE WILL BE PUNISHED WITHOUT MERCY! It is written in thick red felt-tip pen, and underneath Isak has drawn a bear with two crooked horns on its head.

Laura reads the notice for Molly. She says the drawing isn't a bear, it's a devil.

Erika is at the sink, rinsing out her bikini. She rolls her eyes. She can't generally be bothered to play with Laura and Molly. Sometimes Rosa offers five kronor to whichever big sister will mind Molly while she goes to the mainland or gets on with housework. Erika hasn't got time. Erika's seeing Marion or Ragnar or going to the shop for an ice cream or something. Laura says she hasn't really got time, either, but she needs the money.

Molly studies her father's drawing and says she doesn't think it's a devil. She says this although she has no idea what a devil is.

"It's a bear," says Molly.

"It's a devil," says Laura.

"It's a bear," says Molly.

"Bears don't have horns on their heads," says Laura, pointing to the horns.

"Those aren't horns—they're teeth," says Molly.

"Nobody has teeth on their head, silly."

"Oh yes they do!" says Molly.

"Well, bears don't. I've never seen a bear with teeth on its head."

Molly loses her temper. "But I have!"

Erika takes Laura's arm and tells her to stop it. Laura says Erika isn't the babysitter. Erika can mind her own business while Laura does her babysitting job.

Erika shrugs.

Laura points at the picture again and says to Molly: "It's a devil with horns."

"They're teeth! They're teeth!" screeches Molly.

She sits down on the floor and beats the drying cupboard with her fists.

Erika wrings out her bikini and leaves.

Laura says: "I know Daddy a bit better than you do, so I know the sort of pictures he draws."

She jabs her index finger at the drawing.

"And that is not a bear."

"I couldn't care less about you. It's a bear, and all bears have teeth on their head!"

Day after day of sunshine. Hot in the air, hot in the sea, hot in the grass. It's almost too hot to have her blue dress on. It's best to be virtually bare. Just panties and undershirt. Or a bikini. It's Molly's birthday soon. She's going to be five. She wants a bikini for her birthday.

Molly knows it's possible to swim yet at the same time not to be able to swim. It's hard to explain to Rosa and Isak. They say either you can swim or you can't. They say when it comes to swimming, there are no two ways about it. They say on no account are you allowed into the sea when you're only four years and fifty-one weeks old and not sure whether you can swim. Isak grips her in his arms and lifts her high in the air and spins her around.

"You do as I say! Otherwise I'll never put you back down again."

Isak calls her a blue flower. It's not because she is a flower, but because she has a favorite dress that is blue.

Molly's tummy and head feel all light and wobbly, and Molly laughs out loud and Isak spins her even faster.

Molly knows Isak doesn't understand what she means. He hardly ever does. He's a giant and she's a blue flower. The most important thing is that she knows she can swim and yet not be able to swim. That's why Molly goes into the water only when nobody's looking. She goes down to the beach. She takes off her dress, folds it up neatly, and puts it on a rock. She lies down in the water, on the stony bottom, and lets the waves wash over her.

It's the summer of 1979, the hottest summer since 1874. It said so in the newspaper. It's July. Molly can count to ten. She can count to a hundred and yet she can't. In Molly's room hangs a calendar with pictures of kittens. Every evening, Molly crosses a day off the calendar. She draws a big red X over the day that's just gone and will never come back, maybe only in Heaven, where everything happens over and over again. That's what Isak says, at least.

Putting X's on the calendar is one way to be sure time is going by. The other way is to sit under the grandfather clock in the living room and watch every time the big hand moves, which it does once a minute.

When the big children go swimming, Molly stands on the beach looking on, shouting HOY HOY HOY. Erika and Laura and Ragnar and Marion and the others splash and play and have fun and wave to her.

Whenever one of the children vanishes underwater—it happens

sometimes; a wave comes and the child vanishes into the wave—
Molly stretches her hands up to the sky and shouts HOY HOY HOY
so loud that the child pops up again, every bit as alive as before.

In four weeks, which is time that goes by, Molly's mother will wash
her dress and hang it on a string outside the bedroom window in the
flat on the third floor. Molly's mother has no laundry room, and she
has no drying cupboard, either. Molly lives with her mother in a flat
in Oslo. Molly doesn't live on Hammarsö.

Laura has told her that one day a long time ago, when Molly was
a baby, she sat in her carriage outside Isak's door and screamed and
screamed until Rosa and Isak had no choice but to open the door and
bring her inside with them. Molly's mother tells her on the telephone
that that is not what happened.

"You're as welcome on Hammarsö as your half sisters," her
mother says. "Next time Laura says anything like that, you tell her to
stop talking rubbish."

One day, Molly sits by herself on the floor in front of Isak's grandfather clock, determined to sit there until it's time for her to go back
home to Oslo. Or at least until it's her birthday. She sits on the floor
for ages. Time goes slowly when you watch it. As she is sitting there,
a bird flies into the living room. There are three windows in Isak's
living room and only one of them is open, and the bird flies in
through the open window. The bird is small and gray and buzzes
around the room like a wasp, only worse because it's bigger than a
wasp. And suddenly it bashes its head against one of the closed windows. THUMP! Molly gets up from the floor and runs toward the
bird, cupping her hand.

"Come here, little bird! Come here!"

But the bird doesn't hear her; it launches itself at the closed window again. THUMP! And another THUMP! Then it does a poo.
White bird poo runs down the closed window. The bird whirls past
her and Molly falls to her knees.

She shuts her eyes tightly, covers her ears and whispers: "Help! Help! Help!"

The bird flies up toward the ceiling and perches on top of Isak's writing desk. It isn't moving now. Molly is still on her knees on the floor, peeking at it through splayed fingers. It's all gone quiet now; all she can hear is the tick of the grandfather clock. She decides that if she squeezes her eyes shut and counts to ten, it will fly away without crashing into anything. She squeezes her eyes shut.

"One—two—three—four—five—six—seven—eight—nine—ten."

She opens her eyes.

The bird is still there.

A living gray blob on top of the writing desk.

She wishes everything could be back to normal so she could sit down and watch time passing and be bored again. But nothing can be normal while the bird is inside.

Molly gets up slowly, goes cautiously over to the windows, and opens first one, then the other.

"Look over here, little bird! Look over here! Out you go!"

The bird looks at her. She's not sure it can see her, but it seems to be looking at her. She doesn't want it to start flying again, buzzing wildly from wall to wall and bashing its head against the closed window and pooing. But she doesn't want it just perched up there on the writing desk, quietly looking at her, either. She doesn't want it to be so scared, at least not while she's the only one who knows it's so scared. Surely it could fly off and be scared somewhere else, where she wouldn't have to look after it. No one expects Molly to look after all the birds in the whole world. It could be birds that have gotten their wings covered in oil and can't fly and lie dying on the beach; that happens all the time. It's sad, but not so terribly sad. It could be birds that get eaten by other birds or fly into other people's living rooms or get stuck in the branch of a tree. They are not Molly's problem. If Isak or Rosa or Erika or Laura had come into the living room, she would have been able to run away and then this bird wouldn't have been her problem, either. But as things stand, it is.

Molly and the bird are alone together. Suddenly it takes off and flies straight at her, hurtling toward her. She raises her arms to shield her face and screams, shutting her eyes tightly.

It's that noise again. THUMP!

"Please! Fly away! Fly away!"

Molly is crying now.

And then suddenly: nothing. Complete quiet. She looks up at the writing desk. It's not there. She looks around. The bird has gone. It isn't here any longer. It has flown out one of the open windows, and it was Molly who opened them.

Molly saved the bird and now it has gone.

It no longer exists.

Molly hop-skips through the woods, in and out among the trees. She's got new red sandals. When it's as hot as it is now, it's better to have sandals. The problem is, your toes stick out, and if someone's got scissors that are sharp enough, they can chop off the whole lot. Every single toe. That's what Laura says. Not that Laura (who's got some sharp scissors like that) would chop off her little sister's toes, when she was asleep, say, and not even wearing sandals, but there are certainly other people who might do it. Ragnar, for example, and Ragnar also has a horned head. Not two horns like in Isak's drawing. But one.

One night when Molly was lying in Laura's narrow bed, Laura switched on the bedside light and whispered: "If you look carefully at Ragnar, you can see he's got a brown lump on his forehead. Once, that was a big horn, but Isak did an operation and cut most of it off."

"I don't believe you."

"It's true," said Laura.

"And then what?"

"When Ragnar's mum was having him, it nearly went horribly wrong. They couldn't get him out of her because of the horn."

Laura clasped her throat and made a dreadful noise, then the blue in her eyes vanished upward and her eyeballs were totally white.

"And then?" said Molly.

"And then," said Laura, "when Ragnar was a year old and had learned to walk, his mum took his hand and went with him to Isak and asked him to do the operation. But although Isak's a doctor, he couldn't get rid of it all."

Molly hop-skips in and out between the trees in the woods. The bikini she has asked for as a birthday present will have polka dots, just like Erika's, and the cake Rosa makes will be decorated with wild strawberries—and Erika and Laura will pick them. As for Molly, she will sit on a red cushion and eat chocolate pudding all day. Isak says so.

If Molly isn't at home when Rosa starts cooking dinner, which she does at half past four—an hour and a half before the meal is served—her sisters have to go and look for her. Sometimes they can see her a long way off, hidden behind a tree, because Molly is very good at hiding but also not very good. Sometimes they can't see her. Sometimes she doesn't answer when they call. She's usually wearing the blue dress, so that's what they hope to catch a glimpse of. The dress is completely washed-out and only just covers her bottom. This summer, Molly is allowed to take part in the Hammarsö Pageant. You really have to be six to take part. But Isak says Molly can be in it even though she's only four years and fifty-one weeks old. Rosa is going to make her a dress of purple velvet and she will stand in the middle of the stage and sing, and when she has finished singing she will do a low curtsey to the audience and say:

> *And now that night is falling*
> *The full moon is bright as day*
> *We are halfway between light and darkness*
> *And halfway through our play.*

Erika can hear Laura calling her, but she pretends not to. She is sitting on her unmade bed, reading a letter from Ragnar. There's something he wants to tell her face-to-face, he writes. *Meet me in the hut!* It is taking some time to read the letter, because he has written the whole thing in the secret language they used to speak when they were younger. There was music on the radio—the Jam, the Stranglers, the Boomtown Rats—but they have interrupted the music to bring news of the terrorist attacks at Spanish beach resorts. Erika looks up from her letter for a moment, listens, and turns back to the letter . . . *Three Finns and one Swede have been killed . . . Tourists are bathing in their own blood on the Costa del Sol.*

"Erika!" Laura calls from the kitchen.

Erika doesn't answer.

"Where are you?" calls Laura.

Erika burrows under the quilt and puts the pillow over her head. Other voices.

"Erika! Erika!" calls Rosa.

And then her little sister's high voice.

"Erika, you've got to come right now!" Molly calls.

Erika presses the pillow down harder over her head and waits for someone to open her door and find her. (Open her door without knocking! Nobody ever bothers to knock, in spite of the sign DO NOT ENTER WITHOUT KNOCKING! Isak is the only one who ever knocks.)

"Erika!" calls Laura.

"Erika! Erika!" shrieks Molly.

"Erika, can you come at once! We need you!" calls Rosa.

Erika throws aside the quilt. It's too warm lying like that. Tonight she's going to sleep naked with just the quilt cover and put the quilt under the bed. Rosa doesn't like you taking your quilt out. She thinks you should keep it on even when it's hot, for some unknown reason. But this is the hottest summer since 1874, and even Rosa, admittedly against her better judgment, lets you open enough windows to create a draft in the house. Rosa usually can't imagine anything more threatening to her family's well-being than a draft in the house.

What the local paper claims about its being the hottest summer since 1874, Isak says can't possibly be true. Isak says there's no need to go any further back than 1971 to find the same prolonged high summer temperatures.

"Erika, you've got to come!" calls Laura.

"Come on, Erika, you've got to come and help!" calls Rosa.

"ERIKA!" shrieks Molly.

Erika sits stock-still in bed, listening to the voices outside, voices from the living room, voices from somewhere out on the veranda. Then a quiet knock comes at the door.

"Erika," says Isak, and she visualizes him bending his great head to the door so she can hear what he is saying.

"We need you now. You've got to sing. Can you open the door?"

Erika gets off the bed and drags herself across the floor. Over her bikini bottoms she's wearing a fitted white shirt that she thinks looks good against her brown skin. Her hair is long and tangled; it comes down below her shoulders now. Laura's hair is longer.

Erika opens the door, leans against the door frame, and looks at her father. He smiles when he sees her. She smiles back.

Erika remembers she has been chewing gum and quickly swallows it before opening her mouth to speak. Isak doesn't like girls chewing gum. He says it's unbecoming.

"What can I do for you?" she says.

"A funeral," says Isak.

"Who's died?"

"A sparrow," Isak says.

He smiles again.

"Molly's been so sad ever since she found it; we really didn't mean for her to find it."

"Birds die, and five-year-olds find them and cry," says Erika.

"She's been looking forward to the funeral," her father says. "I think it was Laura's idea."

Isak holds out a little wooden cross.

"I made this."

"All right, all right," says Erika with a shrug. "I'm coming."

Ragnar's hut is equipped so he can survive almost anything except an atom bomb or a nuclear explosion in the east. When he was smaller, he was scared of all that stuff, plutonium and explosions and bombs, and to comfort him his mother said Sweden would never be hit by an atom bomb and wiped off the face of the Earth, because Sweden was neutral and campaigned for peace on Earth. Ragnar knew better: nobody escaped the atom bomb. Yet he still tried to imagine a completely ordinary Sweden in a world that was otherwise entirely blotted out. The thought was not particularly edifying. Ragnar doesn't brood about the atom bomb so much anymore; he can't do anything to defend himself against it, after all, and if there's war that may be just as well. Total Annihilation! Global Death! Ragnar thinks about other dangers (because on Hammarsö, nobody's neutral—it's perpetual war), so the hut is conceived not just as a place to be, with Erika, for example, but also as a fortress not unlike the old ruined forts on the eastern side of the island. Except his fortress is built of wood, not stone. One day, maybe next summer, he's going to build a fortress of stone. Work is already in progress. In the evenings he collects big stones on the beach, loads them into a supermarket cart he stole from the shop, hauls them through branches and brush to the hut in the woods, and stores them either under his camp bed or outside, all around the clearing.

The hut's main advantage is its location. It stands in a little patch of open heath beyond a virtually impenetrable forest of pine trees, dense juniper bushes, briar roses, and dark green, overgrown deciduous trees. Nobody uses this path, nobody ventures to this part of the forest. And why should they, when there are so many other, prettier woodland paths to take, inland to the open, flowering heathlands, or down to the sea? They would only scratch themselves on the thorns, stumble and fall in the brushwood and get bitten by ticks and horseflies and other disgusting creepy-crawlies. It's the perfect hiding place, and he has everything he needs: a stock of tinned food that, as long as he doesn't quite eat his fill every day (actually, the feeling of fullness only comes half an hour after you've eaten, he read somewhere), should last him three weeks. He has thirty liters of water, forty-seven bottles of Coca-Cola, and ten bottles of Pommac (which is the worst-tasting soda in the world, here intended for situations when everything else has been drunk and all hope is gone). He has five collectors' ring binders of *The Phantom* and *Superman,* complete sets. He has two working flashlights, a good tape player he got from his mother on his birthday, and his favorite cassette tape of the band Television. He has a box full of new batteries and another of potato chips and cigarettes and matches. On one wall there's a film poster of Robert de Niro as Travis Bickle, signed by Puggen—that's a birthday present from last year, too. He has a sleeping bag, an extra blanket, and a threadbare brown teddy he hides behind the stones under the camp bed whenever Erika comes to see him. He has plates, cutlery, glasses, and cups for two, and a flower-patterned oilcloth for the camping table.

Ragnar has a part in this year's Hammarsö Pageant. It wasn't his idea; he thinks the whole thing is pointless. But his mother went to Isak and said this time he'd better make sure her boy had a part for once.

Ragnar initially had no idea what Isak meant when he rang one evening and said they were looking for an angel for this year's production and hoped he might oblige.

"Why me?" asked Ragnar.

"Because it would be fun," answered Isak. He was playing Wise Old Man, he added.

At that Ragnar started laughing.

Isak also said that his daughters were all playing wood sprites; even Molly had a part this year.

"And Erika?" asked Ragnar.

"What about Erika?" said Isak.

"Is Erika in it, too?"

Isak did not mention to Ragnar that his mother had come to him, begging him to include her boy in the play. It was Erika who told him about it a few weeks later. Ragnar had said he couldn't understand why he'd been offered a part all of a sudden. Isak calling him, being all nice and welcoming. He didn't get it. And so Erika told him the truth, that Ann-Kristin had come to see Isak, begging on his behalf.

He could visualize the scene: his mother at Isak's door—ugly and shabby and old. And Isak not even inviting her in for a cup of coffee. TO HELL WITH HIM.

Ragnar turns up for every single rehearsal in the garage. They are all there, dressed as wood sprites and angels and old peasant women. Marion, Frida, Emily, Pär, Fabian, and Olle. Erika makes faces at him when nobody's looking, and sometimes takes his hand and gives it a squeeze. Erika smiles when he says his lines, a verse that starts with the words *I am an angel from the north.*

Marion doesn't say much. She chews gum and reads her lines. It's just ten days to the opening night in the community center. Palle Quist shouts at the pianist, who has overslept for the fourth rehearsal in a row. Isak Lövenstad, in a fake white beard, can't get through his second monologue. The leading lady, Ann-Marie Krok, is in the early stages of senile dementia (they say) and is confusing this year's with last year's lines. Palle Quist sits down on the floor, puts his head in his hands, and shouts, NO! NO! NO!

Marion runs one hand through her black hair and smiles at him. "Hi, Ragnar."

He looks at her and she doesn't look away. She rolls her eyes and shrugs, to show how idiotically everyone's behaving—Isak, Ann-Marie Krok, Palle Quist.

"See these people?"

He nods. They can see the same things. Ann-Marie Krok starts crying and runs offstage and out of the garage. Palle Quist rushes after her. Marion leans right up close to him and whispers: "That's my grandmother. They all want to be young and beautiful."

Ragnar nods. In a moment of jealous intimacy he thinks he will tell Marion what he is planning. She would understand. She's the only one who would. Not even Erika would support him or understand (Erika has been chosen to sing and is taking the whole play much more seriously then she lets on), but Marion hates this spectacle as much as he does. Ragnar wants to tell her he's thinking of upstaging this whole stupid pageant. Instead of saying his cringe-making angel lines, he's going to read something quite different. He's going to declaim a manifesto. On opening night he's going to appear to them as a real angel! Not a fairy-tale angel in white, but a terrifying angel of death! An angel of truth and darkness!

I reckon that'll make them shit all over themselves sitting there in the community center, he wants to say. But he keeps his mouth shut. He looks at Marion. She runs her hand through her hair again.

She says: "See you, okay?"

She is on her way out, but turns and gives him a smile. She has big, almost black eyes.

"Okay?"

"See you," says Ragnar.

The funeral procession moves slowly down to the sea: first Molly wearing a long black shift, quickly whipped up for her out of some old dress material that Rosa had right at the back of a cupboard; then Laura and Erika side by side, Erika with *Hymns Ancient and Modern* in her right hand; then Isak with the fake white beard, holding the wooden cross high; finally Rosa with a picnic basket of fruit cordial and buns. Laura is pulling a spade along behind her. The dead sparrow lies on a bed of white cotton wool in a shoebox from the Nordiska Kompaniet department store.

Erika has promised her father she will sing at the funeral—she can hardly refuse—but as soon as it's over she's going to run through the woods to Ragnar's hut. She will lie on his bed and wait for him. She misses him. It's all so difficult. She can't tell anyone, can't tell Marion, Frida, or Emily. At the very mention of Ragnar's name, Marion sticks her finger down her throat and says, YUCK! Then Frida and Emily stick their fingers down their throats and say, YUCK! Marion would really like Erika to pair up with Fabian with the thick tongue. *You'd be good together, I just know it, so go on, kiss him!* and Erika does a bit of making out with Fabian, just to keep Marion happy.

The funeral procession draws close to the sea. Molly is holding the shoebox in her hands, carefully. She is not crying now; she is preoccupied with keeping her balance and not tripping over the black shift, which is a little too long. She has insisted on wearing her best shoes, new black patent-leather ones, bought on the mainland. The idea was for her to wear them for the first time on her fifth birthday, and again in the Hammarsö Pageant. After that they were to be packed in tissue paper and put in her suitcase and taken to Oslo. There, Molly's mother would unpack them and put them at the back of the wardrobe in Molly's room to await the next big occasion.

"Best shoes," said Rosa, "are only supposed to be worn on special occasions; they are supposed to hurt and to give you blisters."

Rosa said, too, that the shoes would get scratched and wrecked if Molly wore them on the beach. But Molly cried and said she wanted her new shoes for the funeral, they were black and went with the black shift, and although Rosa said no, and no again, Isak said it would be fine. And it is Isak who makes all final decisions.

Molly has told her sisters to dress up as well. Laura said there was no way she could be bothered to dress up for a rotten dead bird, and that made Molly start screaming.

"Can't you just be nice for once," Erika hissed at her sister. "Can't you? Is that so hard for you?"

Laura shrugged.

Erika put on the costume she was going to wear for the Hammarsö Pageant, which Rosa had just finished making on the sewing machine. It was a thin white cotton dress with lace on the sleeves and a white ribbon belt. Erika wasn't exactly sure what a wood sprite looked like, but you couldn't go wrong with white lace and ribbon, Rosa said.

Anyway, the most important thing is that she's going to sing. Not just now, during the funeral, but in the Hammarsö Pageant. Palle

Quist had asked Erika, Marion, and Frida to audition for the big closing number, and he had chosen Erika.

"You sing like a little angel," Palle Quist said, and Erika looked across at Marion and Frida and knew they would make her pay for those words, for Palle's admiration; she could see it in their eyes, in their sneers. She didn't know exactly how, but they were bound to make her pay. They would make her look stupid or ban her from the rock or force her to walk alone to the shop every day for a week to buy ice creams and Cokes for everybody. Something! Marion couldn't care less about the Hammarsö Pageant; that was what she said: I couldn't care fucking less about the goddamned play; but she had auditioned to sing even so, had made eyes at Palle Quist and tossed back her long black hair. And then he gave the part to Erika.

The beach below Isak's house is long and bleak: nothing but stones and thistles and the occasional defiant yellow beach flower. The stones are four hundred million years old; many of them are entirely flat, as pale and silky smooth as the palms of Molly's hands. It is the hottest of all the hot days, but down on the shoreline the wind is touching everything that can be touched and set in motion— Molly's black shift, Erika's white dress, Isak's fake beard, Rosa's long hair. It must appear a strange procession to anyone happening to see it from a distance. They step or dance or balance across the stones and the sun burns in the sky. Suddenly Isak halts, raises his head, and cries: "Stop! This is it. This is where we shall bury the dead bird!"

Molly hands out felt-tip pens to everyone from the pen set in Rosa's basket. She asks them to write on the shoebox.

"To the bird," says Molly. "And maybe to God."

"Why?" asks Laura, and rolls up her eyes.

"*Because,* silly!" whispers Erika.

"I'll write mine first," says Isak.

Sometimes Erika tells Ragnar she's coming to see him and then gets on her bike and goes to Marion's instead. Sometimes she goes on her bike to see Emily, who is really Marion's best friend, or to see Fabian with the thick tongue. She knows it drives Ragnar crazy when he waits for her in the hut and she doesn't come. He wrote her a letter saying she mustn't tell him she's coming if she's not.

Erika misses him when they haven't seen each other for a while, but when they're together, she just wants to get away.

It's as if Ragnar is always with her. She'll find herself imagining him standing just a few steps away, watching her. Like now, here on the beach. Everything she does, everything she says. After the funeral she's going to run and find him. Then he'll kiss her and undress her. She's often embarrassed by what they do together.

Making out with Fabian now and then doesn't count for anything. His tongue fills her whole mouth, and once it made her feel sick, but she blamed it on something she'd eaten, so then they played Yahtzee and shared a packet of chips instead of kissing. That would never have happened with Ragnar. For a start, being kissed by him doesn't make her feel sick; she moves closer to him and takes his hands and puts them on her breasts, between her legs. She pulls him onto her and feels him lying there on top of her and wants it never to end. But she doesn't want him to take it so seriously. They lie on the camp bed and touch each other's faces, each other's eyes, noses, mouths, cheeks, and Ragnar sometimes says, We're alike, Erika, you and me.

Last time he got out a pocket mirror. They were lying together on the camp bed; she had pulled the blanket up to her chin, suddenly not wanting him to see her breasts. He angled the mirror so both their faces were reflected in it and said:

"You can see it, can't you? We look like brother and sister."

Erika took the mirror from him and threw it under the bed. It didn't break. She said she'd like a Coca-Cola. Or some chewing gum. Or something nice to eat.

Ragnar sometimes says: Don't leave me! And that just makes Erika want to get up and run away from the hut and never go back. She almost hates him then, hates him because she was missing him just before.

. . .

Molly wants everybody to write something on the shoebox. She has written her name in big, sloping letters, like this: *MOLLY*. And now she wants the others to write other things.

"Can't I just write my name, too?" asks Laura when Molly gives her the shoebox.

"No!" says Molly. "You have to write more."

"But you've only written your name," says Laura.

"Yes, but *you* have to write more," declares Molly.

Laura rolls her eyes. "But why? Why must I write more when it's *your* funeral?"

Rosa tugs Laura's plait and tells her to buck up and do as Molly says. A cool wind is blowing across the water; they all lift their heads and shut their eyes, letting the wind stroke their faces. It lasts only a second or two. Molly stands up on tiptoe and stares straight at Laura. The wind rustles the black shift. She says: "You have to write more! Writing your name isn't enough."

Laura takes the shoebox and writes swiftly:

> *Thank you for the world so sweet*
> *Thank you for the food we eat*
> *Thank you for the bird you killed*
> *Let it spurt out blood and gore*
> *Rest in peace, AMEN*

Rosa looks over her daughter's shoulder and says: "Oh, Laura, no!"

Isak bends over the shoebox and reads. His earlobes flush red and he raises his hand to his fake beard as if he wants to tear it off.

"You little brat," he whispers to Laura. "Shall I cut off your fingers now or later?"

Laura eyes her father defiantly.

"But it's true!"

"What is?" he hisses.

Laura shrugs.

"About the bird."

"What does it say?" shouts Molly. "What did Laura write? What did Laura write?"

"Nothing," says Rosa tersely. "Laura hasn't written anything."

"But she's GOT TO!" shouts Molly. "She's GOT TO write something."

Isak pulls himself together, raises a hand, and says:

"Hush, the lot of you. Hush! Quiet! I must ask you all to be quiet now. It's time for us to bury this bird."

"Finally," mutters Erika.

"Come on, Molly," says Isak.

He takes his youngest daughter's hand in his.

"HOY! HOY! HOY!" screams Molly.

"Come on, Molly," he repeats. "We must all be quiet now."

Without meeting Laura's eye, Isak carefully takes the shoebox from her and passes it to Rosa.

"Now you write something," he says to his wife.

"I'll try," says Rosa. "And then we'll have a picnic. I've got lots of nice things in the basket."

Rosa writes: "Little bird, now you are flying to Baby Jesus in Heaven."

Rosa passes the box on to Erika.

Erika writes: "Dear God, bless all the people and birds here on Earth, best wishes, Erika."

Erika passes the box to Isak.

Isak writes: "We went not namelessly away / Our life was to give name."

When Erika catches sight of Ragnar, half hidden behind a tree, she doesn't know how long he has been standing watching them. He is a fair way off, there in the clearing in the trees, where the woods stop being woods and start being beach instead. She doesn't know how long, but she has sensed it, sensed that Ragnar is watching her. Every time she raises a hand or takes a step, it's as if she is doing it for him.

. . .

What do you think of the way I raise my hand? What do you think of the way I move along the beach? Am I beautiful in this white dress with this ribbon belt? Am I, Ragnar?

She raises her hand, partly to wave to him, partly to shade her eyes from the sun. It's that time of the afternoon when the light is at its whitest. Everything is white and glaring. You have to screw your eyes up really tight to see anything at all. Ragnar isn't waving back. It's not her he's looking at. He's looking at Isak. That's hardly surprising, thinks Erika, because Isak does look very odd—at least if you're seeing him from a distance, as Ragnar is. Isak is standing on a rock out in the water with his fake beard fluttering and his arms raised to the sky. He is speaking. It's a kind of sermon.

Erika turns back to Ragnar. He doesn't notice her. She tries to wave, but Ragnar is looking only at Isak. He is standing quite, quite still behind the tree, staring at her father.

Isak is the wicked king from the land of Dofeatovhok who has bewitched the island and everyone who lives there—the people, the sheep, the cows, the trees, the fish. He has an ear as big as the tall windows of the community center. He hears everything. Every sound. The slap of the flounder against the stony seabed. Fir cones opening. Your breathing as you run away through the woods. And everything he hears, he writes down in a book he hides in his house. In the grandfather clock? In the writing desk? Ragnar will defeat him, find the book, burn it, and free the king's daughters. When Isak is dead, they will live in the secret hut in the woods and rule over land and sea themselves. But first, you must tell me everything about him: what he does in the morning, in the afternoon, in the evening, in the night when you all think he's asleep. To kill him, I need to know him as a son would know him.

Erika and Ragnar are almost fourteen now. There is something between them, something serious that must be kept secret. No one must know about it. No one.

Isak stands on the rock out in the water and raises his arms to the sky and says: "Dear God, who reigns over Norway, Sweden, Denmark, and large parts of Hammarsö, take this little bird in Your hand and give it a place in Heaven."

He signals to the others to shift stones and dig a hole. Rosa grabs the spade Laura has put down on the ground and does as Isak says. Rosa is strong; it doesn't take her long. Rosa can do things nobody else can or has the stamina for. Put the chains on the car tires. Make a soufflé. Dig a decently deep grave. Isak climbs down from the rock, wades through the water, and comes back up the beach. When the hole is deep enough, the shoebox is placed inside it. Everybody except Laura helps gather stones and fill in the hole again. Finally, Isak wedges the little wooden cross between the most attractive stones, which have been arranged on top.

"Now we'll all stand in a circle and Erika will sing," he says.

They form a circle. Erika, Isak, Rosa, Laura, and Molly. Erika opens the hymnbook. Just before she starts, she turns to see if Ragnar is still there, behind the tree.

Isak takes her hand and squeezes it. He leans close to her.

"He's not there," he whispers.

Erika looks at her father.

"He's not there," he says again.

"Whisperers are liars," mutters Laura.

"Shhh," says Isak.

"SHHH," shouts Molly. "Now Erika's going to sing for the bird."

Erika lets go of Isak's hand, takes a breath, and sings:

> *Safely, safely gather'd in*
> *Far from sorrow, far from sin;*
> *No more childish griefs or fears*
> *No more sadness, no more tears;*
> *For the life so young and fair*
> *Now hath pass'd from earthly care:*
> *God Himself the soul will keep,*
> *Giving His beloved—sleep.*

Erika knows her voice won't let her down. So she sings as loudly as she can. She wants Ragnar to hear her. He's running through the woods now, through juniper and bramble thickets, along the path that isn't a path but just a thin stripe in the earth, running and running and running until there is scarcely any air left in him. And her voice doesn't let her down.

Marion has a big bright pink beach bag and in it she keeps everything she needs to be Marion. Hairbrush, mirror, lip gloss, lipstick, Coca-Cola, tampons, *True Life Stories, Smash Hits,* contraceptive pills (Marion's fifteen now, so she's reached the age of consent, according to Swedish law), bikini briefs, T-shirt, towel, battery-driven tape player, battery-driven vibrator (or massager, as it's also called) that buzzes noisily when you hold it in your hand, and then her Blondie cassette, which she's played to bits. It's the only one she wants to listen to, and though Erika has cassettes of the Jam and the Boomtown Rats, Marion refuses to play any tapes but her own. Of all Marion's friends, Erika is the most awkward and the one most often punished. She feels unsure of herself among girls. They make her feel little: she isn't one of them; she doesn't toss her hair like they do, doesn't wiggle her hips like they do when they walk. But she has one advantage over Frida and Emily, and that is being the only one who can salvage the Blondie cassette when it gets all tangled up in the tape player, as it often does. Especially when they're lying on the rock, sunbathing. Suddenly it groans and goes quiet and then Erika has to coax out the long, light brown tape that has wound around itself and wind it carefully back into the cassette with the tip of her little finger. This requires technique, plus experience and patience. Marion has none of those things. Every time the music stops playing, she picks up the tape player and shakes it. When that doesn't help, she sighs and gives it to Erika.

"You'll have to fix that," she says, and dives into the water.

Marion wants to listen to "Sunday Girl" all the time, never anything but "Sunday Girl." No one's allowed to borrow Marion's tape player. No one would ask to, anyway. You don't ask Marion if you can borrow her things. Marion borrows things all the time, from Frida and Emily and sometimes from another girl she knows called Eva. But that's different. From Erika, Marion has borrowed a scarf to tie around her waist, a hair clip, and a new white blouse that Erika said her mother bought her before she came to Hammarsö.

This is your birthday present, but you're getting it in advance, which means you WON'T be getting a parcel from me in the post, Elisabet had said as she wrapped the blouse in red tissue paper.

Erika senses it's an honor to be allowed to lend her things to Marion. It makes her the chosen one, the one with priority over the other girls. That's how it is with the scarf. That's how it is with the hair clip. Marion leans close to Erika, rests her head on her shoulder, and says: "You and me, Erika! We're the best, closest, greatest friends in the world!"

Marion's skin is warm. She smells of apple. She has long slim arms you can fold yourself into.

Erika unties the scarf from her waist, loosens the clip from her hair, and gives them both to Marion.

"You're an angel, Erika. Thanks so, so much!"

Marion says she wants to borrow Erika's white blouse to wear for the singing audition with Palle Quist. Erika had really intended to wear it herself. It accentuates her breasts nicely, and she wants

Palle Quist to see that, but when Marion is going through Erika's wardrobe and spots the blouse on its hanger, she exclaims: *I want to try this on!*

It's raining, they can't sunbathe on the rock, and Marion has decided that with Frida and Emily's assistance she will spend the day in Erika's room, throwing out everything no longer worth keeping: clothes, magazines, books, pictures, toys. Erika perches on the edge of the bed and says nothing. That's the rule. She's not allowed to protest or to express any opinion about what is being taken out or jettisoned.

"We're doing it for your own good," says Marion, raking through everything that was hidden in the old toy box under the bed. A teddy bear, a doll, two issues of *Look and Learn,* four Nancy Drew books, and a photograph album with pictures of Isak, Rosa, Erika, Laura, Molly, and Ragnar in it.

"You've got to learn to sort out your stuff and get rid of everything you don't need," Marion says.

Before Marion throws out the album she leafs quickly through it and looks at the photos. She sits on the floor with Frida and Emily. There are not many photos.

One of them shows Isak with a hose in his hand, spraying water. He is making a monster face and clearly trying to scare his daughters, who are running around on the grass among the fruit trees, looking as if they are squealing with delight. Another picture shows Erika and Laura in the long grass in front of Isak's house. It's from the time when they still played together every day. Now Erika is too big to play with Laura. A third picture shows Erika with her father. They are sitting on the stone wall, legs dangling, skinny Erika and enormous Isak. They both have brown top hats on their heads. Their arms are folded and they are beaming at the camera, making roguish faces.

"God, you look really stupid in this picture," says Marion.

Frida and Emily giggle.

Erika giggles, too.

"Yeah, my dad's kind of stupid," says Erika, thinking that he definitely isn't but it's absolutely vital to say he is.

Erika wants to tell them that when she was younger, she and her father used to play a game in which she was Oliver and Isak was Fagin. But Marion has no doubt not read *Oliver Twist* or seen the film, and you can bet she'll say *Pathetic!* or *Mental!* or *Stupid!* whatever Erika says.

There's a picture of a much younger, even spindlier Ragnar in his Niagara Falls T-shirt.

"That's pathetic," says Marion, pushing the album away.

"Psycho boy!" says Frida.

Emily rolls her eyes and turns expectantly to Marion.

"This album clearly has got to go," says Marion.

She picks it up from the floor, holding it between thumb and forefinger as if it is a dead mouse, and thrusts it down into the garbage bag.

This, too, is a kind of honor. It confers honor, the fact that Marion wants to spend a whole day in Erika's room clearing out her stuff, but when Marion goes through the closet and insists on throwing out the red anorak with the SAVE THE RIVER badge, Erika says no. Saying no to Marion might as well be saying yes to punishment, but Erika doesn't want to throw out the anorak.

"I don't want to throw that one out," Erika says.

"Why not?" asks Marion, looking at her with eyebrows raised.

"I wear it a lot."

"I know. And I don't think you should," says Marion.

"We're doing this for your own good," says Frida.

Marion holds the anorak up in front of her. Seeing it like that, through Marion's eyes, Erika thinks it looks worn-out and frumpy.

"It's just really ugly," says Marion.

"But I don't want to throw it away," objects Erika.

"Okay, whatever you say," says Marion.

She lets the anorak fall to the floor and goes quickly and carelessly through the rest of the clothes in the wardrobe. She's lost interest by now; Erika's things are no longer of any concern. She's got to go home for dinner soon, she says. So do Frida and Emily.

Erika feels embarrassed. To save the pathetic SAVE THE RIVER anorak from the garbage bag, she has provoked Marion's wrath and by extension Frida's and Emily's.

And then: "I want to try this one on!"

Marion has found the hanger with the white blouse. She wrenches off her own T-shirt and stands in front of the other girls half naked. Frida whistles quietly. Marion jokingly spreads her arms wide and bows as if receiving applause for her striptease. Then she turns to the long mirror. Her back is slender and brown; her shoulders are broad. Her long black hair is fixed up in a loose knot at the back of her neck.

"You're gorgeous," whispers Erika.

It slips out. She looks quickly at the others to make sure they haven't heard her.

Everyone is looking at Marion's reflection in the mirror.

Marion laughs and puts on the blouse. She leaves the top few buttons undone.

"Can I borrow this for a few days?"

Erika nods.

Marion turns away from the mirror and gives Erika a brief hug.

"We've got to go now," she says, and nods in Frida and Emily's direction.

The half-full garbage bag is left lying on the floor. Later, Erika wonders whether to throw it out or retrieve all her things and put them back in their places. She decides to throw everything away except the photo album. It's nothing but a load of old junk, after all.

The next day, the sun is shining again and Marion, Frida, Emily, and Eva are lying on the rock, sunbathing and listening to "Sunday Girl." Erika is standing on the beach a little way off, looking at them and waiting for a sign.

This is the rule: if the sun is shining and Marion doesn't ring in the morning and say *Come with us to the rock* or something like that, Erika takes her things down to the stony beach. Usually Marion waves to her and calls *Come sit with us out here,* and then Erika wades out to the others with her towel, suntan lotion, magazines, and Coca-Cola. But this time, Marion doesn't wave. It's happened before. Erika stands on the beach looking at the girls on the rock, and Marion pretends not to see her. She's still furious with Erika for what happened with the anorak. Or it might be for something else. Erika isn't sure. Erika only knows she's done something stupid. With her beach things under her arm, she turns around and goes back home. Maybe it was the photo of Ragnar in the album. Erika doesn't think so. It's such an old photo. She can't be punished for old pictures. Everybody has old pictures. She thinks about what she and Ragnar do together on his bed in the secret hut. Those aren't old pictures. They are now. *Psycho boy!* Erika looks back at the rock one last time before she walks onto the path that leads away from the beach and straight to Isak's house. She knows they won't wave to her. Marion stands up, a towel around her torso, and stretches her arms toward the sun; Frida, Emily, and Eva sit bending over something. A magazine, perhaps. From a distance, they look like long shadows.

The porn magazines Marion pinched from her father, Niclas Bodström, and sometimes she sits on the rock under the sun, surrounded by the other girls, reading aloud from the "readers' confessions." Erika thinks the stories in Marion's father's porn magazines are rougher and thus more thrilling than stories like this she has read before. The pictures of naked girls parting their legs or thrusting their bottoms at the camera are all exactly the same, and none of the girls wastes much time on them. No, it's the stories they eagerly turn the pages to find.

Just a few days after Marion cleared out Erika's room, Marion and Erika are lying alone on the rock. That hardly ever happens, but today it has. Frida is standing on the beach, staring at them and waiting for a sign, and Marion laughs and says: "Look, there's Frida. Shall we ask her to come over, or say fuck it?"

"Fuck it," says Erika, feeling the sun suffuse her with warmth.

The two of them pretend not to see Frida, and eventually she goes away and they have the rock and the beach to themselves. Marion reads aloud from one of her father's magazines and they both snicker, and Erika edges closer and lies beside her stroking her stomach, her thighs, between her legs. Her bikini briefs are made of a thick, soft material and Marion has lots of hair between her legs; Erika has seen it on several occasions. Marion likes taking her clothes off in front of the others, displaying herself, soaking up the small, silent sighs of admiration. She has more hair than Erika, more than the other girls. It's like running your fingers over a bumblebee. Marion pretends not to be aware of what Erika's doing and carries on reading out loud. Erika unties the bikini briefs and puts her hand right on the slit. Marion is warm and honey-wet, and Erika rubs with her hand cautiously to and fro, and her hand gets warm and honey-wet, too. Everything is soft and easy and wet. Just the sun, the sea, and Marion here beside her. Erika sticks one of her fingers into Marion and Marion giggles, and wriggles her backside a little, but carries on reading. Erika rubs harder, and simultaneously puts more fingers into Marion. Marion puts down the magazine, shuts her eyes, and yields to Erika's hand. Erika looks down at her face. It isn't so pretty now: the mouth is half open and the cheeks very red, the black hair trailing down her neck like stinging jellyfish tentacles. Erika holds her breath, pokes one finger deep into the slit, and pulls it out again. Then she stops. Erika sits still with her hands on her lap and looks down at Marion, who is moaning and writhing.

Marion whispers: "Don't stop! Please! Don't!"

It's an entreaty.

Erika laughs.

"Why are you laughing?"

Marion's voice is so low, she can hardly hear it.

Erika shrugs.

"I was only messing around."

Marion shuts her eyes again and Erika rubs her hand to and fro along the slit, rubs hard, until Marion's breathing grows louder and faster; there's a little gasp, and the whole thing is over. She knows it's over when Marion suddenly turns away and lies down on her side with her legs pulled up under her. No cries and moans like the girls in her father's magazines. No howling. Marion turns away and lies on her side, and when Erika tries to touch her, she slaps her hand away.

"Get lost."

Erika sits there on the rock and looks down at her: the slender back, the pale backside, the long brown legs. Marion is shivering; she's cold. It's one of those days with scorching sunshine one minute and clouds the next. Everyone's going around saying they can expect thunder. The waves beat against the rock. Erika finds a big sweater in her bag and puts it over Marion's shoulders, and Marion takes the sweater, pulls it over her head, and sits up. Her black hair is tangled, her eyes are red-rimmed.

"GO!" she screams, not looking at Erika. "Didn't you hear, I told you to fuck off! Get lost! You fucking slut!"

Molly isn't allowed to get up in the morning until the man on the radio has finished talking about what's going on in the world and another man has read out the temperatures for all of Sweden. The magic word is *Borlänge*. When the temperature man has declared what kind of weather the people of Borlänge may expect that day, Molly can get up.

Today is Molly's birthday. She's five. She wants a bikini. One like Erika's, with polka dots. Isak says you don't always get what you want. She might end up with a globe instead.

"There are hard lessons to be learned in life," says Isak.

Molly has a radio in her room, on her bedside table. It's small and oblong and gray, with a long aerial sticking up. Sometimes you have to twist the aerial to get a good sound. Molly knows how to do that.

The man on the radio says: *Wage earners' investment funds were the most controversial issue of the 1976 election campaign and led to the Social Democrats' fall from power. As this year's election approaches, wage earners' investment funds have been consigned to the political wilderness, but that particular bear is unlikely to sleep in peace indefinitely.*

Molly sits up in bed and yells: "HELLO THERE, RADIO MAN! Bears never sleep!"

Molly wonders if she'll get up even though the temperature man hasn't started reading out the temperatures. This is the rule: the temperature man might say *Borlänge seventeen degrees Celsius* and before that he might say *Kiruna twelve* and *Luleå fourteen* and *Sundsvall nineteen,* but it's only when he gets to *Borlänge seventeen* that she's allowed to get up and run in to Isak and Rosa and shout at the top of her lungs BORLÄNGE SEVENTEEN! and hurl herself into their bed and tug at the quilt and jump up and down without Isak's getting angry and bellowing that she's to take herself back to her own bed and go back to sleep.

Birthdays are no exception, Isak told her yesterday evening.

Night is still night and day is still day, even on your birthday.

Molly has asked Laura if bears absolutely, definitely exist, and Laura says they do, and they can attack at any time. She shows Molly a newspaper article about a bear that has torn lots of sheep to bits. Laura reads out: *The idyllic scene in this beautiful northern valley has turned into a desperate hunt for corpses.*

"What's a hunt for corpses?" asks Molly.

Laura shrugs. She shows her sister a picture of three mutilated dead sheep. Next to one bloodied sheep stands a farmer with a rifle slung over his shoulder.

Rosa says there are no bears on the island, but Laura says Rosa's lying because she doesn't want to frighten her.

"Grown-ups always lie to little children," says Laura.

"About what sorts of things?" Molly asks.

"They lie about world war and murderers and nuclear power stations and atom bombs and disarmament and fucking and cancer and death and God and Jesus and the Virgin Mary and everything. They lie about everything, get it?"

Molly is quiet for a moment. She eyes her sister.

"But they don't lie about bears," she says.

Laura groans.

"They lie about everything! Everything!"

The truth is, at night, when both the yellow ferries between the mainland and Hammarsö are lying still and the ferrymen are asleep in their beds, the bears slowly swim across the sound, one after another, in a long, long row. They paddle through the water like dogs. They have thick, shaggy white coats and sharp teeth and black eyes. Laura says God exists and God sees everything. Molly knows that. Jesus died a long time ago, so did Granddad and the bird that crashed into the window and other birds that crashed into other windows and the kittens the caretaker in Oslo flushed down the toilet. They all live in Heaven, with God, who sees everything.

Laura says it's important to pretend she's not afraid of the bears, because if God sees she's afraid, he'll cancel her birthday and then she'll have to stay four for a whole year longer and maybe forever, for all eternity.

"God punishes everybody who's afraid," says Laura.

Molly gets out of bed, pulls the blue dress over her head, creeps out of her room and along the hall, and unlocks the front door. Then she runs down to the sea, and the wind blows around her ears, and she shouts to the wind that she's Molly. I'M MOLLY! she shouts. HOY, HOY, HOY! The waves roar. Molly can swim although she can't swim, so she takes off her dress and dips her toe in the water. It's cold. She's sure the man on the radio hasn't said *Borlänge* yet; he hasn't read out a single temperature. It's terribly, terribly early in the morning. Isak would definitely call it night. Molly kneels down and the cold water comes up to her bottom; it laps at her and it's cold and the sun sparkles on the horizon. The rough stones in the shallows open up an old gash on her knee, but it's been reopened so many times that it doesn't hurt anymore. Molly isn't afraid of anything. I'M NOT AFRAID OF ANYTHING! she shouts, and looks up at the sky.

She puts her hands together and prays.
Most of all she wants a polka-dot bikini.

Erika is lying on the rock in the sea with Marion, Frida, and Emily. And Frida has brought a magazine, an even dirtier magazine than those Marion steals from her father. The new magazine actually belongs to Frida's brother Evert, who is eighteen and doing his military service. This raunchier one has mainly pictures and hardly any stories.

"Let me show you! Let me show you!" Frida says eagerly, fending off all the girls' hands grabbing at the magazine and trying to see.

Frida turns to a picture of a woman lying on her side on the floor and being taken frontally by one man and from behind by another, while a third is kneeling over her face. Frida holds it up so they can all see and then passes it to Marion, who passes it to Erika, who passes it to Emily. Erika looks at the picture and giggles and feels a tingling inside her. To be utterly filled like that. Totally blocked up and torn apart at the same time. Outnumbered and mastered and powerless.

"Take a look at that, Erika!" whispers Marion, who is sitting next to her.

The other girls look at Erika and snicker.

"That could have been you," Frida says in a low voice.

"You could have been screwed by Fabian on one side and his twin brother on the other side," says Marion.

"While you sucked Pär's cock," says Emily.

"Pär's mine," says Marion, with an ominous look at Emily.

"All right, Ragnar then," says Emily. "While she sucks Ragnar's cock."

"Yuck!" says Marion, and sticks her finger in her mouth, in and out, and makes a face as if she's about to throw up.

Erika giggles. She doesn't want to giggle; all this stuff they say isn't worth giggling at, all this disgusting stuff that spews out of them every time they say Ragnar's name—it's like spitting on him—but she giggles anyway. It's like that time, a few days ago, when they were looking through her old album and saw the photograph of her and her father and she said: My dad's stupid. She didn't want to say it, but she said it, even so. She doesn't feel able not to. Marion puts an arm around her and says she's having a party later in the week and lots of people are coming. Not just Fabian and his brother, but older boys, Frida's brother's friends, all on their military service. Erika can feel Marion tickling the back of her neck and bending over her and licking her ear. She thinks of the picture of the woman being taken from the front and the back and in her mouth, and there's a tingling between her legs.

"NOW!" says Marion suddenly.

Frida grabs Erika's arms, pushes her down onto her back, and holds her there. Emily pulls off her bikini briefs, forces her legs apart, and holds her there.

"No," giggles Erika. "Don't do it."

Marion goes over to her beach bag and fishes out her vibrator.

"Please, no," giggles Erika.

She can't stop giggling. Marion approaches slowly and looks just too comical with the buzzing vibrator held out in front of her and an expression on her face (eyes half closed, pouting lips) that's supposed to suggest the horny woman in the magazine. It *is* comical. It's like being tickled, and Erika can't keep herself from laughing. She laughs and laughs and laughs. She wants to sit up and recover, but Frida is gripping her wrists and Emily her ankles, and Erika can only writhe there, pinned at each extremity, her legs parted. Now they're all laughing. Frida at her head, Emily at her feet, holding her down. Marion with the buzzing vibrator. Erika on her back with her legs splayed wide. They laugh and laugh, and the more they look at one another, the more they laugh, and it's impossible to stop. Marion tries to recompose her incongruous face, but can't do it. Her face dissolves into more laughter. She kneels down in front of Erika and moves the vibrator toward her, and Erika laughs and shouts: "No! No! No! No! Not that!"

Marion laughs, too, and pushes the vibrator into her, hard, and the pain is like being gored and speared and Erika stops laughing and screams *No! Ow!* But Marion carries on spearing her, and Erika screams and struggles against Frida's and Emily's hands. They keep her pinned and everybody's laughing.

"Do you want it up your ass as well?" shouts Marion.

Frida and Emily try to roll Erika onto her stomach, but Erika manages to pull herself free, screaming at them to stop.

She's crying now.

The three girls look at her inquiringly.

"Oh, come on," says Marion. "It's only a bit of fun. You were laughing as much as us."

Erika has found her bikini briefs and wrapped a towel around her body. She doesn't want to cry. There are so many tears. But she doesn't want to cry in front of them. So she takes a deep breath and forces herself to smile.

She says: "I've got to get home for dinner, okay?"

Marion looks at her. She's still got the vibrator, buzzing, in her hand, between thumb and forefinger. Everyone can see the traces of blood. Erika looks down at the ground. Nobody says anything. Marion flings the vibrator into the sea.

"There, it doesn't exist anymore," she says with a shrug.

Frida and Emily giggle. Erika turns away, doesn't want them to see the tears streaming out of her. The shame is like vomit.

"Gone! Gone!" whispers Marion.

She takes Erika's hand in hers and carefully wipes away the tears.

There are still seven days until the opening night of this year's Hammarsö Pageant, with the working title *An Island in the Sea*. Isak and Ann-Marie Krok have both failed to learn their lines. Quite a few of the young people are not turning up at rehearsals; the heat wave continues.

Palle Quist is not happy with the title *An Island in the Sea*. Too humdrum and inconsequential, he thinks, not least because all islands are by definition in the sea. So he lies in his bed night after night, twisting and turning and trying to think of a better title, all the while knowing that he desperately needs his eight hours' sleep—because without sleep he will never be able to pull together this year's production, which already has more problems than anticipated. The leading lady, Ann-Marie Krok, is clearly suffering from senile dementia, and Isak Lövenstad, in his role as Wise Old Man, has not even once managed to get through the crucial long rhyming poem that rounds off the play and is concerned with not only the dead and their longing for life but also the final confrontation between God and Satan. It is a vital monologue! If Isak Lövenstad chokes on opening night, the whole play will be ruined and that loathsome young summer critic wannabe from Örebro will have more than enough ammunition to massacre the playwright's thoughtful endeavor when writing his review in the local paper.

It is a difficult time for Palle Quist, who has so many things to worry about as he lies awake at night. He worries about the pianist, who—out of sheer devilry—regularly oversleeps, so the actors have to practice their songs without accompaniment. He worries about black-haired Marion, who skips rehearsals and chews gum or just laughs her way through her lines. He worries about his scenery, which is now being completely sabotaged by the caretaker of the community center. The caretaker maintains that for safety reasons it is impossible to make a hatch in the floor, which—with a great rumble!—would open up and let out the wood sprites. The whole point, said Palle Quist, was for the wood sprites to come out onto the stage *as if they really were streaming from underground realms!* The caretaker, a tanned, weather-beaten man with blue eyes, a stub of cigarette in his mouth, and a sow in labor back at his farm, had sighed and said he could not authorize any such damage to community center premises and declared that Palle Quist would have to assume all responsibility if any were done. He further considered it his duty to remind Palle Quist that the Hammarsö Pageant was but one of the ongoing programs of the community center that summer, and just imagine what would happen if they all came and demanded their own hatches in the floor and God knows what else. With the sow about to give birth, the caretaker, being extremely short of time, remained intransigent on this and all other points of scenery—and visions of wood sprites streaming from underground realms utterly failed to move him. Just the opposite, in fact. The bastard, who had doubtless never read a book or seen a play in his entire life, was incapable of entering into or being carried along by, much less undertaking himself, any daring leap of the imagination, and he made

Palle Quist feel stupid and ridiculous in his big flowing clothes, his long artist's scarf, his proud beard, and his faltering magnum opus, now so hopelessly close to its premiere. So at night he lies tossing and turning, staring into his own inadequacy, his joints, his muscles, and his head aching, and more than ever he hates the puppy from Öre-bro, the critic with the pretentious German surname, whose sole mission in life seems to be to ridicule, trivialize, and destroy him. And once he is lying in bed and staring at the ceiling, unable to sleep, he starts thinking about Ragnar, the skinny boy in black with the birthmark between his eyebrows, the boy who stares morosely at him or sneers ironically when given instructions and lets a kind of trembling death throe run through his body every time he reads his line *I am an angel from the north!*

"Dear Ragnar. My dear friend . . ."

Palle Quist furrows his face in friendly concern.

"The idea is not for you to shake and gasp for air and feign the spasms of a dying man. You're an angel. The idea is . . ."

Palle Quist hesitates.

"The idea is . . ."

Ragnar fixes him with a look and says: "So the idea is what? . . . You've really got me curious now!"

"The idea is that the angel—that is, you!—is *life itself*! And as a symbol of life, you mustn't frighten the audience with those death spasms, but *embrace* them! Like this!"

Palle Quist throws out his arms, hugs Ragnar, and cries happily: "I AM AN ANGEL FROM THE NORTH!"

He lets go of Ragnar, looks at him and smiles.

"See what I mean?"

Ragnar smiles churlishly but does not answer.

There is nothing about the thin boy's smile remotely reminiscent of *life itself,* and Palle Quist muses bitterly, as he does whenever encountering any resistance, great or small, that his play is going to be a total disaster.

In all fairness, it was not *his* idea to give Ragnar the part of life itself. *He* is not at fault, and that is important to Palle Quist. Neither Ragnar nor Ragnar's mother had contacted him about the possibility of a part before the tenth of May deadline had passed, and Palle Quist was therefore under no obligation to write the boy into the play. It was Isak who insisted.

"But why?" Palle had said.

"Because . . . ," replied Isak, faltering. "Because this is something I must ask you to do, and which you simply cannot refuse. The lad must have a part!"

Deep in his heart, which is big and capacious and beats for the meek of the world, Palle Quist is a defender of children. He sits on various committees in Stockholm devoted to promote the UN's Year of the Child and the importance of children's rights. Still, he finds Ragnar an irritating individual. He is forever running off to the toilet and disrupting rehearsals. His hand shakes, his small, small hand, apart from everything else that is peculiar about him. But instead of accepting Palle's concern, for Palle is one of the few to show him any, Ragnar pushes him away. Palle Quist has reached the limit of his strength. He knows very well how important it is to show care for other people, regardless of who they are or how they look or where in the world they come from, and Palle is not one to stint in demonstrating his good nature: touching, comforting, hugging, or offering the encouraging word. But Ragnar is a thankless child. He shows no signs of gratitude much less for his inclusion in this year's Hammarsö Pageant, or for the generosity and warmth with which Palle Quist has enfolded him. He has done all he can for Ragnar, ungrateful whelp!

Not so much as one unforced smile in return.

It's hopeless. It's all so hopeless.

And Ragnar runs along the strip of land by the sea with a train of children after him. He runs and runs. What year is it? What month? What day? Everything that happened last year is happening again this year, and never ends. Nothing changes. All he can hear is their shouts and his own breathing. In. Out. In. Out. In. Out. The worst thing that can happen now is that he might get a stitch. Then he'll have to stop and squat down and try to throw up. Run through the pains in his stomach. Ragnar doesn't want to stop. He doesn't want to be sick. He doesn't want to surrender to them. And so he breathes steadily. In. Out. In. Out. He runs faster than the lot of them, and now and then when he's on top of the world, he stops and waves to them and jumps up and down and shouts something, just to annoy them. They catch him only once in a while, and then it's as if they have been longing for him, because it is a kind of longing, this: they long to embrace him, hug him, consume him, pummel him, rip him to pieces! When Frida grabs his hair and bangs his head against a stone wall, he knows it's not the last time and he doesn't cry then, or when they strip his clothes off in the woods, sit him on a tree stump, and stand around him in a ring and jeer: *weakling, wimp, mongrel, cunt licker, bastard, faggot, psycho boy, thicko, stupid.* It happens only once in a while, but when they get him they are insatiable, unstoppable, he is their fondest, the most beloved, and when they run out of words to shout they simply start again, because everything that has happened happens again, everything that has been said once is said once more; it never ends. When he was ten, Marion closed her eager hands around his dick and pulled and pulled at the foreskin and shouted at him that his penis was barely a scrap of skin and not the size of real boy's. She pulled and pulled and pulled until it swelled and started bleeding as girls do and that made him cry and beg her to stop. Marion! Marion! Marion with the long black hair! Once she sat on the back of his big yellow ladies' bike and they rode together along the winding lane to the shop to buy ice cream, and then he taught her how to ride the bike, because she hadn't known how before he showed her what to do. He gets beat up by the boys, blows and kicks and punches in the face, and then it's over until the next time, when they force him to drink horse piss, rub dog shit into his hair and call it shampoo, force him to French kiss a girl called Eva who starts crying almost immediately, so after that they leave her alone. He's the one they can't get enough of. That's the way it is. Ragnar, their loveliest, their dearest. He is the one they desire. Ragnar, the blessed. He runs and runs and runs and only once in a while they catch him.

Ragnar can hear his breathing, an even in-and-out.

They are way behind him now. He can still hear their shouts. And laughter. But the distance between them just grows, and soon they are gone and he is utterly alone and now free.

The plan had been to celebrate their fourteenth birthday together in the secret hut. They were going to meet at seven in the evening and swap presents and drink Coca-Cola and share some leftover birthday cake. Erika and Ragnar had agreed long ago. It wasn't really a thing you needed to plan, Ragnar said. Ever since they were eleven they had celebrated their birthday together in the hut. Just the two of them and nobody else.

Erika didn't think you had to keep doing the same thing year after year just because. And people did need to make arrangements with each other.

She had lots to do on her birthday, she said, and she wasn't sure if she and Ragnar would still be celebrating their birthdays together in the secret hut when they were, say—Erika took a deep breath—twenty-five or thirty or something.

That brought the tears to Ragnar's eyes, and he took her hand and said: Please say we will.

Ragnar cries many times that summer, and Erika doesn't know what to do. One time she holds him. Another time she puts his hand on her naked breast and kisses his eyelids. The third time she rests her head on his shoulder, and then he rests his on hers and they sit like that until he has finished crying.

There isn't much to say. She knows they beat him up. She knows they torment him. But it's mostly just horsing around. Even Ragnar says they're only joking and it doesn't matter much and, anyway, she can't stop them. She can't say that she and Ragnar are a sort of couple. She can't say it.

She tries picturing it, though. Erika pictures herself opening her mouth and saying that she and Ragnar are together and that the others have to leave him alone.

"Just lay off him!"

She pictures their faces: Marion, Frida, Pär, Emily, Fabian, and Olle. The silent laughter. The looks. Then she'll run into them on the beach or on the way to the shop or at the community center and Marion and Frida or Frida and Emily or Marion and Emily will come up to her, stand right up close—as close as they possibly can without actually touching her—and then start a conversation with each other. If Erika says anything, they'll pretend not to hear. If she looks at them, they'll look straight through her. If she jumps up and down and screams or crumples to the ground or starts singing, they'll just carry on talking to each other. She'll be thin air to them. She's seen them do it many times. But they're only kidding. It's not that serious. Even Ragnar says they're only kidding. They mean no harm.

"Father."

"Yes."

Isak looks up from the newspaper.

Erika says: "They won't leave Ragnar alone."

"Why not?"

"I don't know."

"What do they do?"

"They fight."

"They did in my day, too."

"Your day?"

"When I was young."

"Father, you don't understand."

"I get what you're saying, Erika, but boys will fight. They always have."

"It's just as much the girls."

Isak laughs.

"Ragnar ought to kiss the girls instead."

"You don't understand."

"What is it then? What is it I don't understand?"

"They say things."

"What do they say?"

"I don't know. Disgusting things."

"Well, I expect he asks for it."

Erika looks at her father.

"What do you mean, asks for it?"

Isak gets up from his armchair, folds the paper, and puts it on the table. He says: "There's something about him . . . something about his eyes. He's got dog eyes."

About the fourteenth-birthday celebrations: Erika has to tell Ragnar she can't meet him at seven o'clock in the secret hut after all. It's the day before the big day and Rosa has given her permission to invite some friends over. For a sort of party, on the veranda.

She doesn't say that she finds that a more tempting prospect than sitting in the hut with Ragnar.

Hearing the news, Ragnar is quiet. Is he going to start crying again? Erika looks at him. She wants to say: It's not just *your* birthday. It's mine, too. It's for me to decide what I feel like doing. Listen to me! It's only a day, Ragnar! It's only one stupid day among other stupid days! She wants to shake him. Shout at him. Make him listen. You're so . . . you're so . . . you're so . . . heavy!

She says: "You can come, too, if you feel like it."

Ragnar gives a little laugh and shakes his head incredulously.

"No. But thanks anyway."

They are sitting beside each other on the camp bed in the secret hut, sharing a Coca-Cola. Ragnar in black trousers and a black Tom Verlaine T-shirt. On his head an old hat pulled down over his forehead hiding the birthmark between his eyebrows. He inherited the hat from his dad, he says. Erika knows nothing about Ragnar's dad. She doesn't know if he's dead or alive or sick or married or divorced or has just shoved off to Australia. It's the evening before their fourteenth birthday and they are sitting on the camp bed in the secret hut and Erika really wants to leave—she wants to be anywhere but here, feels as if she's been sitting here for years—but he takes her hand and she just continues sitting there. His is a little kid's hand. Ragnar has always been thin. Slender wrists. Thin legs. The boy with matchstick legs, they used to call him.

Once, a long time ago, Erika and Laura lay in the long grass and saw a thin boy in an I'VE BEEN TO NIAGRARA FALLS T-shirt running toward Isak's door. He was running with a flock of other children after him. Erika tries to remember. Where did the other children come from? Did she know them then? Wasn't it just Ragnar running, that time? She remembers Ragnar collapsing on the doorstep and Isak opening the door with a great bellow and lifting him up in his arms and carrying him indoors. It was only many hours later that they saw him again; they had been lying waiting forever, shifting repeatedly because of the sun. And when they finally saw him down by the house, they got up and ran after him. The boy first, with Erika and Laura behind him.

"HEY YOU . . . WHERE ARE YOU GOING? . . . WHY DID YOU RING OUR FATHER'S DOOR? . . . WHAT'S YOUR NAME? . . . WHAT DID OUR FATHER SAY TO YOU?"

"I've got to go," says Erika, and she gets up from the camp bed.

"Don't go," says Ragnar, squeezing her hand.

"I've got to."

Ragnar says: "I don't want to be alone. Please."

Erika gives him a hug and whispers: "Bye then."

She looks at her watch. It's late. Nearly eleven.

"Just an hour left of being thirteen," she says.

Ragnar gives her a smile. He is still sitting on the camp bed with his dad's hat pulled down over his eyes. He raises his hand and waves, doesn't look at her.

"Happy birthday!"

Erika nods back.

"You, too," she says, and runs home.

Having them at her house. Marion, Frida, Emily, Pär, Fabian, and Olle. Seeing everything through their eyes: the white limestone house by the sea is small and messy and old-fashioned; like everything died sometime in the sixties; Isak is just an old man and Rosa is fat and stupid with dust on her brain—must she keep coming out onto the veranda, saying *More lemonade? More hot dogs? More cake?* as if they were ten? And that's not all. Laura sits gorging herself on hot dogs and yakking away even though she knows she has no business being there.

Laura promised her, she vowed not to show herself for as long as the party lasted.

These are Erika's friends.

As for Molly, nobody pays any attention to her. She's sitting completely still under the table on the terrace, wearing the cloak that makes her invisible to everyone but Erika. Her sister gave her the cloak for her birthday. The cloak of invisibility is actually a red anorak with a SAVE THE RIVER badge on the arm. Erika didn't have time to buy Molly a present, or she forgot. In any case, she then came up with the idea of the cloak of invisibility. Molly pulled it over her head right away. It came down to her ankles and really could be called a cloak. A poppy-red cloak. Molly twirled around and shouted: *Am I invisible now? Am I invisible now?*

And Rosa and Isak and Laura gasped and took turns to reply:

"Where's Molly?"

"What's happened to Molly?"

"Has Molly vanished?"

And when Molly threw off the anorak and shouted *Here I am!* they were all equally astonished and said: *Oh, there you are!*

Molly sits quite, quite still under the table in her poppy-red cloak of invisibility, listening to all the voices, and now and then Laura throws a bit of hot dog or cake onto the floor for her. Like she's a dog. But she isn't a dog. She's invisible.

Laura knows she promised to keep away from the birthday party, but Marion with her ravishing hair stretched out a hand as she passed the table and stroked Laura's sweater and said it was nice, and so then Laura sat down beside her instead of going for a walk down to the beach as she'd intended. And nobody minds. Only Erika. Not the others. Erika always wants to keep her out of things. Imagine if they knew that Erika's really paired off with Ragnar and not with that boy called Fabian. Imagine if they knew what Erika and Ragnar get up to when nobody's looking. Ragnar, of all people. With the horn on his head and the squeaky voice and black clothes.

The first present is from Frida, followed by presents from Marion and Emily. The boys have brought presents, too. Fabian's is a fancy box of chocolates from the mainland and Erika reads out the card: *To Erika. Roses are red. Violets are blue. The stars are shining and so are you. Happy birthday! Best wishes from Fabian.* They all laugh. Even Fabian. Erika blushes and gives him a hug and says wow thanks and she had no idea he liked her so much. She rests her head on his shoulder.

And then suddenly:

"Erika is Ragnar's girlfriend!"

Laura says it out loud, and they all go quiet and look at her.

Erika gets up and sits down again.

"Get lost, Laura," she says. "Just get lost."

But Laura doesn't get lost. She says: "Erika sneaks out of the house at night and goes to his hut in the woods and they make out all night."

They all look at Erika. For a moment everyone around the table is utterly silent. Nothing but the roar of the sea and the screech of gulls and a warm wind caressing their cheeks.

Fabian lets go of Erika's hand and Marion sticks her finger down her throat and says EWW! Then they all start laughing again.

"Get lost," Erika whispers to Laura.

"No!" says Laura.

"It's not true," Erika tells them. "She doesn't know what she's talking about."

She turns back to her sister.

"You little brat!"

"I was only kidding," Laura whispers. But when everyone turns away from her and starts talking to one another again, she says: "I was only kidding. But it's true all the same. Erika and Ragnar are going out."

Marion tugs Laura's plait and asks: "How old are you, anyway?"

"Nearly thirteen," says Laura.

"She's *eleven,*" cries Erika, and groans. "Get lost, Laura!"

They all look at her. They all look at Laura.

She says: "And I know where his hut is!"

Erika rolls her eyes.

"Everyone knows where his stupid hut is."

"Not me," says Marion.

"I don't, either," says Frida.

"Time for a trip to the woods," says Fabian, and they all laugh.

They all laugh. They get up from the table and laugh. They run around the house and off into the woods and along the path and left onto another path, laughing and screeching and yelping, and twenty-five years later Erika isn't sure who is showing them the way. Erika herself, walking or strolling or sauntering with the others, arm in arm with Fabian, calling *No, no, go left here, around the bend there, through those bushes,* or Laura, running ahead with her long, dancing plait, or Molly in the ankle-length, poppy-red cloak of invisibility, hop-skipping, scampering, cheering. The woods get thicker. The path peters out and is just a thin line on the ground. You can see someone has been that way before, but it's hard going. In the end, only Molly is walking upright. She marches on like a little red soldier. The rest have to hunch under branches, climb over logs, hold the bushes aside. They prick themselves on thorns, they scrape their knees, but they make it through the undergrowth and out into the clearing. Laura puts a finger to her lips. No laughter now. No voices. Not even Molly says anything. She hop-skips back into the woods and lies down behind a bush, gets up again and lies down behind a different bush.

Outside the little lopsided hut stands a supermarket cart loaded with stones. Nothing out of the ordinary otherwise. A patch of green heath. A crooked tree. The hut, looking as if it might collapse at any moment. Erika takes a few steps forward, away from the others, stops, and stands utterly still. She hopes he is not there. She clasps her hands and whispers, *Please let him not be there.*

Marion comes after her and stops beside her.

"Do you think he's in there?"

Erika shrugs. "I don't know."

"Are you going in to see?"

"I don't know."

"I think you should go in and see."

She puts her arm around Erika and Erika rests her head on Marion's shoulder. But that isn't what Marion means. She doesn't mean for them to stand there in the clearing with their arms around each other. Erika feels a hard shove in her back. A shove forward.

"Go and see," says Marion.

. . .

When Erika opens the door and sees Ragnar sitting on the camp bed with his hat pulled down over his eyes, her first reaction is to think he's been sitting there since the night before. It's virtually pitch-dark inside the hut except for a lit candle on the table in front of the bed. He's wearing a new Jimi Hendrix T-shirt.

"Hi," says Erika.

Ragnar looks up. She can see his face—eyes, nose, mouth—in the candlelight.

"Hi," says Ragnar.

"Happy birthday," says Erika.

"Happy birthday," says Ragnar.

"New T-shirt?" asks Erika.

"From a friend in Stockholm. It came in the mail today. It's Jimi Hendrix," says Ragnar.

Erika nods.

Ragnar looks down at the floor again.

"How come you're here, Erika?"

Erika looks at him. She breathes in, ready to say something. And then she starts to cry.

Ragnar gets up from the camp bed, shoves her aside and goes to the door. He opens it and looks out.

"Fucking hell," he says. "Fucking hell, Erika."

Then he runs.

Ragnar runs, runs through the woods. He has almost no head start because they ambushed him this time, so he takes the shortcut down to the beach. His breathing is uneven. He tries to breathe evenly, but can't. He will end up with a stitch. He will have to stop and crouch down, but there's no time. Some of them are already right behind him, only ten or twenty meters away. He breathes. They are certain to hear his breathing now. They have his scent. The woods open out and he runs onto the wide, deserted stony beach and down to the sea, and the sea opens out, too, and he runs into it and it receives him, the most beloved.

· · ·

Molly runs and hops through the woods. It isn't very easy when you're wearing Erika's ankle-length, poppy-red anorak. Every now and then she trips and scrapes her knees. It isn't only because of the anorak. It's also because it has got dark. *Borlänge* means day, but this is night. The others have run ahead and she is going to find them. They didn't wait for her. They didn't see her. But it's not because she's wearing her cloak of invisibility; it's because she was hiding behind a bush.

Now she emerges onto the beach.

Now she comes to a complete stop and looks.

Now they are all throwing stones at Ragnar in the water and screaming to one another.

Now she raises her face to the sky and shouts HOY! HOY! HOY!

And Erika will never be able to say who started to throw stones. Ragnar runs along in the shallows, the water splashing around his feet, and suddenly he turns and shouts HA HA HA HA and waves his arms, and they all laugh and wave their arms and shout HA HA HA HA, too.

It's as if they are all joining in the same big sing-along. Some call, others respond. Ragnar dances his way backwards, out to sea. The water comes up to his hips. He puts his hands up in front of his face and shouts at them.

"No! Don't do it! Don't! Stop!"

But who started throwing and who threw the stone that hit him on the forehead before he collapsed there in the water, nobody can say.

IV

Summer, Winter

"I think we're in for bad weather tonight," said Rosa, going to shut the three windows facing the sea.

Isak looked up from the paper.

"It couldn't last," he said.

"What couldn't?" asked Rosa, without turning around.

"The heat," said Isak. "It couldn't go on like that."

A strong wind had already sprung up, and Rosa had to pull the windows toward her to get the catches to fasten. A branch knocked against the outside wall; the waves were frothy white and gray. She stood there, looking out over the stony beach.

"I'd better put the bikes in the garage," she said.

Isak was sitting in one of the two armchairs in front of the television and Rosa was standing with her back to him, looking out the window. He felt as if he could disappear from it all and nest in her broad back, the tight floral summer dress and the big gray woolen cardigan she had hanging from her shoulders every evening.

He said: "But it isn't raining yet, is it?"

Rosa did not turn around; she stayed by the window.

"No, but look at those clouds."

She pointed to something outside.

"It's already getting dark. This time yesterday, we were sitting outside drinking wine, but tonight it feels like autumn all of a sudden."

Isak glanced at the grandfather clock that stood ticking to itself in the corner. This living room, he thought. This clock. The armchairs. The television set. The writing desk. The pine table with the blue china vase. In the evenings, Rosa sometimes says she's going out for a walk; she says she wants to be by herself for a bit, so she goes out after she has put Molly to bed, Molly who is not her own child but Ruth's. After a while she comes back with a handful of wildflowers. Red, yellow, white. She fills the china vase with water and puts the flowers in the water. Nothing must change. Be fixed up. Painted over. Scraped off. Here, everything must stay as it is, and none of them will have to talk about what has been or what is to come. No. Here, very quietly, they will eat their meals, watch television programs, say their kind and tender good nights to one another every evening. Here they will grow old and die together, without disturbances or demands, quietly and without guilt.

"Are the children back?" he asks.

"Yes."

"Was the birthday party a success?"

"Yes."

Then, on reflection, "Well, I think so, anyway."

Rosa sighed and pulled the gray cardigan more tightly around her. Isak wanted to rest in her face, her eyes, the corners of her mouth, her cheeks.

She said: "I'd better go and see to those bikes."

Night fell, a storm blew up, and the storm wanted nothing better than to wrench up trees, boundary walls, and houses that had stood there so long, refusing to be torn to pieces. The island had weathered worse storms, those who had always lived there would say.

Erika crawled out of bed and crept into the hall; she thrust her feet into Isak's green Wellingtons and unlocked the front door. The wind whipped at her nightdress and hair, lifted her and carried her down to the sea. She fell and hurt her knees, and that scared her. First because of the fall and then because of the sound of her own thin voice. It wasn't a terrified, shout-above-the-noise scream, it was almost nothing, and she rolled around and up into a sitting position. It was dark and she wasn't able to pick out the grit and dirt that had gotten stuck in the gashes, and there was sticky blood all over her hands, knees, and nightdress. She got up and ran on; ran and hobbled and fell and got up and ran again. She waded out into the waves and stood upright with legs planted far apart, her feet firmly in the Wellingtons. She opened her mouth and the wind tore at her and she wanted to shout louder than it, make it be quiet. But what should she say? What should she shout now that she was standing here, wet, shaking, with bloody knees and hands and nightdress, gooey, sticky blood? I HATE YOUR FUCKING TOM VERLAINE T-SHIRT! she cried. She screamed. And the sea beat at her and pulled her down and she remembered him saying all you had to do was surrender yourself, let yourself fall backwards, that was the bravest thing they could do. He also said that when it is as dark as this, a light shines across the sea (it was a natural phenomenon here on the island, with a name she couldn't remember), and she was standing in that light now, and perhaps he could see her, perhaps he was standing a little way off in that clump of trees where the woods stopped being woods and became beach instead, standing half hidden behind a tree. The beach was black and stony, and she had no idea how long she had been standing in the waves, in the rain, but she could feel him watching her. Every time she raised a hand or took a step it was as if she were doing it for him, and she took a step toward him and he said I don't want to be alone, Erika, please, don't go.

And the rain fell from the sky and everything grew heavy, wet, gray, sludgy, and the thunder rumbling in across the sea also brought the power cut that nobody noticed until the next morning. It was night and people were asleep. Those who were awake didn't turn on the light.

Molly lay beside Laura in the narrow girl-size bed, and they were both awake because a bumblebee was flying in spirals across the room, from wall to wall. Outside, the storm raged and the thunder boomed, but it was the bee that was keeping them awake.

"You've got to go to sleep now," said Laura, and she began to cry.

"Poor Laura," said Molly, and patted her sister on the head.

Laura curled up in the bed and put her arms around her sister's small waist. Then she whispered: "You don't understand. We can never get up again!"

"I think we can," said Molly. "We can get up tomorrow when the man says *Borlänge*."

Laura cried and cried.

"You don't understand. You don't get what I'm saying. You don't understand what's happened. We can never get up again."

"No," said Molly.

Laura let go of Molly and sat up in bed, looking sternly at her sister.

"But you must never, never, ever tell anybody what happened on the beach."

"No," said Molly.

"If you say it to anyone, they'll come in the night when you and your mummy are asleep . . . and they've got keys to every door in every country, so locking the door won't help."

"Who'll come?" Molly interrupted.

"The hunters," said Laura. "And once they've unlocked the door, they'll find their way to your mummy's room and kill her by shooting five bullets into her head."

Molly started to scream.

"Shhh," whispered Laura.

Molly put her hands over her ears and went on screaming.

Laura dried her own tears, held her sister close, and rocked her slowly back and forth in the bed.

"Shh, Molly. Shhh. It'll be all right. You just can't say anything."

Ann-Kristin walked up and down in the cold house she had taken over from her parents. Looked out at the sea and waited for Ragnar, who had stormed off and not come back home. It had been the usual argument, the same words they always exchanged. He said he was going to sleep in the hut in the woods. She said he should come home and sleep in his room. They had had dinner, steak with béarnaise sauce, ice cream with chocolate fudge for dessert. That was his favorite meal, and afterward they ate birthday cake, just the two of them, and watched a comedy on television, a film starring Goldie Hawn. They had sat beside each other on the brown sofa in the light from the television and watched the film and laughed quite a lot. He said he had really liked the dinner, the cake, and his presents, but then he had announced he was going to the hut to sleep. She said no and then he said *I'm fourteen, Mom,* and stormed out, slamming the door after him. And now here she was, looking out the window, watching for him, listening for his steps outside.

Palle Quist, who lived in a house not far from Ann-Kristin's, sat in a chair, trying to relax enough to go to bed. When he saw the lightning flash in the sky and heard the crash of thunder a moment later, he thought that was just his luck. The sun had shone all summer, the hottest fucking summer since 1874, and here came the rain, the wind, the thunder and lightning, right on cue for his premiere in two days. It would ruin everything! God was against him. Now he certainly wouldn't get to sleep.

Nor would Isak, thinking about the work waiting for him in Stockholm and Lund, wishing he never needed to leave this house, this island. It was here on Hammarsö he wanted to be. Without friends, without children, without colleagues, without patients, without anything. Just him and Rosa. In total peace and quiet. She was breathing deeply and evenly beside him. She always slept well. She turned on her side, pulled the quilt over her, switched off the light, said good night, and slept until seven-thirty the next morning, when she would open her eyes, ready to tackle a new day. That's what Rosa was like. He nudged her in the side. Because there was something else bothering him. Not just the fact that they would soon have to leave the island. It was something else. Something he couldn't really put into words. Rosa turned over and looked at him, sleepy and inquiring. He did not usually wake her when he had trouble sleeping.

Isak said: "Maybe I should just pull out."

He sat up in bed, breathing heavily. Rosa yawned and gave him her hand.

Isak said: "I shall never remember my lines."

Rosa patted his hand as if he were a little child, and said: "I think you ought to sleep on it. It's not that important."

He said: "I don't want to make a fool of myself. That's all. I don't want to make a fool of myself."

She shook her head and smiled. Then she shut her eyes and went back to sleep. As for him, he sat there staring out into the darkness. He wondered what she would say if he nudged her again. Would she be cross? How many times could he wake her in the course of a night before she got cross with him? Rosa, who never got cross. Or only once, when Molly was born. That time, Rosa said she was leaving him, moving away from the island, going away forever. He had never seen her like that. He was a bad father. He was a bastard. They would reproach him when they were grown up. Erika, Laura, and Molly. Their mothers were already reproaching him, not Rosa, maybe, but Elisabet and Ruth, and not only them, but also a retinue of other self-righteous women who considered they'd been done wrong. *You're a deserter, Isak! You're a cold son of a bitch! You're a liar!* Yes, yes, so what? So what? But he had his work and his work was the most important thing; his work filled him and liberated him and he had promised himself once, long ago, that even though he was a bastard privately, he would be the best in his field professionally, and now he was. Isak Lövenstad was the best in his field. Yet still this need to nudge Rosa and wake her to ask her . . . what? Ask her what? What had he forgotten—what was it that was bothering him? The fact that they would soon have to clean the house, pack up, move back to the city? The fact that he would make a fool of himself as Wise Old Man in this year's Hammarsö Pageant? Yes, yes, all of that. But there was something more. Isak sat up and looked at the flapping curtains. He got out of bed and went over to the window in his bare feet, unhooked the catch, and pulled it toward him. Then he stopped and looked out. Later—when he was trying to tell Rosa what had happened as he stood in front of the closed window looking out at the storm—he would say it was as if an angel had come to stand beside him and whispered in his ear. He had an idea, a premonition, a sudden and unexpected thought, namely that he must go to fetch his child. So much water everywhere. So wet and cold. So battered and broken. It was vital for him to set off right now and not go back to bed. There was a light over the sea. That was where he should go. He could visualize his child's face and himself touching that face and the child going calm and quiet. Isak strode out of the bedroom, through the living room, and out to the hall. His Wellingtons were gone, so he put on his running shoes and his big green raincoat. He opened the front door and the storm bellowed at him. If Laura, who was lying awake in another part of the house, had seen him then, she would have said he bellowed back. But no one saw him and he strode on, like a giant or a huge animal, away from the house and through the woods and down to the stony shore.

When he saw her, already some way from the beach, wearing only her nightdress and heading out into deeper water, he thought in desperation that he was already too late. There was nothing he could do. He sped up and ran out into the sea, the rain and waves beating against him. It was too late. It was too late, and he grabbed hold of her, pulled her to him, lifted her up in his arms, and carried her to shore. She was shivering and crying, saying nothing. Isak said nothing. She was shivering. She was crying. He stroked her face with one hand and said *No more now, no more now.* He lifted her and carried her along the beach, through the woods, and home. He took off her soaked nightdress; she was thin, just a child, for God's sake, he thought, she was just a child; he dried her with a towel and found some dry pajamas that really belonged to her sister Laura. Then he put her to bed, pulled the quilt up over her, and sat on the edge of the bed.

Isak didn't know what else to do. She tried to talk to him, tried to tell him something, but her voice was too weak. She hadn't the strength, and he whispered, *No more now.* The power of lucid thought had deserted him and he felt exhausted. So he began singing nursery rhymes he hadn't known he knew or had even heard, and that seemed to calm her, and he sang and stroked her hair until she stopped shivering and he was quite, quite sure she was asleep.

Laura nudged Molly, who had almost fallen asleep beside her. (She was still having little hiccups at irregular intervals.)

"Listen!" said Laura.

"What?" whispered Molly.

"Father's singing in Erika's room."

Molly listened, and smiled cautiously in the dark.

"Bom bom bom," she whispered. "That's what it sounds like. Bom bom bom."

Laura put her arm around her and pulled her close.

"Bom bom bom," Laura whispered back.

And the waves washed back and forth with ever greater force and Ragnar came loose from a net of seaweed and sea grass in which his foot had gotten tangled. He floated up to the surface and was flung ashore and then out to the depths again, in to the shore and out to the depths, until in the end he was borne by a wave and laid out almost tenderly on the beach (in a small hollow scooped by stones and fossils four hundred million years old) so that someone would soon find him.

But it was going to take time. Morning came and afternoon came and when the storm finally abated it was succeeded by cold, torrential rain, and Ragnar lay quite still in his hollow, saturated with the water that had flowed through him; pale and dead. Many stayed indoors that day and the beaches were empty; no girls on the rock; everything was purling, cold and gray, and only Ann-Kristin went from house to house, asking if anyone had seen her son, but no one had.

Other mothers and fathers—Marion's mother, Pär's father, the mother of the twins Fabian and Olle—opened their doors and looked at her, inquiring, indifferent, wondering, and shook their heads.

"You haven't seen him since yesterday evening, then?"

"He tends to run off sometimes, doesn't he?"

"Have you called the police?"

.   .   .

Palle Quist also had a visit from Ann-Kristin that morning.

"I hope Ragnar plans to show up this evening," Palle Quist said to her. "We're having a complete run-through."

He quite simply forgot to ask if she wanted to come in out of the rain, dry off, warm herself by the stove for a minute, have a cup of coffee. And no, Palle Quist had not seen Ragnar. Neither had his daughter, Emily, as far as he knew, but he would ask her when she got up.

"But he's progressing," he said. "Ragnar is progressing. It's so good, Ann-Kristin! Tell him that from me when you see him, and tell him it's good! We mustn't lose momentum now, even though the weather has turned."

When Ann-Kristin collapsed in a heap outside Palle Quist's house and began to sob, he had already shut the door.

From Palle Quist's house it was not far to Isak's, but she had dreaded ringing at that door and asking about her son. It was Rosa's cold stare; it was the fact that Isak had told her long ago to keep away, and she had kept away. She would ask to speak to Erika. She wanted to say: Where is Ragnar? Where is he? You know where he is, don't you? But when she had run and stumbled all the way to the blue-painted door beyond the long, white grass and rung the bell, and Isak had opened the door and was standing there in front of her, huge and brilliant and terrible, she cried out through the tears and rain: "I can't find the boy!"

It would take a few more hours for them to find him. Molly sat in front of the grandfather clock, tracking the movements of the big hand across its face, while the rain rippled down the panes of the three closed windows. The big hand moved once a minute: to think that a minute could take such a long time. Molly wanted to go home to her mother in Oslo, she wanted to get away from the white rails in Rosa's drying cupboard, get away from the bears who swam across the sea at night when the ferrymen weren't keeping a lookout, get away from Laura and Erika, who were suddenly just sleeping and sleeping, like princesses behind a hedge of thorns. They simply wouldn't get up. Rosa said the change in the weather had left them feeling poorly.

In the kitchen, through the wall from the living room, Ann-Kristin and Rosa sat facing each other across the table, under the blue lamp. Ann-Kristin was crying silently. Isak was talking on the telephone. As he put the telephone back on the hall table, he said that the police were on their way, but that it would take them about two hours to reach the island and everyone was to carry on searching until then.

Ann-Kristin looked up, meeting first Rosa's eyes, then Isak's.

"But doesn't Erika know anything?"

She didn't believe it. Did nobody know where he was or where they had last seen him?

"Doesn't Laura know anything?"

Ann-Kristin demanded to talk to one of them, preferably Erika. Weren't Erika and Ragnar going to celebrate their birthday together? They always had before. Did Isak know that? She lowered her voice. Did he in fact know what good friends Erika and Ragnar were?

Rosa interrupted.

"Erika had her birthday party here yesterday," she said. "On the veranda! There were lots of them here, but not Ragnar. He wasn't invited, as far as I know."

"Wasn't invited?"

Rosa went on: "Friendship between children of that age is so unpredictable; one minute they're bosom pals, the next minute they're not talking to each other anymore."

Isak said: "I'll go and wake Erika. She was ill late last night, after the party, but I'll wake her and ask her when she last saw him."

He moved toward the door, but then turned and said: "Ragnar has a hut . . ."—Isak was groping for words—"a secret hut in the woods."

He gave a little laugh and looked at Ann-Kristin.

"You know where it is, I imagine? You've checked he isn't just in the hut?"

Ann-Kristin lifted her head and looked at him.

"Of course I've been to the hut," she whispered. "It was the first place I looked. The hut's empty."

So much water everywhere.

Water through his clothes, water through his skin, water in his lungs, water dripping from his hair. He lay in the hollow, in brackish water, in rain and sea, and the stones that surrounded him were as smooth as the palms of a little girl. When they finally found him that afternoon, he was heavy to the touch, heavy to carry.

It was two foreigners, two women from Adelaide, Australia, who saw him lying there. They had been on Hammarsö for the whole of July, enjoying the scenery, which reminded them more of places in Africa than of Scandinavia. This was their last day on the island, and they had decided to brave the rain and go for a long walk along the stony beach.

They acted swiftly and silently. One woman crouched down, bent over him, listening for his pulse and heartbeat, although she knew he was dead. She stroked his hair to one side, patted his cheek, and closed his eyes. Then she put her arms around him and pulled him to her. She got wet and cold, and many, many years later, when she was old and not far from death herself, she would remember the dead boy with the thin wrists as the rain bucketed down. She nodded to the other woman. They lifted him—the boy was not very big, but he was heavier than they expected—and they carried him between them along the stony beach and through the woods until they reached a house, though they did not know who lived there, and knocked on the door.

. . .

Ann-Kristin was still sitting in Isak and Rosa's kitchen when the telephone rang. Rosa took the call.

Erika stood in the doorway in Laura's pajamas, rubbing her eyes. Her body was heavy and sated with sleep.

Rosa spoke quickly and quietly, saying what had happened, what had been said on the phone, how they had found him, where he was now; her voice went on and on, she used many words.

Ann-Kristin raised her head and looked straight at Erika. They regarded each other for a long time: the woman on the chair and the girl in the doorway. Rosa's voice droned on. Then Ann-Kristin opened her mouth as if to scream, but no sound came.

Rosa stopped talking; and then it was quiet.

One after another they were interviewed by the police and fed hot chocolate and Cokes and dry cinnamon buns that grew big and doughy in their mouths. The rain had abated, but the day that was turning into evening was cold and gray, a sign of impending autumn. Everyone was talking about the change in the weather. They were all present. Marion, Frida, and Emily. Eva was there, and Pär, Fabian, and Olle. Their parents were there, too. The police interviewed them one by one, in the community center. They all agreed it was a tragedy. A deliberate accident, someone called it, and that phrase, *a deliberate accident,* seemed to stick. No one said straight out that Ragnar had killed himself, but why else would he have been down there when the storm was at its height?

"It can't be viewed as anything but a deliberate accident," said Marion's father, Niclas Bodström.

What did Erika tell the police through a mouthful of bun?

"Ragnar was sort of . . . a bit weird," she said.

She chewed and chewed on the bun and talked at the same time, gesturing, pointing, crying, and chewing bun, which expanded in her mouth and was impossible to swallow.

"We weren't usually with him," interjected Laura.

Marion, Emily, and Frida nodded. The boys looked at the ceiling or at one another, anywhere but at the girls, who did the talking.

"He was just unbelievably weird," repeated Erika.

And afterward! By the time the police had talked to everybody who knew him (and no one knew him particularly well, they said), by the time the ambulance had taken him to the mainland and a kindly islander had offered Ann-Kristin a place to rest, a bed to sleep in, so she wouldn't be left on her own, it was late in the evening and everyone agreed that this year's production of the Hammarsö Pageant would have to be canceled because of Ragnar's death. Palle Quist's entire team had gathered in the community center. The coffee and hot chocolate had all been drunk, the buns eaten, the evening's rehearsal canceled because of the police interviews.

They couldn't possibly think of doing the play now, not under current circumstances, thought Frida's mother, who was involved in this year's production as both a costume designer and an extra.

A great, heavy, long sleep was descending on everyone.

Palle Quist put his head in his hands and wailed: "It's terrible. Terrible!"

Someone nodded, someone shook her head. But then Palle Quist had an idea. He had been sitting with his head in his hands saying *Terrible, terrible* all evening. Now he raised his head and stared out through the big vaulted windows that overlooked a heath covered in fiery red poppies. The community center was known for those windows, and for its view. It was strange. The weather had turned again, and the evening was now as mild as a Swedish summer evening can be, and light. Yes! Yes! Palle Quist allowed himself to be seduced by the light and heard himself say tentatively, inquiringly, because he was still not sure whether one could say what he was about to say:

"But what if we *don't* cancel the performance?"

He cleared his throat.

"If we were to go ahead with the performance, as a . . . as a . . ." Palle Quist racked his brain for the right word: ". . . as a *tribute* to Ragnar?"

He was met by a wall of sleep: sleepy faces, sleepy looks, sleepy hands fending him off. No one, except Frida's mother, could be bothered to answer.

"Palle," she said, and repeated what she had said earlier in the evening, "we can't think of doing the play now. Not under current circumstances."

Palle Quist nodded. It was what he had expected. They would change their minds. His work, his magnum opus, would not go to waste. He would allow time to work to his advantage. Everything, he thought (no, he knew!), would look different after they had all had a night's sleep.

Isak went first, with long, heavy steps. The woods were dense, but the night was light. Her father's back was bigger and broader than the blackboard at school: you could write things on it, Erika thought as she walked behind him. And the great, fair head with the great, brilliant brain. What was he doing with it all? She imagined an explosion of forgetting and grief.

Just before she fell asleep the previous night, she had opened her mouth and told him everything. The words had tumbled out of her, every word a stone four hundred million years old, and he had put his finger to her lips and said *Hush, little one,* and carried on singing.

First Isak, then Erika, and then Laura. Isak chose the shortcut through the woods. It only took ten minutes if you hop-skipped or ran or took long, straight strides like Isak. Rosa was waiting at home with tea and freshly baked bread and wild strawberry jam.

Molly lay sleeping in her room.

When Rosa tucked her in, she said: "No more of this getting into Laura's bed at night. It means neither of you gets any sleep."

Molly shook her head.

"Good night," said Rosa.

"Good night," said Molly.

But Molly would not sleep. She lay in her bed that evening, aware of the smell of freshly baked bread. She had helped make the uncooked strawberry jam while the others were at the community center, and been allowed to taste it before going to bed. As she lay there, she heard Rosa pacing up and down the kitchen. She heard Rosa sigh, heard her crying, heard the tick of the grandfather clock in the living room. She heard Isak, Erika, and Laura come home; she heard a door slam, footsteps in the hall, voices. All this Molly heard. When Isak opened her door a crack and looked in, she pulled the quilt over her head and became a snail in its shell.

Isak closed the door again.

"Hoy hoy hoy!" whispered Molly, trying hard to think of lollipops.

Someone is playing, someone is shouting, someone disappears under the water, and then they pop up again, one way or another. Molly pushed the quilt off her face. She wasn't a snail anymore.

"And for once I was right," said Palle Quist to his friend Isak as they had a cup of coffee together the next morning. "For once!"

After a long night's sleep, they had all (everybody involved in any way in the production of *An Island in the Sea*) informed him, one after another, that, despite the horrible tragedy, they wanted to go ahead with that day's dress rehearsal, and the premiere the day after.

"I mean . . . for once!" he repeated.

Isak said nothing. He did not appear to be listening.

"I think it's for the best," ventured Palle.

Isak nodded.

"Finishing what we've started, I mean."

Isak nodded again.

"And it will be a tribute," said Palle Quist.

He had given up trying to engage his friend's attention and was talking more or less to himself.

"A tribute to Ragnar and to life. I think Ragnar would have appreciated that, in spite of everything. God bless him."

In his review of that year's Hammarsö Pageant, *An Island in the Sea*—written and directed by the Social Democrat and energetic enthusiast Palle Quist—the impudent upstart from Örebro, the one with the silly name, expressed the view that it was time to take a break. Next summer, he wrote, enjoy the summer, enjoy the sunshine, enjoy the sea, and enjoy the special, beautiful natural world of Hammarsö! The best thing about this whole dismal amateur performance, he continued, had been the cinnamon buns and saffron pancakes served at intermission.

The audience was on the whole more indulgent than the reviewer from the local paper; it allowed itself to be carried along by the storyteller, by the sea nymphs and wood sprites, by Ann-Marie Krok's halting meter and Erika's singing.

Somebody said afterward that the youngest member of the cast looked like an angry little troll. The audience was unaware that Molly did not want be in the play. Molly wanted to go swimming.

But Rosa and Isak said she had to be in the play. She could go swimming afterward, or the next day, but she had practiced all summer and couldn't just back out at the last minute. She had a responsibility to everyone, Rosa said.

Molly stood squinting on the edge of the stage for a long time, and most people thought she had forgotten her lines—she was only a little girl, a small, skinny figure in a purple dress—but finally she opened her mouth and hurled the words toward them, one after another, loud and furious:

> *And now that night is falling*
> *The full moon is bright as day*
> *We are halfway between light and darkness*
> *And halfway through our play.*

And it could have been a success, thought Palle Quist the night after the premiere. They gave only one full performance. There was no encore performance the day after, as there had traditionally been. It could have worked. But there was something missing. Something that went wrong. He had been obliged to cut Ragnar's monologue, and he mused for a moment on the strange, angry boy who had never wanted to play the part as written. He wondered how Ragnar would have performed in front of an audience: Would he have done anything differently? Then Palle put the thought to the back of his mind. Because it wasn't that. It wasn't Ragnar. It wasn't even Isak. The closing monologue in rhyming verse had been not only about the longing of the dead for life and God's confrontation with Satan but also about the whole political situation . . . the fleeing boat people in Southeast Asia, the terrorist attacks in Spain . . . the crucial election campaign in September . . . yes, everything! Everything! The sort of life people wanted to live—that was what it was about! It was the best, richest, most pregnant monologue he had written in his life, it was charged with meaning, brilliant and unconstrained.

But Isak had ruined everything.

Isak had ruined everything.

And then there was something else, something he couldn't put his finger on, something missing. The reviewer was right. He was through being a playwright. He didn't give a damn! Next summer he would just relax and enjoy himself.

"Come hither and hear what I have to say, for they call me wise!"

The stage was dark and silent. The animals were sleeping. The wood sprites began to hum and the bird tamer, clad in green, played the flute. It was a simple, pretty tune. Then Isak made his entry from stage left, dressed in a black cloak and fake white beard, with a large leather-bound book under his arm. When they saw him, the wood sprites stopped humming, the bird tamer laid down his flute, and Isak positioned himself center stage and cleared his throat. He looked out over the audience. He cleared his throat again. He saw their faces and froze. He felt giddy, and as if he were going to be sick. He knew that Now! Now! Now! Now! it has to happen and I can't do it, can't do it. He heard someone in the audience fidgeting, someone coughing, someone saying: Hurrah for Isak Lövenstad! He bowed and smiled at the man who had shouted hurrah and thought, If I don't say what I've got to say now, it will be too late. Everything swam before his eyes. It was cold. He had no choice. Or anything to lose. Not anymore.

Isak bowed again and then he spoke; he spoke loudly to be sure everyone would hear him.

"I apologize."

Isak felt a great, heavy fatigue running through his body, as if he were underwater and could no longer resist; it would be nice to get home to Rosa.

"As I say, I apologize."

He took a breath. It was over. He said: "But I seem to have forgotten my lines . . . I do not know what I am supposed to say."

He gave a third bow.

"So I shall go now."

All the suitcases were packed and lined up in the hall—Isak's big green one, with room for his papers and folders and books, Rosa's and Laura's practical black ones, Erika's little blue one, and Molly's big red one. Molly had the biggest suitcase of all. Molly's case stood there in the hall, lording it over all the others, and when Isak went to lift it and carry it out to the car, he gave a loud groan. Not wanting to hurt his back, he decided to drag it after him through the front door to the open trunk. Molly, wearing the blue dress that just about covered her bottom, hop-skipped back and forth between his legs until in the end he had to ask her to go and sit in the car and be quiet. All the bed linen had been washed, ironed, folded edge to edge, and neatly piled in the linen cupboard. Rosa had been up since three o'clock on the last morning to get the house ready for their departure, and at eleven the drying cupboard was switched off for good that summer. Now it was empty and dark and cold in there. There was nothing hanging on the drying rails. Not Molly's blue dress, or

Isak's socks and shirts and trousers, or Erika's polka-dot bikini. The sheet of paper with the picture of the horned devil and the warning THIS DRYING CUPBOARD IS NOT TO BE USED BY CHILDREN AFTER SWIMMING! ANYONE WHO BREAKS THIS RULE WILL BE PUNISHED WITHOUT MERCY! was still on the door, fixed with a bit of sticky tape. Rosa had considered taking it down; it was in her nature to tidy, clean, clear out, and sort, and she liked to leave clean, smooth, empty surfaces behind her—yet, without really being able to say why, she left the sign there. The floors had been vacuumed and then scrubbed with green soap; the windows had been cleaned and covered with thin fabric to protect everything from the light and to stop anybody who happened to be passing that autumn from looking into the living room (at the armchairs, the grandfather clock, the writing desk) and perhaps getting the urge to break in. Her duster had touched everything in the house that could be touched; Rosa had stood on the top rung of the ladder; she had gone down on her knees and lain flat on her stomach; she had compressed herself into a little ball—not a single hook or sill or corner or patch of floor, under a wardrobe or bed, had been missed. The toilets had been scrubbed and scoured with blue cleanser, and when she had finished that (about two hours before it was time to go), nobody was allowed to go to the toilet again except once, just before they got in the car and drove off, and when you pulled the chain that last time, the water in the toilet was still blue. A final afternoon meal comprising cold meatballs, boiled potato, salad, and homemade lemonade was served, and consumed quickly around the kitchen table, and by then there wasn't much to say to one another. The people around the table, a man and a woman and three children, had, as the house would have attested if houses could bear witness, already left. The house had washed them out of itself and remained standing there, clean and shut and uninhabited, ready for quieter and darker days and nights.

Isak was at the wheel, with Rosa in the seat beside him. In the back sat Erika, Laura, and Molly. As the car passed the gate and the field of long grass, Erika turned around and saw the white limestone house disappearing from view in the back window. She said nothing. Neither did anyone else. Molly sang a song; that was all. *A memory, a memory, the stars are sweet, a memory, a memory, and the sky is blue.* Now the journey was the important thing. First the twenty-minute ferry crossing to the mainland. Then the tedious car ride to the airport. Then the flight itself. And finally the arrival at Fornebu in Oslo, where Erika and Molly would be met by their mothers, Elisabet and Ruth.

It was Erika's job to look after Molly the whole way, because Isak, Rosa, and Laura would be taking a different route, by car back to Stockholm.

They found they had Ragnar's mother's blue Volkswagen Beetle in front of them on the ferry. She was sitting alone in the car. Erika couldn't see her face, but noticed she had long, thin gray hair (Erika couldn't remember it having been that long, or that gray) and a big gray sweater.

Rosa said quietly: "Don't you want to go over? Say something to her?"

"Who?"

Isak's answer was brusque and dismissive, but Rosa went on: "Ann-Kristin, Isak! She's sitting there, in the blue car."

Isak looked straight ahead.

"Why should I? What would I say?"

Rosa said: "I don't know. That would be up to you."

Isak shook his head.

"No," he said. "I don't want to. I've nothing to say."

It was now, at this time of year, that Hammarsö's summer guests cleaned their houses, dismantled their garden furniture, stowed away their barbecues and barbecue equipment, hammock cushions, blankets, and oilcloths, cleaned out their fridges, jettisoned half-empty milk cartons, messy packs of butter, half-eaten casseroles and veal roasts, hot dogs, depleted packs of cold cuts, and cartons of eggs nearing their sell-by date. It was a shame to throw food away, but what could they do? The food couldn't be left to rot, and it was too much bother to take it back to the city. And it was now that cars were crammed full of dirty clothes (because not many people had laundry rooms as Rosa did, with washing machines and drying cupboards), carryalls, plastic bags, large towels that had once been a luxurious white but were now grubby and gray and lay squashed up against the back window alongside bits of tent, cardboard boxes, tricycles, typewriters, golden retrievers, and cats that in some cases would be let or thrown or lured out of the car in some unfamiliar place far from the island, far from the city, and left to fend for themselves.

In Oslo, Molly lay in her mother's arms and slept heavily. Every morning after they had got up, her mother said: "Give me a twirl, Molly! Let me see. I do declare you've grown some more in the night again!" And Molly laughed loudly, jumped down from her chair and spun round.

Yes, it was now that the island was emptied of people, the ferries no longer shuttled so regularly to and fro, the shop kept shorter hours, and the beaches lay deserted.

Hammarsö's permanent residents could finally stretch their arms skyward and feel the clear, sparkling sunlight warming their bodies, their skin, their hands, their fingertips; warming them all before the autumn came in earnest sometime in November, with its catacombs full of wind and rain and darkness.

And fresh storms came. The wind rampaged over the stony beaches, over the rock in the sea where young girls had played and sunned themselves, over the closed shop and the deserted roads. It forced its way into the houses, into the beds with the rolled-up mattresses, and into the corners that were no longer clean, dusted and redolent of green soap. If anyone had accidentally found themselves going down to the white limestone house sometime during the autumn (though nobody did), they might have asked themselves why Rosa had troubled to get down on all fours and clean and toil and sweat—hadn't it all been in vain? There were black heaps of dead and half-dead flies on the windowsills. Admittedly many of the flies would come to life and start buzzing again when Simona looked in some-time in January to check on the state of the house. The flies would be swatted and swept out into the snowdrifts, but she wouldn't find all of them, and, anyway, new heaps would form on the windowsills after she had gone. There were mouse droppings in the kitchen, in the bread basket, under the refrigerator, beside the telephone, and a real, live mouse was living in the cupboard under the sink. The mouse was living well, because Rosa had forgotten to empty and clean a shelf of snacks. Cheese puffs, among other things. Eventually, as the snow drifted down, it became almost as cold inside as outside, and when the wind decided to show its strength by knocking over Big Dick's son (who was now well over seventy) on the road, causing damage to his hip so he had to start walking with a stick like other old men, it whistled and howled in people's houses, and Isak's was no exception. Fluff scudded over the floors from one corner to another: balls of fluff rolled and flew and gamboled and reshaped themselves into more balls of fluff and still more again; and then the darkness rolled in over the island, over sea and sky and heath and field; into Isak's house, through cracks and holes and fissures and the slit between the curtains that never quite met when they were shut. Nothing remained untouched by the winter darkness. Not the armchairs, or the grandfather clock, or the blue china vase.

When the cold was at its most intense—the residents said it was the coldest winter since 1893—the water froze in the pipes and they burst; and when the snow melted around early April, the water flooded out over the floor of the bathroom, the kitchen, and Rosa's laundry room. Simona had come for the second time that year (mainly to swat a few overwintering flies, she thought, because there was no point dusting while nobody was living there), but when she unlocked and opened the door, the stink of mold and fungus and rot rose up to meet her, and when she stepped over the threshold, the water came up to her ankles.

"What an old dump this place is," muttered the plumber who was summoned. "Did they just forget to turn the water off?"

Simona shrugged her shoulders. She said: "It seemed they were in a hurry to get to the mainland."

There was water running and dripping and seeping and gushing both outside and in. The sun shone through the dirty windows that Simona was sure to get around to cleaning one day, but not now.

The daffodils had just begun to poke through the ground, and soon the hepaticas would be showing, too.

"What rusty old junk!"

The plumber was lying on the bathroom floor with his backside in the air, shaking his head. Simona sat at the kitchen table, smoking. She said nothing.

"The floor'll have to come up. This is a job for a carpenter. And a painter. The whole place will need repainting."

When Simona rang Isak, he barely had time to speak to her; he said he couldn't come and see to it all himself, he had so much to do at the university—he was in Lund now—and Rosa was very busy in Stockholm looking after Laura, who was having problems at school. Laura didn't want to get up in the morning, didn't want to go to school. Depression, the school psychologist said. At twelve! Personally, said Isak, he felt like shooting school psychologists, the whole damned lot, but Rosa said that as long as he had his work at the university, he should leave the child rearing to her, and maybe she was right. He would be grateful if Simona would kindly take charge of all the work on the house and send him the bill—and if she could pay the electricity and telephone bills, too. He would arrange for money to be transferred to her account.

The plumber lay flat on his stomach and sniffed the floor. He said: "It's not just this latest water damage, though that's bad enough—believe me! This is old rot. I'm guessing all the joists will have to be replaced."

He pulled himself up to a kneeling position again.

"It'll cost you . . . hell of a job . . . he's only got himself to blame . . . but I suppose professors can afford it."

The plumber grinned. His teeth were lily yellow from two packs of cigarettes a day for fifty years. In a year's time he was going to retire and move north.

On Hammarsö they said he was a good man.

Simona stubbed out her cigarette and smiled. She was thinking that when the hepaticas flowered—and they generally flowered in profusion around Isak's house—she would pick a big bunch and take them home with her. There was nobody to notice they were gone, after all.

Simona wiped up all the water in the kitchen, bathroom, and Rosa's laundry room, though there was actually no point cleaning or tidying anything now—the house was going to be renovated in due course, in any case, or sold, so she dragged a black trash bag after her from room to room, throwing in any rubbish she came across: everything from a dead mouse in the cupboard under the sink to a drawing long ago fixed to the drying cupboard. Simona tried to read the words under the drawing, but the faded felt-tip pen was impossible to decipher. The plumber mended the pipes and the carpenter pulled up some floorboards, looked down into something that to judge by the expression on his face was a bottomless pit of damp and rot, and announced it was going to take a heck of a long time and cost a lot of money.

He said: "These old houses don't just take care of themselves."

When Simona rang Isak in Lund, he sighed and said it would have to wait. He didn't have the money at the moment. He didn't know when they would be back. No, there would be no summer holiday on Hammarsö this year.

When autumn came, the permanent residents told one another there had never been so many tourists on the island as this year, and even though it had poured rain for the last two weeks of July and been cold and chilly all summer, the shop's revenues were up twenty percent and the campsite had never been so full of RVs and tents.

One summer, a few years later, Palle Quist was asked if he would be writing and putting on a new play anytime soon. A married couple came up to him at the hot dog stand. He remembered them. They had always made appreciative comments after those revues in the seventies. The married couple, she in a bright floral-patterned bikini and he in baggy swimming trunks, regarded him expectantly. Palle

Quist shook his head and said it was nice of them to ask . . . but no, he didn't think so.

"Though, who knows?" he said as they turned to walk back to the beach. He suddenly felt more cheerful than he had in a long time.

"Who knows?" he called after them. "Maybe next year."

Simona went from room to room, whistling. She had a face like a shriveled red apple. Her hands were big, brown, and callused. She pushed a broom around the bathroom floor, killed flies that had revived on the windowsills, ran a duster over tables and cupboard ledges. The rot must have spread up the walls by now, she thought, but she had got used to the smell, and even grown oddly to like it. All houses smelled of something and this house smelled of rot and sea. She could come here and be in peace, sit at the kitchen table under the blue lamp and look at the snow falling on the plot of ground outside. She could sit here in complete silence and smoke a cigarette without anyone asking her anything or wanting her to do something for them. Why shouldn't she be able to take a break now and then?

Occasionally she made herself a cup of instant coffee or lay down on the bed in one of the children's rooms. She liked the room of the eldest girl, Erika, best. Simona had unrolled the mattress and found a quilt in the linen cupboard, and the first time she lay there she thought she might stay there for good, in that unfamiliar room with the torn floral wallpaper and the old, faded film posters, lie there in the cold, unfamiliar bed and just be. Nobody could find her. Nobody could hear her when she shouted or screamed or sang loudly and joyfully.

What was more, she was getting paid for it. Isak made a deposit into her account every other month for her services watching over the house, keeping it clean, and contacting him if anything came up. Simona lay in Erika's room; it was hard work lying down, hard work getting up, but when she finally got the opportunity to stretch out her old bones, really stretch them out, it was as if a song ran through her. She opened the bedside table drawer and found a pile of girls' comics. She gave a little chuckle, heaved the whole pile onto the bed, and started to read.

Not many tourists came to Hammarsö in winter, and those who did would never have called themselves tourists. They would never have set foot on the island in summer, either. Because then, the island was not itself. In summer, Hammarsö bloomed and grew beautiful, charming, alluring, but it was all dissimulation. *Look at me, how beautiful I am in this pale evening light, how beautifully I dance with red poppies in my hair.* No, those who came in winter loved the island for its gray-striped, stony landscape; its inconsolable cold wind; its long nights; its deserted road, plunged into darkness; and its empty beaches. In winter, the sky and the landscape were one, either white, gray, or black. Unchangeable. Immovable. And only if you dared take off your hat and bare your ears to the cold would you hear all the sounds of the island. The sea was always there. You could not avoid hearing the sea. But there was the sound of the forest, too, of the wind in the treetops and of heavy winter shoes on packed snow, of someone breathing in and out so his frosted breath streamed from his mouth. It was the sound of someone who knew the way and lithely negotiated bushes and thickets, went in among fir trees weighed down with snow. And there, at the end of the path that was not a path or even a line on the ground, since everything was covered in snow, lay an open white meadow. Here he stopped, the one who came to the island in winter and picked his way among bushes and thickets in the forest—he stopped and stretched. He had had to walk bent double and even crawl to get here, and just as he extended his arms to the sky, the sun broke through the cloud cover, making the snow sparkle and glisten and burn—the snow on the ground, in the trees, on his wet face, and in his wet hair.

And the sudden, sharp white sunlight forced him to screw up his eyes to avoid being blinded, but when he opened them again he saw at once that it was still there. The lopsided hut with snow on the roof was still standing. And outside the hut, in the deep snow, a supermarket cart full of stones.

When she rang Isak sometime in the spring, Simona said straight out that if he were really considering living here again, he would have to have the house thoroughly renovated. Or else he would have to sell it. Things simply couldn't go on as they were.

No, they couldn't, said Isak, and he told her he had become a grandfather. Erika had had a daughter. Well, yes, it was tremendous news, of course. He was in Lund and she and her baby and husband were in Oslo, so he hadn't seen the little girl yet. But he had gone to the effort of arranging for the best specialist in Oslo, an old friend and colleague, to be on hand during the delivery. But Erika hadn't wanted a doctor there, of course. *Father, I want to make my own decisions about the delivery,* she had told him. *I'll be just fine with a midwife popping in, without the slightest interference from your colleagues.* Erika had almost finished her own medical training, so . . . Had he mentioned that to Simona? That Erika had decided to be a doctor, like him? And that the little girl was already three months old?

"Have you sent her a little romper, then?" asked Simona.

"Oh yes. Of course. Rosa sees to all that," replied Isak.

Simona stood in the kitchen in the white limestone house with the telephone receiver in her right hand and looked out over the sea; the rain ran down the windowpane.

She had stopped listening.

"But it is a reminder," said Isak suddenly.

"Ah, yes," said Simona.

"I mean . . . of time passing," said Isak.

"Yes," said Simona.

When they spoke to each other in January, she repeated what she had now said many times: either the house must be fixed up or he must sell it. If it were up to her, she would be happy for everything to carry on as before, with her coming over a couple of times a month and having a cup of coffee, smoking a cigarette, lying on the bed and closing her eyes, and sort of vanishing from the face of the Earth, but her conscience would not allow her to mislead the old man about the true state of affairs. Isak said he would think about it. There was so much going on at the moment. Laura had completed her final year at school with mediocre marks and wanted to travel around the world with some boy called John, and Rosa seemed tired. He could not be away from her so much in the future; he had been away far too much, he said. Rosa was really not very well. She was complaining of pains in various places and didn't get much sleep at night.

Simona sometimes wondered why Isak never mentioned his youngest daughter when they spoke on the phone. He spoke occasionally of Erika and occasionally of Laura, but never said anything about the little one. Of course, she would never ask him—it was none of her business—but she remembered the girl running about in a blue frock and dancing around the grown-ups' legs, shouting something—hoppity, hoppity, hoppity. Something like that. She had heard that the girl had lost her mother many years before and lived with her grandmother. Didn't know where she had heard it. Not from Isak, at any rate. Simona dragged the quilt after her to the smallest bedroom, the one with blue-painted walls, the yellowing calendar with pictures of kittens, and the tatty patchwork quilt on the bed. This was the smallest girl's room. She sat down on the bed but stood straight up again as a cloud of dust whirled up and made her sneeze.

She flopped down into the white basketwork chair by the window and wound the quilt around her. She had forgotten to pay the electric bill and now they had cut off the power supply. It didn't matter. The pipes had burst several years ago, the water was turned off, everything that could happen had already happened, and nobody lived here anymore. Why pay for electricity, for heat and water and light that nobody used? She liked the cold, herself. It had sunk into the walls, the floors, the beds, the cupboards, and even the coffee cup she filled with scalding coffee from the thermos as soon as she stepped through the kitchen door. The cold was what it was; it suited this house, and as long as she had a quilt and thermos with her, everything was all right.

"No, it's not about the house this time!"

Simona rang Isak in the middle of the peak season and told him Palle Quist was dead. One morning he simply didn't get up. His wife called and called for him to come for breakfast, and when he didn't reply, she went into their bedroom and found him lying on the floor. It happens like that sometimes, said Simona. His children were grown up now, after all, and his wife was smiling—but everyone grieves in their own way, of course. The funeral had been in Hammarsö Church. Simona was in no doubt that that was what Palle Quist himself would have wanted. He loved this island. There was a splendid obituary of him in the local paper, she said, headed "Death of an Optimist."

She could send it to Isak in Lund, if he cared to read it.

In Oslo, an old lady and a young woman sat in large chintz armchairs, watching television. The young woman had small hands. Strips of green light flashed across the screen, and a correspondent was shouting BOOM, BOOM, BOOM, straight into the camera; he seemed unable to think of any more descriptive word than that for the rocket explosions over Baghdad. The flat was small and dark, but clean, neat, and smart. The old lady was crying, but not because of the war. Well, maybe because of that, too, but mainly because King Olav V was dead and everyone was so sad, whether they supported the monarchy or not, and because this winter, with its constant threats of war, was harder and colder than all other winters, and because nine years previously she had lost her only daughter. Her grief was constant, like the air she breathed, like the cold water she drank every morning.

"No," said the old lady, making a dismissive gesture with her hand. She just could not face the thought of all this!

"All what?" asked Molly, looking at her.

Her grandmother had been over forty when she had her daughter, and over seventy when she lost her. They didn't talk about it very much, she and her granddaughter.

Sometimes Molly's grandmother would find something in a drawer or a box, a ribbon or a keepsake book, and say: Look, this was Ruth's when she was little. Then Molly would smile and nod, but never say a word about how much she felt the loss of her mother, because those feelings belonged to her alone, and if she spoke of even one tiny memory, told the story, put it into words, it would be diminished by her grandmother's perpetual crying. The memories were not that extensive; they were as small and hard as marbles. Molly was not yet eight when Ruth's car swerved onto the incoming lane. She could remember the scent of her mother's body at night, and a voice singing, *Give me a twirl, Molly, give me a twirl so I can see how big you've grown.* She remembered her mother's hair.

Her grandmother shook her head and dabbed her eyes with a handkerchief. She said: "King Olav couldn't face the thought of this war . . . of this new age . . . not any of it! That's why he died now."

"I think he died because he was old and sick," said Molly.

She got up to fetch a blanket from the sofa and arranged it over her grandmother's legs. She decided she would skip the first lesson at school the next day and buy a big bouquet of flowers. Roses, or tulips perhaps? No, roses! Red roses!

Molly was planning to give a dinner party. First she had rung her sisters to ask if they wanted to come as well, but neither of them was able to. They made excuses. Erika had said it might be better if she and Laura didn't come. Maybe it was time for Molly and Isak (who was passing through Oslo) to talk, just the two of them, undisturbed for once. Yes, why not? Molly had said. I can ask him why I live with the old lady and not in Sweden with him. Erika had said she didn't think that would be wise.

Molly was going to skip the whole day of school and use the time to go shopping, cook the dinner, and make the flat look nice. Neither she nor her grandmother was used to visitors. Molly preferred to go to her friends' houses. Her grandmother's flat wasn't the sort of place you took your friends. Before too long, when she was eighteen and had left school, she would get a job and move out. If she decided to continue her studies, she'd do that later. But tomorrow, she was going to shine. Isak would see how pretty she'd grown. She would take his coat and hang it in the hall cupboard, and then place him beside her grandmother on the sofa and offer him a glass of white wine. *A little aperitif?* she would say, and then they would both laugh and the atmosphere would be lighter. She must remember to remind her grandmother not to start crying. Isak wasn't coming to dinner to hear about Ruth. Perhaps she could give her grandmother a sleeping pill and put her to bed? Molly looked across at her. They were still sitting in their armchairs, watching the war report. Molly stroked her grandmother's rough cheek. The old woman smiled and patted her hand.

Molly took a breath. Here's the plan, Isak! I'll decorate the place with flowers. Roses, no less. I'll serve you white wine that I will buy at the wineshop even though I'm not eighteen yet. I will lay the table with fine white china and crystal glasses and silver flatware and linen napkins, because Grandmother has all those things in her cupboards, and I shall cook for you: you're going to have tomato soup with basil to start, and fillet of beef for your main course, with red wine in your glass, and crème caramel for dessert. I will serve you all that and I won't ask a single question about you or me or my siblings, about why I don't live with you, why you don't want me to, and . . . and . . . Molly often made speeches to Isak in her head, but she never reached the end of them because it might be true that he didn't love her, after all. He gave her a few exhausted hours a year on the condition she kept to the rules: no demands; no emotional blackmail; *spare me the histrionics*—maybe the rage, the silent fury, would strike her one day, as it had others. She remembered him lifting her high, high in the air and saying she wasn't to bathe in the sea because it could be dangerous.

Molly tugged a hand through her hair. It was long and dark and thick. She looked across to her grandmother, who was falling asleep. The old lady often fell asleep in front of the television. Sometimes Molly would wake her and say: Time to get off to bed, Grandma! Then her grandmother would open her eyes, remember how everything was, and gasp *No, no, no,* or something like that. Sometimes Molly didn't wake her completely, but just enough for her to be able to get up from her chair with her granddaughter's support, move across the living room and into the bedroom to slump onto the bed. All with her eyes shut. As if there were an agreement between them that she need not wake up again that evening. When her grandmother was finally lying on the bed, Molly would undress her: first her dress, then her slip and tights, and finally her underpants. On rare occasions she would cast a glance at the old, pale body with its calluses and irregularities and wrinkles and varicose veins. But normally she did not stop until she had pulled a clean nightdress over her grandmother's head and down over her body, pulled the covers up, switched off the bedside light, and whispered good night in her ear. That was what she would do tonight. It was time for Grandma to sleep now, straight through the night. And in the morning they would trim the roses with Grandma's flower knife and fry the fillet of beef together, because Grandma knew exactly how to handle a nice piece of meat. The secret, she would say, is to let the meat rest for the same length of time as it had been frying in the pan. And although it would be Grandma who actually fried the meat, they would agree to tell Isak that Molly had done everything.

Molly raised her hand to stroke the old lady's cheek again, but just then there was an explosion on the television screen. Her grandmother gave a moan and Molly pulled back her hand. *Don't wake up now. Don't wake up now. You can sleep all night.* Molly stood up from her chair and stretched her arms above her head. Tomorrow she would skip her first class. She glanced at the screen. It wasn't the war in Iraq anymore, but close-ups of parents and children, of grieving people; of flowers and pieces of paper with poems and drawings on them; of thousands of lighted candles in the Palace Gardens. She turned off the television and went over to the window. It had started to snow. She opened the window, stuck her head out, and opened her mouth. Snow fell on her lips and tongue, cold and wet, and it made her smile. Snow fell on her cheeks and eyelids. When she stretched out her arms, snow fell on the palms of her hands as well. Yes, she thought. Yes! That was exactly how it would all happen. She would skip first class. Perhaps the whole day. And first thing when the shops opened the next morning, a large bouquet of red roses.

In the winter of 1992, Isak rang Simona. It was evening, and she was at home. Isak had scarcely ever rung Simona's private number before. They had an understanding that she would ring him if she had anything to report, or he would ring her when he knew she was at his house. Simona's house was full of people. Four children, six grandchildren, and three nephews and nieces, of whom the youngest was only a few weeks old; and husband and brother-in-law and sister-in-law and a great-grandmother who still had all her wits about her but could no longer speak. They all needed to be fed.

"Am I ringing at an inconvenient time?" asked Isak.

"Yes," said Simona.

"My wife's dead," said Isak.

"Rosa? My God!"

"She was ill. There was nothing I could do for her."

"I feel for you in your sadness," said Simona.

"It's dreadful," said Isak.

"And Laura, how's she taking it?"

"She's thinking of moving to Oslo," said Isak. "All my daughters will live in Oslo, then."

"I see," said Simona, surveying her own hungry brood.

"I'm thinking of killing myself," said Isak suddenly.

"It's always an option, I suppose," said Simona.

"I can't see any point in going on without her."

"I do know what you mean."

Simona did not know what else to say. The conversation he had embroiled her in now lay beyond what either really cared to discuss with the other.

"But I expect you're wondering why I've called?" said Isak.

"Yes."

"I want to get away from everything here: sell the flat in Lund, sell the flat in Stockholm, and get my house on Hammarsö fixed up."

"It's a huge job," said Simona.

It all went quiet at the other end. She waited.

Then he said: "I want you to know this, Simona. I'm moving to the island for good."

Simona tried to avoid being selfish in deed, but she did occasionally allow herself a selfish thought, and just now it occurred to her that there would be no more presiding over her icy refuge, and just because the old man had lost everything and thought he could regain some of it on Hammarsö. Why couldn't he just stay where he was and let everything continue as before? She said: "You realize the place is run-down? You will hardly recognize the inside, after all these years."

"I know."

Simona looked out the kitchen window. She preferred the view from the other kitchen window. The one that until this phone call had also been hers. She said: "I'll see to getting the heat turned back on and wash the sheets and towels and pillowcases."

Isak mumbled something at the other end and Simona said: "It's the least I can do, make sure you arrive to a made-up bed."

V

The Light over the Water

They had arranged to meet at Hammarsö Rooms and Restaurant, an inn that was open all year and located not far from the ferry terminal, the community center, and the church. They were going to have a cup of coffee and compose themselves before driving the final stretch to Isak's house. Erika opened the door. She had to duck to avoid hitting her head on the lintel. She stepped over the high threshold and into the gloomy lobby. The orange-patterned linoleum floor had recently been scrubbed; it glistened, wet and slippery, with a clean hospital smell. Voices and laughter reached her from a television no one was watching. Behind the reception desk sat a woman, knitting.

"Excuse me," said Erika, taking off her gloves. They were now soaked and had been wet ever since she left Oslo, never really having had a chance to dry although she had draped them over the broken radiator in her hotel room in Sunne, and then again over the back of a chair in a motel room in Nynäshamn. She brushed a bit of snow from her anorak. That was wet, too. Everything she was wearing was cold and wet and suffocating, sticking to her skin.

The woman went on knitting.

"Is the restaurant open?" Erika asked. "Can I order something?"

The woman shrugged.

"I can make you a sandwich and coffee. We generally serve dinner from five. But not today. The restaurant's closed today."

Erika looked at her watch. It was just past two. She was cold again. She was sweating one minute and freezing the next. She wanted to sleep. She wanted to take off all her clothes and be naked, to have a hot shower, to lie in a properly made-up bed.

On the ferry over to the island, Erika had been the only passenger. The ferrymen had waved to her from the bridge and she had waved back. They were old and weather-beaten and looked just as they had twenty-five years before, but she knew they couldn't be the same ones. The ferry was the same, the same throbbing yellow across the water as when she was fourteen, but the ferrymen were surely new.

"Is it possible to book a room, just for the day?" Erika asked. "I'm waiting for my sisters; we're meeting here at Hammarsö Rooms and Restaurant and then driving all together to see our father, who lives here on the island."

The woman shook her head. Erika pretended not to see and went on talking. She could pay for a full night if that helped matters. She just wanted to get out of her clothes, have a shower, and lie down in a warm bed for an hour.

"I'm so cold, I just want to rest for a bit," she explained. "I want to shut my eyes."

The woman shook her head again and said: "I'd gladly have given you a room, dear, but I haven't got one."

Erika sighed. "Don't tell me you're fully booked, because I simply don't believe it!"

"No, not exactly," said the woman. "The hotel's closed."

"I see," said Erika, annoyed.

She felt like saying something snide and unpleasant. This establishment claimed to be open all year but clearly wasn't.

"So! No rooms and no restaurant at Hammarsö Rooms and Restaurant?"

Her voice was shrill; she felt ridiculous.

The woman put down her knitting, raised her head, and looked at Erika. She was over seventy, with a thin face and long hair also thin and gray.

Once, thought Erika, her hair must have been her most beautiful feature.

"That's right," said the woman. "No rooms and no restaurant. But I can make you a sandwich and a hot cup of coffee. And you can sit in the lounge and watch TV or read a newspaper while you wait for your sisters."

The woman indicated a door standing slightly open.

"It's through there. You can leave your rucksack with me, if you like. I'll keep an eye on it."

"Is there a sofa there?" Erika asked. "In the lounge, I mean."

"Yes," said the woman.

"Would it be terribly improper of me to take my boots off and lie down on the sofa to rest for a bit?"

"No," said the woman. "It wouldn't be improper."

Erika's eyes were wide open. Ragnar had his mother's eyes. Everyone said so. He was the spitting image of his mother, Ann-Kristin. And he was Isak's heel.

Erika turned over on the sofa.

They lay close together on the camp bed in the secret hut. He was holding up a mirror. They were comparing their faces.

"I've got my mother's eyes, too," said Erika.

"But you've got Isak's mouth," said Ragnar, "and Isak's hair."

"I don't know whose nose I've got," said Erika. "Maybe I've got my great-great-grandmother's nose."

"You've got my hands now," said Ragnar, taking her hands in his and kissing them.

Erika removed her boots and threw her anorak over a chair and was lying on one of the red velvet sofas in the empty lounge. In summer the room would doubtless be full. People would watch television or have a drink and eat peanuts, or talk to other hotel guests. In front of each sofa was a table with chairs arranged around it. The television set was mounted on a wall bracket, high up, almost at ceiling level. Erika wanted to switch it off, or at least turn it down, but she couldn't find the remote control and hadn't the energy to get up. On the screen, a young girl was jumping up and down, screaming with delight. The audience was clapping. The girl had won something.

Erika opened her mouth and said: "Forgive me!"

She didn't recognize her own voice. Its tone was different. It had something to do with the acoustics in the room. It was three o'clock and the winter light streamed in through the windows. The light was white, hard and bright. It was an ancient light. When Erika visualized her own death, it wasn't dark, but light like this. Light and still. The stillness was also ancient. It had always been there and would always be there.

The girl on the TV screen had been set a new task by the emcee, and it didn't look as if she would succeed this time. She frowned and shook her head. The audience clapped encouragingly anyway.

Erika turned on one side, pulled her feet up under her on the sofa, and cried.

The woman from reception opened the door. She was carrying a tray with some slices of bread and a steaming pot of coffee. When she saw Erika, she set the tray down on a table and put a blanket over her.

Erika took her hand.

"Thanks so much."

The woman sat down on the edge of the sofa.

"If you can get a bit of sleep now, you'll feel better," she said.

"My sisters and I are going to visit our father."

Erika was still crying. She squeezed the woman's hand, wanting to assure herself that it was real, that it was alive, that she was not utterly alone here, left to the mercy of herself and this light.

"We haven't been on the island since we were children. That's why it's affected me like this, I think."

"I know," said the woman.

Erika lifted her head and dried her eyes.

"Do you know him?" she asked. "Do you know Isak? Do you know my father?"

The woman smiled at her.

"No," she said. "I can't say I do."

She slept and woke and fell asleep again. From time to time, she heard the church bells chime. She had forgotten that. She had forgotten that the church bells on Hammarsö rang every half hour. Isak's house was a fair distance from the church, but the shop was right beside it, as were Hammarsö Rooms and Restaurant and the community center with its distinctive vaulted windows.

Often when Erika and Laura went to the shop to get an ice cream or to pick up some things for Rosa, they would hang around there for a while, maybe lie on the heath with all the poppies, and wait for the church clock to chime. Then they could set their watches. Thin watches around slim wrists.

It was a contest to get the time as exact as possible.

They should have been here by now!

Erika sat up on the sofa and looked about her. It was entirely dark, inside and out. The television had been switched off. She had slept for a long time, deeply and dreamlessly. She looked at her watch. It was almost half past five.

They ought to have been here ages ago.

She switched on a lamp, wrapped a blanket around her, and padded across the room in her socks. There was a cold draft around her feet. She located her mobile phone in her anorak pocket. She switched on more of the lamps. There were old photographs on the walls. Most of them were black-and-white. She called Laura's mobile and got her voice mail. She called Molly and got no answer at all. She sent them both the same text message: *Where are you? Let me know!* Then she went over to look at the pictures on the walls. These were personal pictures, mementos of a summer long ago: adults and children on the beach, by the kiosk, with hot dogs and ice creams in their hands, at the community center and in the shop. There were many pictures of a wedding. The reception had been held here at the inn, after a ceremony in Hammarsö Church. The bride in white had flowers in her hair. She was smiling for the camera. Erika went from photograph to photograph to see whether there were any faces she recognized, but she recognized nobody.

Erika was lying on the sofa again, and the silence was older than the light, older than the darkness.

She sat up. *I've got to call my kids.*

Ane didn't answer, but she sent a text. *Hi Mum @ cinema cant talk now. Luv :-)*

Erika dialed Magnus's number—it didn't matter if he was annoyed, as long as he answered, as long as she could live in his voice for a brief moment. She had wanted to ring him every day since he went off on the school trip to Poland, but she had restrained herself, put one hand over the other. Let him grow up; he isn't yours twenty-four hours a day forever.

Magnus answered straightaway.

"Hi, Mum."

He sounded almost pleased to hear from her, but she could have been mistaken. Perhaps he was just being polite. There was screaming and bawling in the background. The class wasn't in Poland any longer. They had been in Berlin all day and now they were spending the night at a hotel in a town whose name he couldn't remember. It was great in Berlin; he'd like to go back there again. Tomorrow they were going to two more concentration camps, Sachsenhausen and Ravensbrück, and then they had the long bus ride home. Magnus paused for breath.

"Was there anything else you wanted?" he asked. "I've really got to go now."

Erika wanted to hold on to him a bit longer.

"What was Auschwitz like?" she asked. "It must have felt terribly"—she searched for the right word—"it must have felt terribly powerful."

"It was packed with tourists," he said. "People all over the place, and somebody asked where they could buy something to drink. I couldn't really take it in, everything that happened there. That happened there a long time ago, I mean."

"It's not that long ago," said Erika.

"No, but I've got to go now," said Magnus. "Bye."

Erika put the mobile phone down on the table. Then it was all quiet again.

The church bells rang six. Erika went to the window and looked out over the dark landscape. It had started snowing again. It would be best for her to leave her car at Hammarsö Rooms and Restaurant and go the rest of the way with Laura and Molly in Laura's car. Laura's was the more powerful car and she was the better driver. The snowplow certainly wouldn't have cleared the road all the way. Erika shut her eyes. She had never seen the white limestone house surrounded by snow. When she was a child coming to Hammarsö it was always summer, and she always seemed to arrive when the lilacs were in bloom. The lilacs bloomed later on Hammarsö than in Oslo, so every year she saw two lots of flowers; it was like having a double spring. And when she got to Hammarsö and the lilacs were in flower and it was a whole year since she had seen Isak, a whole autumn, a whole winter, and a whole spring, he would always be sitting waiting on the bench outside the house. Rosa's car would turn in at the gate and rumble down the slope, and Isak would be sitting on the bench, waiting. He wasn't waiting for Laura. He wasn't waiting for Rosa. He saw Laura and Rosa all year round. He was waiting for Erika. And when the car finally came to a stop outside the house, she could wrench open the door and run into his arms and up.

"Daddy!"

Into his arms and up. Like running up a set of steps, up and up and up, and the steps just kept going up, never ending.

When Rosa died, there was no one to comfort him. Isak turned around and around and bellowed. Where was relief to be found? Laura couldn't cope with having anything to do with him just then.

I can't do it, Laura told Erika.

Isak wanted to sit on the settee and hold her hand and stroke her face and tell her she was like her mother. She had her mother's eyes and her mother's hair. And that was the last thing Laura wanted.

"He was grieving for a woman and I was grieving for a mother, and we couldn't both grieve together. The very thought of that sort of intimacy with him! Isak should have realized that."

Erika could not comfort him, either. She went to visit him in Stockholm on one occasion and they went to a restaurant near his flat for dinner. The restaurant was virtually empty. Erika drank a glass of wine. He drank water. His hands were shaking, and it occurred to Erika that he could not carry out his work with hands that were shaking like that. The restaurant played the same song over and over again: a slow, mournful pop song. Erika knew the song and told Isak the name of the woman singing, but immediately regretted it. He did not care what the singer was called. They could hear laughter from the kitchen. Isak ate a few mouthfuls; it was like eating stones, he said. He put down his knife and fork, looked at Erika, tried to smile, and said: "It's wretched, the whole thing."

A few weeks later, he sold his flat in Stockholm and the one in Lund and moved to Hammarsö for good. He resigned his professorship at the university. It was over.

"I haven't done anything practical with my hands for a long time," he told Erika on the phone, "and now I'm going to put my house in order."

After that, nobody heard from him. He moved to Hammarsö and fell silent. In the end, Erika rang Simona.

"Is he still alive?"

"Yes," said Simona. "He's renovating."

"All on his own?"

"Yes. Basically. He's getting a bit of help from a carpenter and a plumber. Two old codgers who've lived on the island all their lives. They all have coffee together. I think it's because of them he's taken up smoking. But he's doing most of it by himself; basically, he's on his own."

"My father started *smoking*?"

"Yes."

"What else does he do?"

"He goes to church every Saturday evening to listen to the summoning bell for Communion. But perhaps he's always done that? He sits quite still in the back pew and listens to the church bells; then he goes out again."

The door to the lounge opened.

"Erika, is that you?"

Erika turned. Laura and Molly were standing side by side in the light from the open door. Each wrapped in a big anorak. They still had their hats and gloves on. They were smiling at her, both with rosy red cheeks.

"You made it," said Erika, feeling the relief wash over her.

To start with, they sat together around the table in the lounge, surrounded by all the photographs.

The woman from reception brought more sandwiches and more steaming hot coffee.

"These are my sisters," Erika said to the woman.

The woman set down the tray and said hello; then she went out, closing the door behind her.

"Who's she?" said Laura in a low voice. "I feel as if I've seen her before."

"She works here at the hotel; she's the receptionist," said Erika. "She put a blanket over me when I was cold."

Molly stood up from the sofa and went over to the window. She stood there, looking out at the falling snow.

"One time, many years ago," she said, "I stood by the window like this and, just like now, I was thinking I would be seeing him soon. I'd cooked a big dinner, bought red roses, but he didn't turn up, of course. Canceled at the last minute."

"Have you been in touch with Isak today?" Laura asked Erika.

"Yes," said Erika. "I spoke to him this morning."

"Is he pleased we're coming?" asked Laura.

"No," said Erika.

"Is he afraid we're coming to confront him or something?" asked Laura.

"I don't know. He says he's too old."

"Too old for what?"

"Too old to entertain three daughters, I assume," said Erika. "He insisted that we should turn around and drive back home. Me and you and Molly."

"And what did you say to that?"

"I said that we were coming regardless of what he thought, and that he wouldn't need to entertain us. I said I was bringing some videos and we could watch those if we couldn't think of anything to talk about."

Molly was still standing at the window. She turned to her sisters.

"But we've got lots to talk about," she said.

"Yes," said Erika, "but I think we'll have to leave most of it unsaid."

Erika and Laura got to their feet and went to join Molly at the window. They all looked out at the snow. The clock struck eight. Beyond the church lay the sea.

"Look," said Molly, pointing. "There's a light over the water."

"It's called something," said Erika. "I can't remember what. It's a natural phenomenon here on the island. It glows, then it vanishes, and then it glows again."

Then she said: "I remember it was Ragnar who first showed me. He said you had to make sure not to look away, or even blink, because you're seldom lucky enough to see it. It was as if he thought you could keep the light there by looking at it."

"Yes, right," said Molly.

It was snowing heavily now. Perhaps they wouldn't even be able to get through in Laura's car. Perhaps they would have to walk the last bit, thought Erika.

"Yes," said Molly. "I remember Ragnar. He had a mark between his eyes and a hut in the woods that he'd built himself. Yes, I remember him. His mother was called Ann-Kristin, wasn't she?"

"Yes," said Laura.

"And I remember," said Molly, "a sunny afternoon in the garden outside Isak's house. We were running between the fruit trees. There were apple trees, weren't there?"

"Yes, a couple," said Laura.

"Yes," said Molly. "I remember it being lots. Apple trees and plum trees and pear trees, but maybe I've imagined that? But anyway. We ran in and out among the trees. It was a hot day and I hardly had anything on. Probably just that blue dress. Yes. I had a blue dress that barely came down over my bottom. Do you two remember all that?"

"Yes," said Erika.

"And you were both there," said Molly, "and I was there and so was Ragnar. We ran in and out among the trees, shrieking and screaming. Yes. I don't know how old we could have been. I was much younger than the rest of you, of course, but I remember this vividly. It was us three and Ragnar, and then Isak, too. Yes! Isak had got out a hose and he made a monster face and came toward us and we were shrieking and screaming and running in and out among the trees, and Isak said One-two-three I'm coming to get you and you can't escape, and he sprayed us with water and we got soaked and shrieked and laughed and screamed. *No, please don't come and get us, Mr. Troll, please don't!* I got soaked and I held out my arms to Ragnar and Ragnar lifted me up, but I was too heavy for him so he passed me over to Isak, who hoisted me high in the air and spun me around. Yes! I remember it well."

They were still standing at the window. Erika said: "I remember that day, too. I've even got a photograph in my album at home. But Ragnar wasn't there. He never played with us like that. You've got it wrong. He isn't in the picture."

Molly smiled.

"Well, that must be because he was taking the picture, then," she said. "I haven't got it wrong. Ragnar was with us. We were all there together."

Laura went back to the table with the tray of coffee and sandwiches. She took a gulp of coffee. It had gone cold.

"So," she said.

Erika and Molly turned to face her.

"So," she said again.

"What?" said Erika.

"It's half past eight. Time we got going, don't you think?"

"Can we get through in your car even if the snowplow hasn't gone the whole way?" asked Erika.

"Yes, we can," said Laura, getting ready to leave.

Erika went over to the sofa and folded up the blanket. She stacked the plates and cups on the tray and took it out to the woman at the desk.

"Are you off now?"

"Yes, we're off," said Erika, picking up the rucksack she had left with the woman and slinging it over one shoulder.

"Thank you for being so kind to me," she said.

"You're welcome," said the woman. She looked at Erika. "And take care now," she added.

Erika went back into the lounge and put on her boots, anorak, hat, and gloves. She turned to her sisters. They were already fully dressed.

"We shouldn't just turn around and go back home, then?" she said.

Outside it was dark and white. There was still a light over the water. It was rare, said Erika, for it to last that long. Laura and Molly took the front seats and Erika got into the back. The rucksack and cases were in the trunk. Laura put the key in the ignition and started the car.

And then they drove the last little way to Isak's house, cautiously, through the falling snow.

A NOTE ABOUT THE AUTHOR

Linn Ullmann is a graduate of New York University, where she studied English literature and began work on a Ph.D. She returned to her native Oslo in 1990 to pursue a career in journalism. A prominent literary critic, she also writes a column for Norway's leading morning newspaper and has published four novels. She lives in Oslo.

A NOTE ON THE TYPE

This book was set in Granjon, a type named in homage to Robert Granjon, a type cutter and printer active in Antwerp, Lyons, Rome, and Paris from 1523 to 1590. Granjon, the boldest and most original designer of his time, was one of the first to practice the trade of typefounder apart from that of printer.

Linotype Granjon was designed by George W. Jones, who based his drawings on a face used by Claude Garamond (ca. 1480–1561) in his beautiful French books. Granjon more closely resembles Garamond's own type than do any of the various modern faces that bear his name.

Composed by Creative Graphics,
Allentown, Pennsylvania

Printed and bound by R. R. Donnelley,
Harrisonburg, Virginia

Designed by Soonyoung Kwon